# Lipstick
# & Camera clicks

## D.J. MURPHY

I would consider this book a fun ride. However, I understand that things that don't bother me, may be harmful to others. So, I do want to list things that could be triggering.

Acceptance of differing sexualities is discussed.

Alcohol is used, not abused.

SA is briefly mentioned.

# Playlist

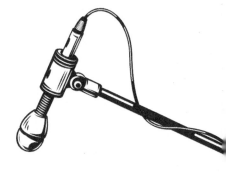

Traitor – Olivia Rodrigo
Special – SZA
Revenge – Mariah the Scientist
Boy's a liar – PinkPanthers & Ice Spice
I'm Fine – Ashe
Drama – Pink Sweat$
Just a Friend –  Mario
Juke Jam – Chance the rapper ft. Justin Bieber & Towkio
Handsome – Chance the Rapper ft. Megan Thee Stallion
Bad Habit – Steve Lacy
Hesitations – Navyug, CORBAL & Shiloh Dynasty
Ex – Kiana Lede
Better – Khalid
My Boo – USHER & Alicia Keys
Imported – Jessie Reyez & 6LACK
Lovers and Friends – Lil John & the East Side Boyz & Ying Yang
Twinz – Kings of Crunk
Snooze -SZA
Back Stabber – Kesha
Run Me Dry – Bryson Tiller
Easy On Me – Adele
Better For You – by siopaolo
Make you Mine – Public
PILLOWTALK – ZAYN
Golden hour – jvke

*To all the black girls who grew up in the era of love triangles and cheesy rom-coms and never got to see themselves. This one's for you.*

# Chapter One

Lying comes so naturally to him, I almost believe it. He doesn't even hesitate; I wonder if he's forgotten what the truth is. How many times will he do it today?

"Are you coming home after your meeting?" I ask as he buckles his watch.

Javi doesn't bother looking at me. "I have to stop at my mom's tonight, so I'll be back late."

Lie number one, and he hasn't even said good morning yet.

"I thought you saw her yesterday?" Reaching for the coffee pot, I turn my back to him. I've never been great at hiding my emotions, and every word that comes out of his mouth makes my jaw tighten.

"I have to help her set up furniture."

Lie number two.

Am I so predictable that he can rehearse these answers ahead of time? Or is he such a pathological liar that making things up is as easy as breathing? "You know we've been dating for almost two years and now we live together, and I still haven't met her." I face him as I pour the steaming liquid into my mug. He finally looks at me with that smile I used to love. His eyes soften and he takes my chin between his fingers,

then places a gentle kiss against my cheek. It takes everything I have not to wipe where his lips touched.

"If my two favorite girls are going to meet, I'd rather make it an occasion. I've never brought anyone home and I want it to be special."

Lie number three. Or should that count as two lies?

I'm not his favorite girl. Couldn't be. That spots already taken and after my social media deep dive last night, I know he brought a woman to meet his mom last week. "Maybe I'll see if Abbie's free." The scent of vanilla fills the air as I add creamer to my coffee.

"Abbie? You know I don't like her. She never knows when to leave." He shakes his head and to his credit, I'm impressed. He doesn't even pause at the mention of her name.

Lie number five is just as easy as the others.

How can he not like her? He took her to meet his mom. They looked super cozy wrapped in each other's arms, with his mother smiling beside them in the pictures she posted. I grip the handle of my mug so tight my nails bite into my palm. Until recently I wasn't active on my socials, so I guess Abbie thought I'd never see it. Javi convinced me appearing single was better for his platform.

"Why don't you reach out to Ryan?" He asks.

This almost sends me over the edge, so I sip my coffee to avoid exploding. It's his fault I haven't seen Ryan in the last month. Now he's acting like he didn't cause that wedge with his jealousy because he doesn't want to be bothered with me anymore.

He shrugs his coat on and takes one last look in the mirror, running a brush over his low-cut fade. Javi's handsome in an adorable kind of way. Round cheeks, perfect smile, golden brown skin and a boyish charm.

"Don't look so upset, Indigo. We'll do something fun this weekend." He leans in and kisses my forehead. "I love you."

Lie number six is the worst of them and it hurts like hell.

My smile feels wrong, like my face is all stiff. It doesn't matter though, because he doesn't notice. The second he's gone, I rub the back of my hand roughly against my face as if that will undo his touch. I pull my phone out of my pocket and open my bank app. The amount I see in my account is the last straw. Can't afford to leave if I wanted to. Abandoning my coffee, I throw myself onto the couch and scream into the cushions. Is this a productive action? No. Does it make me feel better? Not really. But it does clear my head a bit.

How did I get here? I became the person I never wanted to be. Growing up, my mom put her aspirations on hold because my father asked her to and then he turned into someone she didn't recognize. He snuffed out any ambition she had until her light finally faded. She eventually walked away. Went back to school, made the right connections, and landed a high paying job.

I'll always be proud and respect her sacrifice, but there's a part of me that always looked at her past as a cautionary tale. Running my hands down my face, I groan at the thought of having to tell her things with Javi didn't work out. The last thing I want to hear is "I told you so." She never liked him and was angry enough when he encouraged me to go to cosmetology school. My passion is just a hobby to her.

To be fair, she just wants me to have a steady paycheck. However, Javi had been supportive and encouraged me when I was scared to make the leap, which landed him on her bad side. Little did I know cosmetology school would be the start of the end. I'm not sure if I should be grateful I met Abbie there or not. At least she's shown me who Javi really is.

I unlock my phone again, this time pulling up my location tracker. The small blue dot labeled "Javi" is moving the opposite direction of the coffee shop where he mentioned having his meeting.

How many lies is that?

I think that's number seven. How bold can they get? Meeting up without turning off location share is wild. Love is such a made-up delusion. I gave up focusing on what I wanted to do and building my brand to work a job I hated so he could focus on growing his following. He claimed he'd do the same if the roles were reversed.

I scroll through my contacts and my thumb hovers over Ryan's name before I decide to call.

"Indigo?" I can hear the smile in her voice. I look up at the ceiling to stop the tears from falling. I want to break down and tell her everything, but I'm so embarrassed.

"Ryan, Hey. Are you free tonight? I thought I could swing by, and we could catch up."

There's a beat of silence and I chew my lip. Being alone tonight will break me, but I wouldn't blame her for declining. I let Javi's jealousy over my friendship with her brother pull us apart.

"I'm in your area. I can stop by your place instead, if that's cool?"

Relief flows through me. "Sure, sounds good."

"Okay… are you alright? Do you need me to come now?"

She sounds worried, meaning I must sound as crappy as I feel. "No, I'm fine. But I wanted to say I'm sorry for—"

"Indie it's okay. I'm just happy you called. I missed you."

"I missed you too."

"Alright, I'm at a gig and the photographer's calling me." She whispers, "Love you Indie."

Not a lie. In fact, it's the only truth I've heard in a while.

"Love you too."

The line goes dead, and I bring the tracker back up. This time Javi's little blue dot is sitting right next to another labeled Abbie.

Lie number eight.

I've just popped open a bottle of wine when Ryan arriv
the door, she takes one look at me and frowns.

"What the hell happened?" Her bright green eyes s

"Javi's cheating." I'm surprised by how easily the
missed her so much, and she's the first person I wanted t

"Shut the fuck up. Your Javi?" She steps inside and I s
because no, not *my* Javi. I don't think he was ever my Javi

"How do you know?" she asks.

I pull out my phone and bring up the screenshots I
conversations with Abbie before handing it to her. In them
we've grown apart and she co-signs any complaints he ha
While Ryan swipes through the evidence, I head to the
grab a glass.

"She posted pictures online." I add, tipping the bottle ov

Ryan closes the door, following behind me. "What a clown
he now?" Despite her anger, she looks beautiful. Ryan's
simple, but it highlights her high cheekbones and flawless,
tanned skin. Her hair's pulled back in a sleek high bun and her
are on full display in the body-hugging dress she's wearing. S
every bit like the model she is.

"He's on a date, you want to crash?" I'm mostly joking, bu
nods her head aggressively.

"What are we waiting for? Let's go." She takes my glass and
it in the sink. "Lets clean you up a bit." She drags me into my bath
and starts opening the makeup case I left on the counter.

When I look in the mirror, my eyes are rimmed with red an
skin around them is puffy. I reach for the faucet and turn the wate
dip my hands under the stream and splash my face. After drying

ply a little concealer and a light layer of mascara. A little lipstick ays helps me feel more confident, so I add a dark maroon shade.

Ryan hugs me from behind, giving me a tight squeeze. "There's my ."

I've been debating on confronting them tonight, but the thought doing it sends my nerves into overdrive. Even after we clean up and ad out, my resolve is disintegrating.

"What do I say when we get there?" I lock the door behind us and e make our way down the stairs from my apartment to her car parked at front.

"Whatever the hell you want to say, and he's going to listen to every ord." Ryan starts the engine and I text her the address.

"Indie listen, if we get there and you want to leave, just say the word. f you want to make a scene, I support it. If you want confirmation, we'll get it, and if you want a conversation, you'll have it. You don't deserve what he's done to you, and I'm here for whatever decision you make."

My hands shake and the tears threaten to make a reappearance. I've neglected our friendship to focus on fixing what I thought to be minor problems between Javi and me. Until yesterday, I was under the impression whatever was wrong could be mended.

"Thank you, Ryan."

"You'd do the same for me."

I would, in a heartbeat.

We drive in silence the rest of the way. Mentally, I'm trying to psych myself up, so I don't fall apart. Javi screwed me over. He doesn't deserve to get off easy. Abbie either, she was my friend and now she's sleeping with my boyfriend.

When we arrive, we find a casual burger place and choose a table diagonal from theirs. Abbie, unfortunately, is gorgeous. She has milky skin and rosy cheeks. Vastly different from my brown skin. My hand

goes to my thick coils that have a mind of their own. Meanwhile, this girl's hair is pin-straight, not a strand out of place. We're complete opposites in every way. From our looks to our personalities. Abbie's brash, but you never have to wonder what she thinks of you. I liked her honesty. Isn't that some shit?

The lights are dim, adding a shadow over our faces and we're able to hear Abbie laugh at something Javi says over the soft lofi that plays throughout the restaurant. A wave of nausea rocks through me.

"How can she smile knowing he goes home to you every night?" Ryan's lips twist in disgust as she glowers at their table. "She wanted you to know."

Did she? Abbie's arrogant, so when I saw the post, I figured she was overconfident I wouldn't go looking. He wraps his arms around her shoulders, and she practically melts at his touch. He uses his free hand to tap away at his phone. When he finishes, mine pings and I glance at the screen.

**JAVI**

> I'll be at my mom's until late, don't wait up.

Ryan scoffs when she reads the message. Javi slides his phone in his coat pocket and reaches for Abbie's hand.

This is so surreal, like some freak nightmare I can't wake up from. Javi had a string of bad luck, which left me with the financial burden. It's not his fault he got laid off shortly after we moved in together, but while I was out making the money, he started gaining a following online from his video game streaming. We decided together to take a chance, and he was supposed to do the same for me. Now it's time to collect on that promise and he's turning his back on me.

The more I watch them, the angrier I get. Abbie angles her face toward his and he takes her chin between his fingers and kisses her. It's slow and gentle, but it rips my heart to pieces. Ryan sucks in a breath next to me and my vision blurs. Shit, this is embarrassing.

I take a deep breath and remind myself he's not worth it. Pushing back from my seat, I stand and make my way over to their table.

"Hey, what are you guys doing here?" Smiling, I point between them. Javi jerks away from Abbie and hurt flashes across her features before she can hide it.

"Indie, what are you doing here?" Javi asks, his eyes darting between Abbie and me.

Leaning forward, I splay my hands across the table. "I believe I asked you first, babe." I reach for a fry off his plate, popping it in my mouth.

"I was grabbing us a to go order when I bumped into Abbie."

"But you texted me saying you were still at your mothers?" I wave my phone in his face.

The corners of his mouth turn down as he searches my eyes for something. What looks like understanding flashes across his face.

"Indigo, if you have something to say, just say it." He shrugs. Abbie looks unsure of what to do, but raises her chin in solidarity.

We stare at each other in silence. He presses his lips into a straight line, nostrils flaring.

"Indie." Abbie reaches for me, and I give her a look, daring her to put her hands on me. She thinks better of it and lets it drop.

"How long?" I ask, and his expression hardens.

"You're doing too much right now. We're in public." He narrows his eyes at me, always worried about his image.

"You're cheating on me. With the friend you said you couldn't stand. You sat there with a straight face and lied to me this morning." My voice cracks, only making me angrier. My chest feels like a furnace. I've never been so furious.

"I don't know what you think Abbie and I did, but we've only been talking."

An involuntary laugh rolls through me. "I'm not sure if sending dick pics counts as a conversation." My lips turn down in disgust as I look at Abbie. "Some texts you sent were while I was sitting next to you. You asked to come over while I was sleeping."

Abbie ignores me and looks to Javi for help.

"You went through my phone, too?" He shakes his head as if I've crossed the line when he's the one who ran miles past it.

"I sure did. I know everything. You're a piece of shit." Rage is the only thing keeping me from crying.

"If you saw the messages, then why didn't you have enough self-respect to leave? Why follow me? Something's seriously wrong with you." He looks as if I've genuinely disappointed him.

Humiliation wraps around my throat, forcing my words to die on my tongue. This is not how I thought this would go. I thought he'd feel guilty about what he's done, but he doesn't. Not even a little bit. I thought Abbie would be sorry, but instead, she's looking at me like I'm overreacting. My hands move before my brain can catch up and I grab each of their cups and throw their drinks in their faces. Abbie screams, her hair sticking to her face, eyeliner trailing down her cheeks.

"Fuck both of you." When I turn to leave, Javi shouts my name. He demands I talk to him and I hear his footsteps behind me, but Ryan blocks his path.

"Leave her alone." Her tone leaves no room to argue. She catches up with me and when we make it to her car I fall apart. Ryan lets me get it all out. She doesn't judge me for crying over the asshole, but she throws a couple of worried glances my way. It's not so much that we're over. I can handle him leaving and maybe that says something about where we were in our relationship, but it's the disrespect that eats at me.

Eventually, my tears dry up and I sit in silence the rest of the way.

We make it to Ryan's apartment complex and ride the elevator up to her floor. She lives in a luxury apartment in the heart of Los Angeles with River. It's an open floor plan with a pristine white modern couch, marbled tile and floor to ceiling windows. A beautiful granite island centers the kitchen, with a small eating nook off to the side. The décor's minimal, River can't stand clutter, but Ryan has clothes strewn about.

Even though we shared this place before I moved in with Javi, I still feel out of place being here after so long. The smallest room, where I used to live, has been turned into a study. We've been friends since we were little and when their careers brought them to California, I left Texas with them.

Ryan throws her purse on the counter and opens the fridge. "Are you hungry?"

"I'm just tired." I haven't eaten today and I'm paying for it. My stomach feels sick, and a headache is brewing.

At the sound of the doorbell, Ryan's face scrunches in confusion and she curses under her breath. "I had this girl coming over and completely forgot to text her and cancel after you called." She reaches for my arm, and we head toward the back hallway.

"Dating someone new?"

"Wouldn't call it that."

The apartment has three bedrooms, Ryan's to the right, River's room and a small study sit to the left. She opens River's door and drops my hand.

"I can't stay in here." I hate how foreign it feels to be in his room. My friendship with River caused so much tension between Javi and me that I opted to stay away.

"You can and you will. I'm not letting you go back there." She reaches into his closet and tosses one of his shirts to me. "You sleeping in his bed's nothing new."

My face heats and I reach for a pillow and throw it at her back. She laughs and pushes me toward the bed.

"I'll give him a heads up. He can take the pull-out couch in the study." She gives me a tight hug and leaves, switching off the light before closing the door behind her.

I swap my hoodie and jeans for the oversized tee. The blankets smell like River, whatever expensive cologne he's currently wearing. My fingers curl around my phone as I debate checking it again. The idea that Javi's still with her, not thinking about me, makes my heart ache. I take the risk and tap the screen; the glow making me squint.

No new messages, no missed calls.

# Chapter Two

Getting my brain to shut off took forever. It feels as though I've just fallen asleep when I feel two large hands wrap around my wrists, pinning them to my sides. Blinking into the darkness, I see a figure looming above me. My first thought is Ryan must've gotten in bed with me, but when I squint, I realize the shadow is much too broad. It's a man. Still delirious from sleep, I scream. The man's grip tightens, and he leans in so close I can feel his breath run across my face.

"Indie?" He asks and my body stills, "Now what are you doing in my bed?" He breathes in my ear and it sends an involuntary shiver down my spine. The lights flick on and I'm looking up at two beautifully familiar eyes.

River and Ryan look so much alike, yet they have such subtle differences. Ryan has bright green eyes with flecks of brown, her brothers are dark emeralds. Ryan's hair resembles honey-dipped pecans, the gold strands swallow the brown. River's hair is molten chocolate, thick and rich in color. While Ryan's hair falls in neat waves, River's strands bend around themselves forming loose ringlets that frame his face.

One thing they do have in common is the beauty they inherited. They both have the same high cheekbones, full lips, sun kissed skin and long lashes. I forgot how handsome he is. A pang of guilt hits me for neglecting our friendship.

"What's going on?"

Looking past River, I see Ryan in the doorway.

"He scared the crap out of me." I attempt to sit up, but he pushes me back down.

"Are you blaming me?" He cocks a brow.

"I thought you were breaking in." I mumble and look away because his closeness is making me squirm.

"Into my own room?" He smirks and his hair brushes against my skin.

He's got me there. To be fair, my brain's only half working. I glance at the clock on the nightstand and it's close to 1 a.m.

"I didn't expect there to be a woman in my bed. It's not unheard of, but usually I'm included." He's wearing a stupid grin and I feel an uncomfortable pressure in my chest at the thought of how many women he's probably brought here. It's none of my business, but sometimes I forget about that side of his life. He's always been private about his dating.

"Uh, should I leave you two alone?" Ryan smiles with a glint in her eye.

"You were supposed to text him." I throw the accusation at her, and she smiles wider.

"I got distracted." She winks and something tells me whoever was at the door never left.

"Do you mind?" I nod my head toward his hands still wrapped around mine. River slides from on top of me and I realize that he's in nothing but his sweats. His muscles flex under his skin as he moves,

21

and his mouth ticks up when he catches me staring. Warmth spreads through my cheeks and I avert my gaze.

"Why are you here?" He asks, and I remember how horrible my last twenty-four hours have been. Shame causes a tight pain in my chest. First time he's seen me in a month and I've taken refuge in his room. How pathetic I must look right now. Can he tell I cried myself to sleep?

"I'm sorry, I shouldn't be here." Standing, I cross my arms over my chest. His eyes fall to my thighs, and I remember I'm in nothing but his shirt. He clears his throat and looks away; I can feel heat creep up my neck, and I rush to tug at the hem. This isn't how I want him to see me. My crap is now inconveniencing the people around me.

"We raided your closet too. I'll give it back in the morning and get out of your hair now."

I start to leave, but he grabs my wrist. "That's not what I meant." He doesn't let go of my hand. Guilt knocks at my door. I don't deserve his concern.

"What happened?" He asks again, his tone takes on a hard edge.

"Javi cheated on her." Ryan calls from the doorway.

"I'll be gone by tomorrow." I want to clarify that I'm not trying to waltz back in his life after avoiding him.

"You're going back to him?" He drops my hand.

"No, why would I do that?" Honestly, I'm a little offended he would even ask.

"Because he's all you've cared about lately."

"River." Ryan hisses.

His words make me flinch, but he's not wrong. Him being one of the many things I put aside. But I've also taken enough crap today. "You don't have to worry about something that's not your problem. I'll figure it out." I start gathering the clothes I discarded earlier.

"I'm not trying to be an ass." He stands and takes my clothes from me. "Stay. I'll take the couch." He places my things on his nightstand.

"No way, I'll take the couch." I move toward the door, but he grabs the collar of my shirt and I stumble back.

"Take the bed Indie."

I'm too tired to argue, so I do as he says, getting under the blankets while he rummages through the drawers of his nightstand.

Ryan moves to sit beside me, and I rest my head on her shoulder.

The distance that's grown between River and me feels so unnatural. I bring my knees to my chest and pull the blankets up to my shoulders as I watch him.

He grabs something from the drawer and offers it to me. "I thought you might want this. You forgot it when you moved out." It's one of my old silk scarves.

"Thank you." Setting my hair free from its hair tie, I sigh in relief as I massage my scalp with the pads of my fingers.

"You shouldn't cry over someone like him." River says before opening the door.

"Who says I was crying?"

"Your eyes are red." He points out and shuts the door behind him.

"He's right, you know. Javi's not worth it." Ryan wraps her arm around my shoulder.

"I wasn't crying over him, not really. I'm frustrated because I feel lost."

"That's not true. You know what you want to do. Now that Javi's not in the way, it's time to get to work. I'll let you be sad about it for one more day, but after tomorrow, I don't want to hear his name again."

She's right. Feeling sorry for myself isn't helping. "I'll start applying to a few makeup stores nearby. Maybe I can reach out to some of my old classmates and see if they have any leads."

"The best revenge you can take out on someone is success, but keying

23

his car would be good too." She lets her words linger suggestively. We sit in silence for a moment before laughing. Javi would die, he loves that car. It's the one thing he prioritizes over all his gaming equipment.

"While tempting, I think I'll stick with plan A. Breaking the news to my mom's going to suck. If I can't find work before our lease ends, I may have to move back home."

"Indie, you're not going back with Javi. You can have your old room and stay as long as you need." Ryan nudges my shoulder.

"I don't know… It feels awkward. I've been dodging River for a while, and I'm supposed to come crawling back when things don't work out?"

She rolls her eyes. "Listen, he might be annoyed with you, but he'd never push you away. I'm sure he's already got it in his head that you're moving in."

The idea of going back to my mom's is less than ideal. I'll just have to make it up to River to get us back to where we used to be. "It won't be for long. I'm going to do whatever it takes, including avoiding relationships. Never wasting my time on something like that again."

Ryan pushes off the bed. "Don't let that clown put you off completely. There are some good guys out there. One's that would put you first. Sometimes we take chances on people and lose. You still have to play the game."

"This coming from the girl who acts like she's allergic to commitment?"

"You're different from me." She bends and kisses my cheek before shutting off the light.

Waking up to the smell of bacon is a sign that today will be better than yesterday. Hopping out of bed, I slide my legs into my jeans from yesterday so that I'm not walking around half naked. When I make it to the kitchen, Ryan's at the stove. River's already seated and eating, so I take the chair next to him.

"I figured you'd be hungry." Ryan slides a cup of coffee and a plate of eggs and bacon my way. The front of her golden-brown hair is French braided, while the rest cascades down her back in waves. She frowns at me before a slow smile spreads.

"You know what would be fun?" She leans forward on her elbows. "River was telling me about the reality dating show he was hired to work on. Maybe you should apply. How bad would Javi freak if you were on TV dating another guy?" She laughs.

River stiffens next to me. "No." He shakes his head.

"Since when do you do reality TV?" I ask. River works as a producer, but for as long as I can remember, he's avoided that genre altogether because of how unpredictable it can be.

"Someone I work with asked me to do it as a favor. In return, he'll help me meet some people who can look at my script." He shrugs.

"What? River, that's amazing. I didn't know you finished writing it."

"I haven't had a chance to tell you."

The conversation stalls, and I'm reminded of how bad a friend I've been. Sensing the awkward tension, Ryan cuts in, "So what's the show about?"

"Nothing you need to worry about." He grunts.

"I think it'd be fun." She stabs her fork into her eggs.

"Don't push her Ry." River mumbles over his coffee.

"You know what people say, the best way to get over someone is to get under someone new."

"Ryan." River glares over his mug.

"What? People say it for a reason, must be a little true." She takes in another mouthful of food.

"I've got things to take care of at the studio." River stands and pats my head as he passes. We watch him walk out the door and Ryan immediately opens the laptop that's been sitting on the counter. She taps at the keys, then spins it around to face me.

"This is the show." She points at the screen and moves to take a seat beside me.

"The Love Meltdown?"

"Don't judge the name. People go crazy for this show."

"That'll be good for River, then."

"It could be good for you, too." She reaches for the laptop and clicks the apply button.

"You put off building your clientele and brand and this could give you a jump start. It'll be a new chapter."

"I don't know… I doubt I'm what they're looking for."

"Then what harm could it do? If you get rejected, then nothing changes. Plus, they give a weekly stipend while you're there."

The exposure alone would bring traffic to my page, which could lead to more business. I'm also strapped for cash right now.

"I have to get ready for a meeting with my agent. You put in that application." She moves the computer toward me and snags a piece of bacon from my plate.

"Your girlfriend still here?" I ask as I scroll through the questions.

"Not my girlfriend. You just missed her." Ryan leaves and I eye the computer.

Being in front of the camera instead of behind it isn't something I've considered. Honestly, my life is so upside down right now. Doing something I wouldn't normally do might help get me back on track. I guess there's no harm in applying. It doesn't guarantee anything will come from it. So, I click through the questions and it's a welcome distraction.

I'm not sure how long I've been at it by the time I finish. The application was more extensive than I thought it would be. From questions about my favorite hobbies to ones about my mental health background. My cell rings and my mom's photo pops into view. I grimace, but answer anyway.

"Hey Mom."

"Hey baby, I'm calling because I mailed a package to your place, and it says it was delivered. Did you get it?" I can hear her typing away at her keyboard, so she must be working. At least she can't make a scene if others are around. She cares too much about her image for that.

"I'm not home, so I'm not sure."

"Is Javi home?"

The mention of his name makes me lose my appetite. I push the plate away and sigh.

"I'll stop by and grab it today, but don't send anything else to that address. Javi and I are no longer together, so-"

"I knew it wouldn't last. I knew he wasn't any good when he encouraged you not to go back to school."

"I went to school." I bite out.

"I mean actual school, not the makeup thing."

Not even two minutes in and I'm ready to hang up.

"Well, what happened?" Her typing resumes.

"We've decided to see other people."

She pauses and sucks her teeth. "I doubt that's a mutual decision. Indigo, I told you not to follow that boy around. You always make sure you're good first."

"I'm not sure why you think now's the best time to rub it in."

She breathes heavily as if I'm the one frustrating her. "Where are you now? Will you be coming home? Tiffany and I can pick you up from the airport."

Tiffany is Ryan and River's mom. She and my mother are attached at the hip, always have been. The thought of flying back to Texas so my mom can micromanage makes me want to scream.

"No. I'm staying with Ryan and River."

"Oh. You're better when River's around. He'll make sure you get your head on straight, and Ryan's doing so well. I picked up a magazine with her on the front the other day."

River and Ryan can do no wrong in her eyes. They both graduated from top colleges and excel in their careers. Ryan's modeling is as unconventional as being a makeup artist, yet she feels nothing but pride for her. While River's the son she never had, not that she hasn't tried to change that. She's always trying to play matchmaker, but that's not going to happen. It's never been like that between us. Believe me, I found out the hard way.

"Yeah Mom, hopefully I'll eventually be less of a disappointment. I have to go. I'll let you know when I grab the package. Love you." I disconnect the line and know I'll get an angry voicemail from her later, but that's future me's problem.

My eyes gravitate back to the laptop. I'd finished the application before she called, so I move the cursor and hit submit. Leaning back in my seat, I stare up at the ceiling. I'm not letting anything else ruin my day. Positive energy only.

My phone chimes and Abbie's name flashes across the screen.

**ABBIE**

Your stuff's outside the door.

The text accompanies a photo of what I assume is my stuff in multiple garbage bags sitting on the porch.

Motherfucker.

# Chapter Three

My day is quickly going south. I stare at Abbie's message and enlarge the photo in complete shock that Javi allowed this. The garbage bags are a nice touch. What an asshole.

"What's up with you? You look like you want to throw your phone." Ryan asks as she slips her shoes on.

Bringing the message back up, I angle my screen so she can read it.

"Are you shitting me?" She blinks, her mouth hanging open in disbelief.

"It's like we're roommates who ended on bad terms. We had a whole relationship." He doesn't regret what he did at all.

"Give me your apartment key. I'm going to get your stuff after my meeting." Ryan throws her bag over her shoulder.

"Why do you need the key? Everything's outside."

"So he has no excuse to text you again. I'll leave it under the mat." She hands me my purse from the counter. I hand her the key and she shoves it in her bag.

"I'll be back. Don't let this stress you out."

When she leaves, I pick up my phone and delete Javi and I's message thread. I figure looking at all our old texts would be too tempting. Opening my email, I scan my inbox. No responses from the places I applied to earlier this week. I get to work sending my resume to a few cosmetics stores and text a few old classmates for referrals.

This takes most of the afternoon with only a few people hitting me back, letting me know they didn't know of anything but would keep me posted. My portfolio is lacking but I swipe through my photos, looking for some good examples of my work to put on my profile.

"Hey."

The sound of River's voice startles me. I look up and he's standing in front of me with a bottle of lemonade and my favorite chocolate. I take them gratefully and he takes a seat on the couch beside me.

"Have you been sitting here all day?"

I rip open the candy wrapper, "Yeah, I need to find work. Hopefully, I'll hear back soon."

He scratches the back of his neck and looks away. "You don't have to try so hard. I'm not in a rush for you to leave."

A smile tugs at my lips and I feel relief at the thought that he doesn't seem to hate me.

"How fast do you think you can get dressed?" He checks his watch.

"Why?"

"Ryan told me to get you to the beach."

"This late?" The sun's already setting.

"I said the same thing. She yelled that she'd be waiting and hung up."

"I'm assuming I can borrow her clothes. She was supposed to bring mine back from the apartment."

"Unless you want to borrow mine. My stuff looks good on you."

I wave him off. Flirting is a part of Rivers' personality and I've learned not to take it seriously.

It took a while to find something in Ryan's closet that fit. She's taller than me and slim, while my hips make it hard to squeeze into most jeans. Finally, I settled on comfy biker shorts and an oversized gray t-shirt with *West Coast* printed across the front.

It's warm tonight, but the breeze near the water's always cold. I wrap my arms around myself, and River tracks the movement. He reaches between us to the back seat and hands me his bomber jacket.

"Thanks." I mumble as I shrug it on.

"One of us has to be prepared." He smiles and leans against the steering wheel of his truck.

The beach is mostly empty since it's getting late. The sky's a dusky gray and the stars reflect off the water. Wrestling my curls into a bun before we left ate up a lot of our time and we've lost the daylight. After spotting Ryan, we make our way. She has a large blanket spread across the sand, with takeout bags from a nearby chicken spot. She's wearing a pastel pink wig with a large backpack slung over her shoulder.

"Did you drag us here to eat wings? And what's on your head?" River asks.

"I'm not mad about it. I'm starved." When I untie the plastic bag and open the container, the smell of lemon pepper wings makes my mouth water.

"Welcome to Indigo's burning ceremony." She shouts, throwing confetti over me and blowing into a kazoo. Ryan drops her bag to the floor and turns it upside down, dumping everything out.

"Ry, why do you have Javi's stuff?" I put the wings down and look through everything she's taken. Other than some of his clothes, there are photos of Javi and I. We look so happy in them, it's sickening.

"Because we're going to burn it all."

I drop the photo in my hands and my mouth falls open.

"You took all this?" River kicks at the stolen goods.

"Didn't you gift him these?" Ryan holds a pair of sneakers I waited hours in line for.

"I did." I snatch them from her hands. "Ryan, our apartment has a camera at the door. He's going to know you took this stuff."

Ryan hands me a matchbook and points at her shiny wig. "Disguised myself and wore sunglasses." She pulls two more wigs out of her bag, one pastel purple and one green. She plops the purple on my head and the green on River's. Ryan taps the trash can next to her. "Do the honors, Indigo."

I look at River, and he shrugs. He's never been able to stop Ryan when she's got an idea in her head. I light the match and drop it into the trash can, and a small fire builds. I hold the shoes over the fire, they were Javi's favorites. Ryan chants my name as they fall from my fingers and seeing the fire feed off them makes my chest feel lighter.

"Hell yeah." She shakes my shoulders, and I can't help but laugh.

"My girl's a free woman." Ryan shouts into the sky. She pulls a bottle of wine out of her bag, and we pass it between us.

Every time I drop something into the fire, I feel a little more in control. When I found out Javi was cheating, I felt like I lost so much of it. I watch Ryan as she plays music from her phone and dances around the flames. Tonight was needed and when Ryan hands me the wine, I drink, ready to let go of all the stress that's been knotting in my stomach. We pass the bottle between the both of us for a while until River snatches it away.

"You know what's funny about these shoes? None of them are his size. He buys them a size bigger so he can add little heels in them that make him taller." I drop the last pair into the fire.

Ryan doubles over in laughter. "No freaking way." Tears fall from her eyes and her laugh comes out as a wheeze. I do my best to walk over to the blanket, but I trip over my own feet.

"You're both drunk." River laughs while offering me his hand.

I push him away, determined to make it on my own, but the ground tilts and I fall back into the sand. "Okay, maybe I'm a little buzzed." I giggle and River's hands find my waist as he helps me find my balance. When we make it to the blanket, I collapse onto my back next to Ryan. River lies on my other side.

Ryan holds her phone up, wrapping her free arm around my neck. "Squeeze in River."

He does as she asks. Our bodies press together and my skin buzzes at the contact. I'm going to ignore the electricity that pulses between us and blame it on the alcohol. I stick my tongue out and I can feel Ryan putting bunny ears behind my head before the flash goes off.

"I'm going to find a restroom before we leave." Ryan stands, dusts the sand from her shorts and runs off.

"You feel any better?" River angles his head toward mine.

"You want the truth?" I turn to face him, and we're nose to nose.

"Yeah, you're a horrible liar."

Looking into those eyes so closely makes me feel even more off balance. "I feel like I'm not sure what to do next. Javi and I had plans. They mainly centered around him, but they were plans. I also can't help but feel…" Shame claws at me and I let the words die.

River props himself up on his elbow, leaning over me, "Feel what?"

"Unlovable." I drop his gaze and focus on his chest instead. "I know Javi's in the wrong and he's not worth my time or energy, but I thought we had a future. It wasn't all bad, you know?"

"You're the easiest person to love. There's no way he doesn't regret it. He's being an ass because his inflated ego won't let him beg you to come back."

"Javi wouldn't beg."

"If he had half a brain, he would."

My eyes jump to his. I search for any sign of resentment, but there isn't any. "I'm sorry."

"Apologies usually come with context." He lifts a brow.

"I'm sorry for being such a crappy friend. I thought being in a relationship meant prioritizing it over my friendships, and that was wrong."

River doesn't say anything for a while. I lose the battle of wills and break eye contact first. "I'm not mad. I just learned not to let you go again." He brushes sand from my hair, "I'm just saying he mishandled you in ways that will never make sense to me."

"Are you volunteering to take over?" I joke, but River isn't smiling. He opens his mouth to say something, but Ryan stops in front of us panting.

"Indie, I accidentally took your phone with me and it's going off like crazy."

Eager to break the weird tension between River and me, I sit up too fast. I forgot how cloudy my head felt and now I'm lightheaded. She hands me my phone and I swipe up, revealing six missed calls from Javi and three unopened messages.

"What's wrong?" Ryan sits beside me, resting her chin on my shoulder.

"Oh, looks like he made it home." She throws her head back and laughs. My thumb glides across the screen, opening the messenger app.

JAVI

> Really Indigo? This is so immature.

JAVI

> If you're doing this for my attention, congratulations. You have it.

JAVI

> You threw my gaming equipment off the balcony?

"Ryan, you threw his gaming stuff over the balcony?" I slap her shoulder and she laughs even harder.

"I can neither confirm nor deny those details, but if I did that, I would tell you that seeing it shatter as it hit the ground was so satisfying."

"How many crimes did you commit today?" River asks in disbelief.

"Uh, girl you might want to check your social media." Ryan ignores River, peering down at her phone.

Swiping my finger over my screen, I open my account to see *99+* highlighted in red next to the notification bell icon. I haven't posted in forever, but the most recent picture on my account has a flood of new comments. All of them alluding to the idea that I'm obsessed with Javi and am now stalking he and Abbie. People are commenting Abbie's username, but I'm blocked so I log into my old burner account.

When I bring up Abbie's page, the pictures with her and Javi are there, but there's a new post. It's a video and someone at the restaurant caught footage of me throwing drinks in their faces. She still has our old pictures up, so it wasn't hard for people to find my page. Abbie completely manipulated the timeline. She's flipped the script and now I'm the friend who's been pushing up on her boyfriend. I hit the linked tag to Javi's account someone left in the comments. He's made a new post, and my frown transforms into a grimace as I see the accompanying caption.

Javi's sitting on the balcony of his apartment with a beer in his hand, looking into the sunset away from the camera, showing off his profile. A woman sits in his lap, but you can only see the back of her head. The butterfly tattoo stamped on her lower back lets me know it's Abbie.

*Me and mines blocking out the noise. Peace and love to those that need it.*

My anger clears some of the alcohol induced fog. Javi doesn't explicitly confirm anything, but he isn't refuting the comments making the accusation. He has a large following at a little over three hundred thousand compared to my ten thousand, and they're offended on his behalf.

"Now I don't feel bad about trashing his stuff. We're going to ignore him." Ryan snags my phone out of my hands. "All he's done is bring traction to your page, which will benefit you in the end."

"I mean sure, but they're bashing me."

"People follow the herd. It's a hive mind mentality. Right now, it's cool to hate you and they'll continue to follow you and interact with all your posts to do it. Paint the picture you want them to see. Rebrand. People love a good villain anyway, depending on how you play it, they'll switch sides."

I move to stand but my knees feel like jello and my head feels heavy.

"Okay, it's time to get you home." River's hand wraps around my arm, steadying me. "You're not going to make it." He bends down on his haunches and reaches his hands behind him. "Get on my back."

"Nah uh." I'm dizzy and exhausted but not too far gone to recognize having to be carried is embarrassing.

"Get over here, or I'll leave you behind." He calls over his shoulder.

Caving, I wrap my arms around his neck and lay against his back.

He stands and wraps his arms around my thighs, holding me in place. "You okay?"

I nod my head against his back, and his damn scent is everywhere. I'm not sure what cologne he uses, but I hope he never changes it.

"My mom bought me this cologne."

"Did I say that aloud?" My words jumble together, and my eyes feel heavy.

"You did." I can feel his laughter move through him.

He's so warm, I squeeze tighter and nuzzle against his neck, "You feel so good."

His grip on me tightens and I swear his skin turns a light shade of pink.

"That's enough out of you." His voice sounds rough, and I hear Ryan chuckle from behind us.

It takes too much effort to keep my eyes open any longer, so I give up and fall into the best sleep I've had in a while.

# Chapter Four

*I* found work at a local beauty department store and I've been working for a couple of weeks now. The manager here was the only one to offer me a position with my limited portfolio.

"What do you think?" I hold the mirror up to my client's face. It's her birthday, and she has a photoshoot this afternoon. She wanted dramatic cat-eye lashes and shades of gold and brown for her lids. She has cool undertones, so we paired the look with a deep berry colored blush and matching lip.

"Oh my gosh, it doesn't even look like me." She lays a delicate touch to her cheek.

"It helps that you're pretty to begin with." I hand her the receipt and let her know she can pay up front.

I pull my calendar up on my phone to confirm my upcoming appointments. Ryan was right. Javi's' stunt brought me an influx of followers. While the hate is still coming my way, my work speaks for itself and a lot of the people who came to snoop stayed to book. My clientele still isn't consistent enough to branch out on my own, and the pay is low, but it's a start.

While checking my email for new appointment requests, I see a message from *The Real Productions*. I hadn't heard anything after I submitted that application for the reality show and honestly, I'd forgotten about it. Opening the email, I scan the contents, sucking in a breath as I get to the bottom. After the formalities, there is a request to see me tomorrow for an interview.

Exiting the app, I rush to dial Ryan's number.

"Hey, I was about to call you." She sings through the phone.

"I heard about my application from that show."

Ryan squeals her delight on the other end of the line. "I knew they'd call. When is it?"

"I'm not sure if I'm going to go, Ry. I didn't expect to hear back."

"Why wouldn't you go? Live a little Indie, plus you've been complaining about the lack of money coming in. The show matches your wages and gives an additional weekly stipend."

As much as I hate to admit it, Ryan's right. Being on TV would undoubtedly get more eyes on my page and the money wouldn't hurt.

"I guess it's only an interview."

"Exactly, go show them why it'd be a flop without you."

"Fine, I don't know how I let you talk me into these things."

"Because I love you and know what's best."

After hanging up with Ryan, I click the link attached to the email and select my time slot for tomorrow afternoon.

---

Now that I'm here, I regret letting Ryan talk me into coming. Productions rented out a conference room in a nearby hotel. My nerves are getting to me, and I wonder if I chose the right outfit. My dress is long and flutters around my ankles. It has powder blue flowers printed on the fabric and the sleeves puff around my shoulders. The slit of the skirt creeps up my right thigh and I've paired it with beige wedges with straps that wrap up my calf. At least my hair and makeup is always on point. I went with a blue the same shade as my dress for my eyes with white on the inner corner and a wispy lash strip.

"Alright Ms. Johnson, you're all checked in. Someone's coming to take you back." The receptionist's all business, no smile or polite banter.

A woman in a pantsuit comes for me, and I follow her to a hallway. She pushes open the first door we come up to and gestures for me to enter. It seems to be one of the hotel's empty conference rooms. Other than two security guards to my right, there is a table at the back of the space where an older woman and a man who looks a bit older than me are seated. They look up from the folders in front of them when I approach, and I stop a few feet in front of them.

"As stated in the paperwork you filled out, this is being recorded. We have cameras there," she points to a mounted camera behind them, "and there." A second camera's mounted on the wall to my right. "My name's Mary and beside me is Noah." The man nods and everything about him screams Hollywood. From his designer clothes to the fact that he's wearing sunglasses indoors.

"Can you tell us about yourself?" Mary smiles warmly, easing my nerves.

"My name's Indigo Johnson. I'm twenty-three, born and raised in Texas before moving to California a few years ago, and I'm a makeup artist."

"Interesting." Mary says, but Noah lifts his wrist and checks the time on his watch. "What about your family? Are you close?" She asks while still reading the papers in front of her.

"My mom and I—" I'm interrupted by the sound of the door being thrown open. The culprit enters the room and I feel the air leave my lungs. He's the kind of beautiful that makes you want to pinch yourself to make sure you're not dreaming. A face that looks like it was hand carved, all sharp angles and full lips. His dark eyes are storm clouds that latch to mine as he runs his hands through his hair, pushing the curly black strands out of the way. My eyes travel down to his chest. He has light brown skin and the top of his shirt's unbuttoned, but not in a gross flashy kind of way, just enough to pique my interest. The material covering his arms is hanging on for dear life as his muscles tense. My attention draws back up to his mouth, which has formed into a smirk as he approaches.

"You're not supposed to be here." Noah sighs.

"No one answered my calls. Figured I'd drop in. You don't mind, do you?" The mystery man leans against the table and gives me a crooked smile.

"This isn't protocol." Mary grits out.

"Who cares? It's the last one of the day." Noah leans back in his chair.

"Go on beautiful." The man says, still leaning against the table, eyes locked on my lips. I ignore how the look he's giving me makes me feel, all tingly and self-conscious. He's clearly overdosing on confidence, and I can't tell if I like it or not.

"My mother and I are close, even if we don't always agree. She raised me alone until we rented out a room at a friend's house."

"So you grew up poor?" Noah asks.

Irritation flares inside me as pride makes me throw my shoulders back and lift my chin. "We didn't have a lot, but we had what we needed."

"What about dating? Tell us about your recent relationships." Mary sits forward.

My recent relationship is the last thing I want to discuss. My eyes flick to the man still evaluating my every move.

"I recently broke up with my boyfriend. We'd been together for over two years. He was my first real relationship."

"I find that hard to believe." The stranger's eyes travel down my body. I shoot a scowl in his direction, which causes him to smile wider, and I hate the way my heart reacts to the small dimples that appear. What a creep.

"So you're a virgin? Or you were one?" Noah leans forward, pen in hand. Is he wanting to take notes on my sexual activity? "We need to know how to package you sweetheart, the poor thing isn't going to work. We already have a *Cinderella*, but we don't have a virgin." Noah smiles.

"I lost that a long time ago."

"So your boyfriend wasn't your first?" Mr. Way-Too-Full-of-Himself folds his arms over his chest. Yep, definitely don't like him. I can't tell if he's judging me, but I'll never let a man make me feel insecure about what I do with my body.

"No. He wasn't. Thank God for that." The man blinks at me in surprise before laughing, which annoys me more.

Mary cuts in. "We checked your socials and see that you were involved with this Javi guy. He has a large following. Do you often go after men in the public eye?"

"No, I knew Javi before he grew his following." I've avoided fanning the flames and attempting to clear my name to avoid it getting any messier, but now it's followed me here.

"Some girls are good at that, they know which ones to latch on to before a guy hits it big." Noah interjects, a look of displeasure plays across his features. Okay, seriously, what the hell is his problem?

"If we're being honest, I made Javi who he is today. Some men are good at that. They know which women they can suck dry until they don't need them anymore."

Noah's face falls. The man who has yet to introduce himself releases a full-bodied laugh.

"Why'd you break up? The details surrounding your relationship are muddy." Mary taps the paper in front of her which is apparently my dossier.

The heat in my chest returns. I take a calming breath and weigh my words. "People believe what they want. Anything you find online won't paint an accurate picture."

"He also insinuates you destroyed his property. Do you normally have outbursts like that?" Mary shakes her head, her bob bouncing with the movement.

I make a mental note to kick Ryan for that later. When Javi posted pics of the damage, it confirmed the "Toxic Ex" title he'd given me. "At the risk of sounding cliché, it wasn't me."

"You're playing the innocent thing up, but this is the better angle." Noah laces his fingers together and places his hands in front of him.

This conversations officially used up what little patience I had. Javi disrespected me and his actions are still bleeding into my life now.

"I have no reason to pretend to be anything other than who I am. People are obsessed with pushing a narrative and turning it into something bigger than it was."

Noah rolls his eyes. "You're still getting a lot of attention online. This Javi guy has a loyal following. Do you think your current image would be good for the show?"

"You tell me? It doesn't seem like you care if I'm a good person." I raise a brow and Noah gives me a knowing smile.

"It doesn't seem like the situation was that long ago. Do you feel ready to fall in love again?" Mary asks.

I roll her question around in my head. The thought hadn't crossed my mind. Do people even find love on these shows? It doesn't sound like they want real answers anyway.

"I'm ready for whatever comes next. If it's love, then I'm open to it." It won't be, but if that answer sells them, then fine.

"Well, Indigo, I think that's all the questions we have for you. Do you have any for us?"

"I don't. Thank you for taking the time to see me."

Mary smiles while Noah scrolls through his phone, completely checked out. Doing my best to ignore the man still watching me, I turn to leave. I didn't expect to get this far, and based on how things went today; I doubt I'll be hearing back.

"Your troubles with social media and the pressure that comes with it will get worse if you do this. Why would you want to?" The man's voice makes me halt. I look over my shoulder and his eyes are locked on mine.

"I want some control back. If people are going to talk anyway, I might as well give them a show."

"You think you can change the narrative?" He tilts his head to the side, his curls falling with the movement.

"Who says I want to change it?"

The corners of the man's lips hike up and he nods as if dismissing me, so I turn to leave.

I'll be the bad guy if they want me too, but they can hate me while I collect that check.

# Chapter Five

It's been a week since the casting call and I haven't heard anything, which is fine by me. I've been avoiding telling River I applied, but it feels like I'm hiding things from him, so I'm making it a point to bring it up this morning.

"Are you even listening to me Indie?" Ryan huffs into the camera. My phone is propped on the counter while we have our morning video call—well, my morning, her afternoon. Ryan had to leave for Paris earlier this week.

"Your agent had to book your next flight economy since it's a last-minute schedule change and you're horrified to be seated with us regular folk."

"Ugh, Indie. It's a fourteen hour flight from Paris to Japan. I'm 5'10". Do you understand how much pain I'm going to be in?"

"I'm sorry Ry, your problems are a little out of my tax bracket babe."

Her laugh fills the space between us. "I can't believe you haven't heard anything back about the show yet."

"I can. It didn't go well. They were harping on my drama with Javi." Sliding the spatula under the pancake, I move it to a plate and begin

chopping some fruit. "Maybe I don't even have to tell River."

"You used to tell him everything, talk to him."

"Talk to me about what?" The sound of Rivers' voice floats into the kitchen.

"Oop, gotta go." Ryan shouts before disconnecting the line.

"I made breakfast, thought we could catch up."

"Are those chocolate chip?"

"Yep, go sit." I move the skillet to the sink and add fruit on both our plates before bringing them to the table.

"Why do I feel like you're buttering me up?" He drizzles syrup before cutting into his food.

River didn't explicitly tell me not to apply, but he didn't seem to like the idea. So I've been stalling. "Should I not cook for you next time?"

"I'm not opposed to a beautiful woman making me breakfast." He rests his elbow on the table and props his head on the palm of his hand. He's giving me that look that's always made my stomach flip. River may be handsome, but I'll never go down that road again.

*The Becks entered my life when I was five. I was too young at the time to recognize that the life my mom had built for us was falling apart. Most memories of my dad have faded. He was never home. I do remember the fighting. The late nights huddled under the blankets with my palms pressed against my ears, trying to block out the noise. It was impossible, though. It would continue until late and then Mom would climb into my bed. I'd pretend to be sleeping while she cried.*

*This became our routine most nights until one morning she got me dressed like she normally would for school, only she didn't stop at packing my backpack—she had her own bags too. We took a different route than usual and arrived at the biggest house I'd ever seen. A woman with pale skin and brick colored hair answered the door.*

*"Violet." The woman smiled and her eyes crinkled at the edges.*

"*Tiffany, hey.*" *My mom opened her arms, and they pulled each other into a hug while I hid behind my mother's leg. They pulled apart, and the woman bent down and smiled warmly at me.*

"*You must not remember me Indigo, I'm your auntie Tiffany.*"

*Mom explained they were best friends since high school and though they weren't blood related, they considered themselves sisters. Tiffany ushered us into her home and a little boy, who she introduced as her son, was on the floor playing with toy cars.*

"*You guys were inseparable when you were babies. You'd sleep in the same crib and cry when we pulled you apart.*" *Tiffany laughed as she introduced me to River.*

*Even back then, River was a cute kid. His baby fat still clung to him, and his curls were loose spirals falling at his shoulders. Thick curly lashes framed his dark green eyes, and he was missing his front teeth.*

*I remember thinking that River's name fit him perfectly. He liked moving at his own pace, and it was almost impossible not to be dragged into his current.*

"*We're going to be friends.*" *He stood in front of me, toy car still in hand.* "*You're going to be staying in my old playroom. Do you want to see it?*"

*My mom hadn't broken the news that we would be staying with the Becks, and I had a full on, arms swinging, legs kicking tantrum. I remember being upset about the things we'd left behind and my old bed, which felt like a safe space for my mom and me. It felt like being separated from my things was equivalent to my little world going up in flames.*

*When Tiffany and my mom's soothing words didn't stop my crying, River took it upon himself to take my face between his chubby palms.*

"*I'll give you every toy I have if you want.*" *He grabbed my wrist, forcing his car into my hand.*

"*That one's my favorite, but you can have it. We can share my bed too. It's a lot bigger than the one in the playroom.*" *He smiled at me, his tongue poking* through the gap in his teeth.

"I don't like cars." The tears had stopped flowing. His words had piqued my curiosity and my five year old heart was fickle.

"My sister's not home. I bet she has something we can steal." Mischief danced in his eyes.

River was right. We were fast friends. I slept in his bed every night when we were small. It didn't stop as we aged until Ryan said it was weird that we were in middle school and still doing it.

"Aren't you guys getting a little old to be sleeping together?" She asked out of the blue.

"Why would it be weird?"

"Indie, I know my brother's a dork, but he's still a boy." She puckers her lips, applying a pretty shade of pink.

"So?"

"So, he's at the age where girls stop being gross. You guys can't remain naïve forever."

"What do you mean?" I move to sit at the edge of her bed.

"Listen Indie, you're a cute kid, but your body will start to change. Remember the summer our moms had to take me shopping for my first bras? It'll be your turn soon."

Ryan's two years older than River and me. She always felt light years ahead, so the possibility that I would turn into a girl with curves that turned the boys heads the way she did never crossed my mind. The idea that River could be one of those boys was even further off my radar until that moment. The thought of him noticing me opened a door that should've remained closed.

Not long after that conversation, I realized I had a crush on River Beck. I'd grown accustomed to him knowing when I needed him most and making me feel like anything I said or felt was important. This was at a time when my mom was busy with school and work, so having River helped fill that hole.

*Once it was clear that I liked him, I stopped going to his room at night. It didn't help that River lost his baby fat over the summer and while he was always cute to me, the other girls started to notice too. While River became lean and towered over me, the boobs I was promised never came, and I fell behind the other girls in that department.*

*Keeping things from River felt unnatural, and this crush was eating away at our friendship. I promised myself I'd tell him how I felt before high school, but our summer before the ninth grade went faster than I expected. I remember feeling sick to my stomach as I waited for him in the hall. Biting back my fear, I knocked on his door. It took him a while to answer, and I felt my courage fading. Just as I was about to leave, his door opened, the light from his room spilling out.*

*"Hey Blue, what's up?"*

*Blue. I'm not sure when he first called me that, but I do know it always felt right. I liked that it made me feel tied to him in a special way.*

*"We start high school in a couple days." I'm not sure why I chose that as my opener. Nerves, I guess.*

*"Uh, yeah. Are you asking or telling?" He asked, cocking his head to the side.*

*"Telling. What do you think of me?" He cocks his head to the side, so I barrel ahead before he can answer. "Because I think you're my favorite person, and that we owe it to ourselves to give it a try."*

*"Give what a try?" He only looked more confused, rightfully so. I was blowing it and not making much sense.*

*Before I could figure out how to salvage things, laughter erupted from his room. The door was pulled open by one of River's friends. Behind them were two other boys I recognized from his basketball team.*

*"Dude, you're being dense. She's clearly coming on to you." The boy who opened the door threw an arm over River's shoulders.*

*River shook his head. "No, she doesn't, don't tease her." He elbowed his friend in the ribs.*

*"Tell me I'm wrong," the boy knocked River's shoulder. "You haven't told her about Elizabeth?"*

*The embarrassment feels fresh just thinking about it. I'm not sure what I looked like to River in that moment, but I could see the realization hit him and I ran because liking me in that way was clearly something he hadn't even considered. To his credit, he did follow me. He was persistent. I ignored his knocks at my door and the multiple texts he sent asking to talk. My humiliation prevented me from facing him. Unfortunately, we still lived together, so we did eventually have "the talk".*

*"You're my best friend Indigo, you're one of the most important people to me. I don't see you like that, and there's too much going on right now." He avoided looking me in the eye and it wasn't lost on me that he dropped the nickname.*

*"Besides, changing what we have... why risk that, right?" He finally made an effort to look at me and I could tell this was awful for him, too.*

*"I do want to tell you, because I'd rather you hear from me. I'm dating Elizabeth. You guys had a class together last year."*

*"Oh. That makes sense. She's so pretty." It's all I could think to say. My hands trembled, and I did my best to hide them. He frowned and started to say something, but I didn't want to hear it, so I cut him off. "It's okay, hormones suck. Ryan warned me. You're not horrible looking and I've been stuck in the house with you all summer. It's you now. It'll be someone new tomorrow."*

I lied. It was River tomorrow, and the next day and the day after that. My feelings lingered for longer than I'd like to admit. My mom and I lived with the Becks for one more awkward year. Mom finally graduated with her masters and found work that paid well enough for her to purchase our own home. Through everything, River has been my constant, even after I made things awkward and even now when he should be mad at me.

"I've got something to tell you." I push my plate forward and sit up straight.

"I'm listening." He leans back in his seat, folding his arms across his chest.

"Well, you remember how Ryan brought up me applying to that show you'll be working on?" I let me words linger but he's not biting. "Well, I did it. I went to the casting call about a week ago. But it didn't go well. I won't hear back."

He's silent at first, and I fidget under his gaze. "You like your privacy. Why would you want this?"

"The exposure could jumpstart everything. I want to get my own studio and find my own place."

"Being on reality TV isn't easy and the way they manipulate the women..." He shakes his head, "You don't even know how you're being portrayed until it's too late."

"I can handle myself, River."

"Are you doing this because of Javi?"

The threats from Javi's followers have died down a lot. Blocking him on everything helped and thinking of him doesn't hurt like it used to. It's been weeks and I've worked hard to move past it. "This has everything to do with me and what I want to do. I'm over the Javi situation."

"Are you? It hasn't even been a month and now you're trying to date another guy on national television."

An uncomfortable silence falls between us and my hands ball into fists. His words bite regardless of his intentions. My world became a lot smaller while I was with Javi, but I'm still me. Was it that easy to ruin his idea of me?

"You said you weren't angry with me."

His eyes soften and he sighs, "I didn't mean it like that."

"You did." I stab my eggs with my fork. "I genuinely think this could be good for me, but that's only *if* it happens. There's always the possibility they'll pass on me."

His eyes bore into mine. "I want to make sure you thought it through."

"I have." Straightening my spine, I attempt to look more confident than I feel inside.

"Then there's nothing left to say." Something about the way he says it sounds sad.

Great. That went well.

# Chapter Six

After work, I stopped at the bank to pull out cash. It's been over a month since I moved in with River and Ryan, and while they haven't asked, I figured it was time I contribute. Every time I send money to River's account, he bounces it back. According to him, my focus should be getting back on my feet, but the least I can do is pay my share of the rent. I've beat him home so I can hide the cash somewhere he'll find it later.

Even though the study is my old room, it feels unfamiliar. Movie posters cover the walls, from famous documentaries to action films. The pull-out couch is pushed against a corner underneath a window and a desk with a computer sits against the wall next to a closet. It's pristine. River's always been a neat freak. I've taken over Ryan's room while she's out of town, and I'm grateful she's as messy as me. The clock in the corner of the computer screen reads 7 p.m. River starts work before the sun's up and doesn't come back until after it sets. I'm not sure how he functions with the hours he puts in.

I open one of the desk drawers and peer inside. It's empty except for a few books. I pull the cash from my back pocket and hide it underneath

the books and close the drawer.

"How many times am I going to catch you in rooms you're not supposed to be in?"

Spinning on my heel, I find River leaning against the doorframe. He's in a pair of gray joggers and a plain white tee. He's wearing his glasses today, and he pushes them further up the bridge of his nose before narrowing his gaze.

"Oh, am I not allowed in here?" I ask, leaning my hip against the desk.

He pushes off the door frame, dropping his bag to the floor. "You're always welcome. You just look like you're up to no good." He stops in front of me and places his hands on the desk, trapping me between his arms.

"Don't come so close." Breaking eye contact, I glance at the door.

"Why? We're just talking."

I don't have to look at him to know he's smiling.

"We can do that on opposite sides of the room." I mumble and fiddle with the hair tie around my wrist.

"Am I making you uncomfortable?" He whispers and his breath tickles my ear, sending a tingle down my spine. Handsome men are the worst, especially when they know it. He laughs and I push past him, making my escape.

"I came to see if you wanted to grab food, but never mind." The lie rolls off my tongue. When I make it to the living room, I grab my purse. The leftovers in the fridge will have to wait. Before I can leave, River breezes past me, he opens the door and dangles his keys in my face.

"I'll drive." He stands to the side, letting me pass. As I do, he grabs my wrist. "How are you going to do the show if you can't handle my teasing?" He smirks and stalks off toward the parking garage.

Hell, if I know, I hadn't thought that far.

We took River's truck to pick up burgers and a large order of fries to share. We park in front of the restaurant, and I pop the lid off my milkshake to dip my fries inside. The salty, sweet combo will forever be superior. River wrinkles his nose at me as he unwraps his food.

"Don't knock it til' you try it." Dipping more fries, I reach over and wave them between us.

"If you don't take them, they'll drip on your leather seats." His car is as clean as his room, no clutter and freshly detailed.

"I don't want your soggy fries." He reaches for the AC and cuts the air down.

"Fine, have the napkins ready, then." The vanilla ice cream comes precariously close to falling when he caves and wraps his hand around mine, biting into the fries.

"Good?" I ask and he coughs, grimacing as if it's the worst thing in the world. "Oh please, it's not that bad."

"Remind me not to take any new food suggestions from you." He says and his cell lights up from the phone stand attached to the dash. He reaches over and taps the screen, answering the call.

His mother comes into view. Her red hair's a mess of curls, and she runs her hands through them. Her eyes are usually a bright green like Ryan's, but today they're dull and framed by dark circles. Tiffany has always had severe depression and spiraled for a while after the divorce. My mom stops by most weekends, especially once we all left Texas, and I try to call when I can.

"Hey, everything alright?" River straightens in his seat.

"I'm fine. I just wanted to check in." She pauses and turns her smile my way. "Hey Indie, how are you?"

"I'm good Tiff. Miss you, though." Leaning forward, I try to squeeze beside River, so she has a better view of the both of us.

"If you miss me so much, book a flight and drag that one with you. He acts like he's too busy for me." She jerks her head in River's direction.

I've avoided visiting, but she looks so hopeful I can't say no. "I'll make sure to bring him home."

Her eyes light up, and her smile widens.

"My son's going to work himself into an early grave. Please watch over him, he thinks taking a day off's a crime." She tucks her fiery locks behind her ears.

"I'm wrapping up a project and jumping right into the next one. It's not the right time to travel." River shakes his head and Tiffany's smile falters, but she slides it back into place. I'm not sure what's gotten into him. He usually bends over backward for his mom. He's tense and keeps looking out the window as if he's ready for the conversation to end.

Shoving River with my shoulder, I smile, hoping to ease the tension between them. "That doesn't mean we can't make time. We'll look at our schedules and figure it out." She nods at my words but looks at River, who doesn't reassure her.

"I'll stop interrupting your date, then." Tiffany's as bad as my mom.

"It's not a date." River doesn't hesitate to correct her, and his tone is harsh. Didn't know the idea repulsed him so much. It shouldn't bother me, but it does. Our moms joking about this is nothing new.

Tiffany doesn't seem ruffled by it though; she shakes her head mumbling "Wishful thinking" before disconnecting the call.

"What's going on with you? We can do a weekend trip. Two days won't kill you."

He sighs and leans forward, wrapping his arms around the steering wheel. His burger sits forgotten on the console between us. "Why haven't you gone back to visit your mom?" He gives me a knowing look.

Okay. He's got me there, but his mom dotes on him and thinks he walks on water.

"Our situations are different." Twisting in my seat, I bring my legs to my chest and face him.

"They are. They always have been." He breathes and looks away from me.

"What's that supposed to mean?"

"It means you've always been able to depend on your mom. She's always worked hard even when she didn't have much to work with. For a long time, I feel like I've had to play the parent."

River's mom has always been fragile. Her depression is so severe that it's difficult to manage without meds and regular therapy. Her good days are great, but the bad ones come tenfold.

"But your mom-"

"I know." He cuts me off and falls back in his seat, finally looking at me.

"Moving here gave me a freedom I thought I'd never have. When my father left and she..." His fingers curl into fists. "Ryan was struggling, and I think to this day she feels like our parents' marriage failing is her fault. So, when I saw my mom breaking apart in front of me, I knew I couldn't let Ryan see that. She'd think she was the one causing her pain." His jaw tightens at whatever memory flashes behind his eyes. It's no surprise Ryan thinks it's her fault. Her father told her it was when he found out she was bisexual.

"I was a kid tying my mom's hair back as she threw up every night from crying, holding her down to force the meds down her throat and begging her to shower. I picked out her clothes most mornings and learned to help her with her hair so that she'd look okay. So, Ryan wouldn't think our mom was broken by what our father did."

"I didn't know it'd gotten that bad." How could I have lived in the same house and had a completely different experience?

"Ryan needed you. I wouldn't have been able to give her what you did when she was struggling."

"You needed me too." I give his hand a squeeze.

"I turned out alright." He shrugs and pulls away. "My mom's better at managing now, I wouldn't have left otherwise. She was the one that planted the idea in Ryan's head about moving to California because she knew I wouldn't leave on my own." He reaches for his phone and taps the screen, checking the time. "I love my mom more than anything, but the idea of going back feels suffocating." He pushes the key in the ignition and the engine comes to life.

"Is that why you bury yourself in work? So you have an excuse not to go?"

"Maybe in the beginning, but I want to be independent. My mother raised us with our father's money. He still pays for her home and expenses. He paid for our schooling, and I always felt gross about accepting it. I want to stand on my own."

River's always been a bit of a workaholic, so I never questioned it. He never really partied or had close friends after high school. He's dated plenty of women, but they all leave after realizing he has no time to give them.

"Working hard is great, but you have to live a little too. Otherwise, what's the point?" I settle back into my seat, snapping my seatbelt into place while cleaning up my cold fries and melted milkshake.

"Work's enjoyable for me." He shrugs and looks over his shoulder before pulling out of the parking space.

"Do you hear yourself? Even robots need to recharge, you know. There's no way your job could be that fun."

We're interrupted by my phone ringing. I peer at the screen before answering, and it's an unsaved number.

"Hello?"

"Hello, Indigo Johnson? This is Mary. We met at the casting call a while ago. Is now a good time for you?"

I turn to River and mouth, *"It's them."*

He mouths back, *"Who?"* But I wave him off.

"Yes, it's a good time for me."

"Ms. Johnson, I apologize it took so long to get back to you, but we had a hard time deciding. In the end, we appreciated your honesty and think that you would bring something special to the show. Are you still interested?"

I genuinely didn't think I'd get picked. My eyes flick to River, "Yes, I am."

"Great, I'll be emailing over more paperwork. Please have it back to me by the end of the week. We have a quick turnaround time and plan to start filming in two weeks. You were part of the last round of girls we met with, so I apologize if it feels last minute. We'll send a car for you on the first day of filming. All other details will be in the email."

"Thank you. I'll get that paperwork over to you as soon as possible."

"Of course, Good luck Indigo."

The line goes silent, and I look at River. "I guess I'll get to see just how fun your job is."

# Chapter Seven

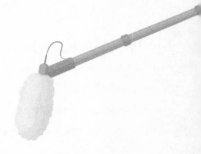

hat about this?" I hold up a classic floor length black dress.

Ryan inspects it from whatever hotel she's staying in, her face way too close to the camera. "I like it. It's simple though, so make sure you pack accessories."

Gently, I fold and place the dress in my suitcase. Ryan's letting me raid her closet for things to wear on the show. "I don't think I can fit anything else in my bag. This has to be enough." Outside of clothes, trying to condense my makeup collection has been a battle all on its own.

"Trust me. It's never enough." She falls backward in her bed.

"This will be our last call for a while. You going to miss me?" I slide a bonnet over my fresh box braids.

"I don't even want to talk about it. You'll be gone and River's going to be scheming to get you kicked off early."

"I'll manage that on my own. I'm going for a good time, not a long time."

"You say that, but this man might woo you."

"Falling in love, especially on reality TV, is the last thing I plan to do."

"Stop saying that. You're way too soft to mean it." Ryan scrunches her nose.

"I'm serious Ry, I've got way too much planned to worry about being in a relationship." Jumping across my suitcase, I use my body weight to flatten it before zipping it closed.

She's silent, so I look up. "What?" I ask as I drag my bag from the bed.

"I'm just saying, I think you can focus on yourself without closing off completely. I'm all for you chasing the bag and reaching your goals, but don't let one rotten apple make you think you have to go it alone."

I cross my arms over my chest. "How many dates have you been on this week? And who's that behind you?"

She turns to look at the lump underneath the blankets she thought I wouldn't notice.

"I'll let love in when you do." I add. Ryan's the most unserious person I know when it comes to dating. She never gets attached, and it's never the same person twice.

"Geez, say it louder why don't you." She eyes the sleeping body, but it doesn't stir, so she relaxes. "You're not built for this life, Indie. You wouldn't make it in my shoes."

"You're right. That's why I'm avoiding it all together."

She looks like she wants to argue further but decides against it. "Yeah, well, I know it's close to bedtime there, but it's breakfast time here, and I'm starving. You got this and remember, you're a bad bitch and no one can take that from you." She blows a kiss and disconnects the call.

My phone alerts me to a text and Javi's name pops up on the screen. I swipe the message away before sliding my phone into my back pocket.

I'm not sure what's changed, but he has been asking if we can talk. Must be trouble in paradise with Abbie, further confirmation that men can be so trash.

Gathering the dirty clothes hamper into my arms, I head to the laundry room. I've been cleaning all day since I leave tomorrow, and I want to leave things the way I found them. When I make it to the laundry room, I drop the basket in my arms and pull out my phone. River and I have fallen into a routine. We work similar hours, so the time before bed's spent watching random B horror films and eating dinner. Tonight is pizza. Chicken and bacon on my side, pepperoni on his. Pulling up the local pizza shops app, I make sure our order is in route. The app show's an ETA of thirty minutes from now.

Once I've got the machines loaded, I hear the front door open, signaling River's return. "The food's almost here. I hope you're fine with pizza." I shout as I make my way to the living room where he's dropping his bag on the island counter.

He yawns into his hands and gives me one of those lazy smiles. "Let me change and I'll meet you back out here."

"If you're too tired, we can cancel." I place my hands on my hips and inspect his face. He looks tired.

"I'm fine. I want to watch the movie." He attempts to head to his room and I side step, blocking his path.

"I don't want you to force yourself."

He rolls his eyes and lifts his shirt over his shoulders. "You going to let me get to my room so I can change, or should I do it here?"

"Grow up." I turn away from him, and he laughs as he passes me. My phone pings alerting me that the pizza's been dropped off earlier than expected. I'll forever be grateful for no contact delivery. I head to the door and grab the goods. Once I return to the living room, I turn on the TV and set the food up on the coffee table. River plops down on the couch beside me with two cans of soda.

"What are we watching?" Grabbing a slice, I eye the bag in his hand. He hands me a DVD case, *Sea slugs: They may move slow but you'll die fast,* is written on the cover.

"Oh, this is going to be good."

"I saw it and knew it'd be right up your alley." River suffers through cheesy horror flicks because I enjoy them.

"This is perfect for our last night."

"I can't believe you're going through with it." He places my drink Infront of me.

"I don't know why it bothers you so much. I'm kind of excited to see you in your element." When I take a bite of my pizza, I'm rewarded with the cheesiest of cheese pulls.

"Will it be me you're focusing on?" River turns to me, cocking his head to the side. I'm now regretting the delicious bite I took because that cheese pull is now dangling from my lips. I, in a very not cute way might I add, push the cheese in my mouth and chew like a starved beast around the steaming bite so I can respond. I hate that nothing I do is ever smooth.

He's laughing now, and I smack my lips.

"Alright, okay. Get it out of your system."

"Eat like that on the show and I won't have to worry about you."

"Are you worried?" Leaning in, I bat my lashes at him. I expect him to push me away, to laugh or make a joke. River does none of those things. His smile wavers and the awkwardness makes me pull away, but his fingers wrap around my arm.

"And if I am worried?" His eyes stay firmly focused on mine, and the intensity in them has me sweating. I reach for his arm and pinch it, forcing him to let go.

"What was that for?" He frowns at me massaging the now red area.

"You were being weird," I huff throwing my hands in the air. "We're like family, so you're used to watching my back, but I promise I've got this."

"I don't think that's the right comparison." The corners of his mouth tilt down.

"Ryan's like a sister to me and you're—"

"I don't treat you like Ryan. Sisters also don't have crushes on their brothers."

"That was a long time ago." My face feels impossibly hot. I've lost control of this conversation.

"I don't see you as my sister. You're my best friend, but you're also a woman. Javi recognized that too."

"Okay, but Javi's insecure. We'd never go there."

"I can't say that for sure. If I were Javi, I wouldn't have wanted you around me either." His eyes rove over my body and I'm acutely aware of how short my pajama bottoms are and how low cut my top is. I don't know what's gotten into River tonight, but honestly, it's kind of pissing me off. I hate that his words have such a hold on me.

"You can stop now. It's not funny."

"Stop what?" He says with a straight face.

"I don't understand you sometimes."

"If you think of me as a brother, prove it." He pops his soda open and takes a sip.

"And how would I do that?"

"Sleep with me." A sly smile spreads across his face.

"Excuse you?" I fold my arms over my chest. He must have lost his mind.

"Not like that," He chuckles and sets his can down, "You and Ryan share a bed all the time. If I'm no different, what's the big deal?"

"Not happening." I reach for my drink, and he moves it out of reach.

"Then tell me I'm right."

He's being ridiculously persistent. Do I think he's attractive? The real question is who doesn't, but River's a line I won't cross. "Fine. I get the side closest to the wall." I shove the movie into his chest and snatch my soda from his hands. He laughs and puts the movie on.

The next ninety minutes are stressful only for me, apparently. River acts as he usually does, commenting on the bad CGI and the over the top acting while polishing off his half of the pizza. While I can't stop thinking about what I've gotten myself into. My eyes keep drifting to him, and I rack my brain for excuses to back out but come up empty. The credits scroll across the screen and my time's up. River turns the TV off and closes the pizza box.

"Ready, sis?" The corners of his lips lift as he packs up.

"Of course. It's two people in a bed. No big deal."

"Right." He arches a brow as if he doesn't believe me.

"It'll be like old times," I stand and grab my cell. "In fact, I'm looking forward to it."

"Are you now?" He tilts his head and his lips quirk up.

"Yep." I rock on my toes and watch as he puts away the leftovers.

"I'll meet you in the room if that's okay?"

He nods his consent. I make a beeline for the bathroom. I inspect my pajamas in the mirror and wish I'd chosen something with a little more coverage. It would be weird to change now, right? Opening the cabinets, I grab my face wash and moisturizer and begin my routine. After brushing my teeth, I make my way to River's room. I hesitate outside his door.

"You can back out if you want." River taunts from behind me.

"Why would I do that?" I throw my shoulders back and open the door. My feet remain glued to the floor until I feel his hand push against my lower back. He brushes past me and heads inside the connected bathroom.

I crawl into bed and get under the covers, trying my best to fall asleep before he makes it back, but my brain won't shut off. My body feels hyper aware of everything. From the sensation of the sheets against my skin, to the scent of his soap embedded in the blankets. I scoot as close to the wall as possible and bring my knees to my chest. The lights switch off and my heartbeat quickens. His body weight causes the bed to bend and my body tilts toward his. Heat radiates off him and I feel his breath against my skin.

I scoot further away. "This is a king-sized bed. Why are you so close?"

"I like to spread out. Why are you running from me?" He reaches his arm around my waist and pulls me against his chest, resting his head against the back of my neck.

"What do you think you're doing?" My voice comes out wispy and my entire body warms.

"You said it would be like old times. I distinctly remember it like this."

"You're remembering wrong." I mumble. His arm remains draped along my middle and his touch sends my nerves buzzing. I squirm in his arms, and he pulls me closer.

"Relax." His mouth is at my ear and my entire body shudders in response.

"I am."

"So it's normal for your heart to beat this fast, then?" He presses his ear against my back.

"Yes, it is." Twisting out of his arms, I sit up and position my pillows between us. "Stay on your side."

He props his head up in his hand and looks over my makeshift fort. "If I didn't know any better, I'd think you were bothered." I can hear the smile in his voice.

"Nope, still not a big deal. Just respect the barricade." Throwing the blankets over my head, I use my hands as a pillow. The bed shakes from River's silent laughter, but he doesn't attempt to remove the wall I've created.

Okay. So maybe I'm not completely immune and brother wasn't the right word, but now I'm not sure how to categorize our friendship. Lately, things have felt a bit blurred and the last thing I need is to make things weird. There's no point in thinking too hard about it since that's a door I plan to keep closed.

# Chapter Eight

The sun peeks through the blinds and warms my skin. A yawn rolls through me and my muscles feel so relaxed. I haven't slept that well in a while. I wrap my arms around the pillows and nuzzle into them, only to find that they're solid. My eyes pop open and I find myself tangled in River's arms. My legs hook around his and I'm nestled against his side, my head resting against his arm.

"Good morning." He's awake, his free hand holding his phone.

"I told you to stay on your side." I slap his shoulder and push myself up to a sitting position.

"Take a better look. You're on my side."

Surveying my surroundings, I find that he's right. I've forced him to the edge of the bed and the majority of the blanket is wound around my body while he's left with a small corner.

"Told ya you were a clinger." The corners of his lips lift, and he runs his hands through his hair. His curls are wild and stand in every direction.

"I set the barrier for a reason." I move to crawl out of the bed.

"You rolled right over them. Every time I moved, you kept coming, so I gave up."

The image of me chasing him in my sleep makes me cringe. "I'm sorry."

"You should be. You may be in denial, but I'm not. Having a woman climb all over me made it impossible to get any sleep."

Heat climbs up my neck, and I glance at my phone. "You should've woken me up." I tap the screen and check the time. It's almost noon. We slept in later than we should have. Waking up in River's arms has me feeling off balance, so I make a dash for the bathroom. Doing the show and getting some space may be good for us.

I've got a couple hours until it's time to leave for filming, so I start my morning skin routine, cleansing and hydrating. The attire today is formal and I'll be wearing black, so I go with a glittering silver on my lids with a classic black wing for my eyeliner and creamy peach lipstick to tie it all together.

After freshening up, I start breakfast. A simple meal of eggs, bacon and toast, with a fresh pot of coffee brewing. River finally walks in and snags a piece of bread off his plate and reaches for the coffee. His hair's gelled back, and he's wearing his signature cologne.

"I can't eat with you. I've got to help set up for filming."

"Oh." Disappointment gnaws at me. It's going to be hard to find time for each other after today.

"Wrap it up. I'll take it with me." He fastens his watch around his wrist, and I reach for some Tupperware in a nearby cabinet.

"When you get onsite, remember: we don't know each other."

When he realized I was serious about joining the cast, he gave me a lecture about keeping our relationship a secret. Not only could it disqualify me, but it could get him in trouble too. This project's more important than his usual gigs, since it could lead to his script being reviewed.

"You don't have to worry about me." Handing him the container of food, I offer my pinky.

"How old are you?" He asks, shaking his head.

"Never too old to seal a promise."

He sighs but wraps his finger around mine and we both bring our thumbs to our lips.

"Now you have nothing to worry about." I sip my coffee and lean against the counter.

"I know you're doing this for your own reasons, and I respect it. Just try not to forget why you're there. The guy they got for this is..." His phone pings, pulling him out of his thoughts. "Be careful Indie." He walks past me.

I watch as he leaves, and then it dawns on me. Why the heck didn't he give me a heads up on who the bachelor is?

A car came for me, as promised, and I was escorted to a hotel. Apparently, we'll wait here and be taken one by one in a limo to meet the man of the hour. People with clipboards and radios bark orders. Cameras swivel around, catching footage, and luggage is being gathered and carted away. The energy in the air is static. All the warnings River's given me play through my head and now I'm hypersensitive to how I might be perceived. From the way I'm standing to the expression on my face—I over think all of it.

A man with deeply tanned skin and a black mesh top steps in front of me. He's paired the top with skinny jeans and combat boots, and his hair's cut low with a perfectly styled pouf on top. "I'm told that you're Ms. Indigo?" He smiles.

"You were told right."

He nods and gestures for me to follow. "I'm Jose. One of the many producers working this circus and you, my dear, will be with me. So, if you have questions or requests, let me know."

"Okay, who's the mystery man I'm supposed to be throwing myself at?

"Ah, except that one." We arrive at one of the hotel's conference rooms. There are chairs set up in the middle of the room and women who arrived before me are seated in some of them. The rest of the women are hovering around a table at the back that has some snacks and drinks available. The room is otherwise bare and the energy in here is no better than out there.

Jose hands me some wires with a clip. "That's your mic. Unless you're asleep, you should have that on. You're lucky number ten, so you'll be the last girl taken to the mansion." He pats my shoulder, then makes his way to the front of the room.

"Alright ladies, listen up. Once you meet the possible love of your life, you'll get two minutes to interact before you're moved into the house. You get one shot to make an impression."

"Can I ask who decided the order?" A woman with long blond hair and ice blue eyes raises her hand.

"No, you can't, number four."

"Bethany." She corrects.

Jose continues as if she hasn't spoken, "As stated in your paperwork, no electronics during filming and your bags will be checked. Days start at 7 a.m. every morning regardless of if we have anything scheduled or not and lights out at 10 p.m."

"7 a.m? Every day?" Bethany interrupts again.

"Yes, number four, I look forward to seeing your enthusiastic smile bright and early. You'll have assigned rooms; your bags will be waiting for you when you arrive. So get to know the girls around you. You might be sitting next to your roommate."

"Roommate? I'll take my own room, thank you." The woman who interrupts this time is lethally beautiful. Her face is all sharp angles with dark wide-set eyes framed with thick lashes. Her inky black hair's pin straight and falls to her waist. The dark color of her hair highlights the pink undertones of her fair skin.

Jose sighs, checking his watch. "And what's your name, number six?"

"Sabrina."

"Sabrina, I love it. I think there's some confusion here. You guys are the contestants. You're here to fall in love. I'm one of the producers. We're here to make that happen. You don't set the rules, but we'll do our best to make your time here comfortable. However, everyone's getting a roommate. No one's above anyone else. Got it, babe?"

Sabrina folds her arms over her chest and nods.

"I'll see you guys on location and welcome to *The Love Meltdown*." He sighs like the short interaction has tuckered him out and leaves us behind.

"The next couple of weeks should be interesting."

Startled, I find the owner of the sultry voice beside me. Her burgundy locs are pulled into a low bun with the front swooping over the right side of her face. She has the kind of lips people pay for, big brown eyes and umber skin.

"I feel like I'm in high-school all over again." A nervous laugh escapes me.

"Girl high school was child's play. Most of the girls seem nice enough, but I'd still watch my back. I'm Cameron, by the way, or you can call me number five."

"Indigo formally known as number Ten." We laugh as a man with a clipboard opens the door calling for number one. A woman with long burgundy hair meets him at the door.

"It's finally starting. I need a drink. It's been a day." Cameron fans her face, nodding toward the food set up. I follow behind her and another man pops his head in asking for girl number two.

"Do you have any idea who we're meeting?"

She shakes her head in response, the gold rings clipped to her locs swing with the movement. "The gossip blogs have thrown out some guesses, but no one really knows." She pours herself a cup of water.

"Want to know who I think it is?" A petite girl with a short pixie cut, sharp cat eyes and sandy brown skin reaches across for a cup. She speaks with a high lilt, dragging her words out at the end. "Big Bandz." She says excitedly.

"The rapper?" Cameron says dubiously.

"Yeah girl, why not? Maybe it's wishful thinking. He's my celebrity crush." She giggles.

"I'm Gabby Ramirez from the Bronx, born and raised." She smiles.

"I'm Cameron Williams from Miami, Florida, baby."

"What about you?" Gabby nods her head in my direction.

"Indigo Johnson from Dallas, Texas, but I live here in Cali now."

"Number Three." A man calls from the door.

"Oh. That's me, ladies. See you guys on the other side." Gabby gives us a small wave.

"So, what do you do for a living?" Cameron asks, still sipping her drink.

"Makeup artist, you?"

"That's cute." She smiles, wrinkling her nose. Something about the way she says it reminds me of my mom and I automatically feel my defenses go up. "I'm a public speaker and I have a book coming out next year about my time in foster care." She waves a hand as if it's no big deal, but judging by her toothy grin, it's something she's proud of. "I try to use my platform to bring awareness to different issues and I'm hoping

I can do that while I'm here too."

Cameron being an influencer automatically sends up a red flag after everything with Javi, but someone who advocates for children can't be all bad.

I watch as they pull Bethany from the room and then turn to Cameron, "I love that. I'll have to check out your stuff after this."

"You should. Have you worked with anyone I would know?" She taps a manicured finger against her glass.

"Probably not. I'm just starting out."

Cameron nods and there's an awkward lull in the conversation and another assistant pops in, calling Cameron's number. They're moving fast and I'm not waiting long before my number's called. When I look up, River's standing at the door. He looks at me like I'm a stranger and I do my best to do the same. We end up at a limo parked at the curb behind the building.

"Someone will come for you when it's time to exit the vehicle." He shuts the door after I get inside and walks off.

It takes a few moments to arrive at our destination. The driveway is long and twists up a hill. The limo comes to a smooth stop and there's a small knock on the window before the door opens. Jose is there with his hand stretched in my direction. I take it and step out with wobbly knees.

Voices come from the radio attached to his hip. He freezes to listen, then relaxes. "Okay beautiful, you ready?" He asks.

"Ready as I'll ever be."

"Alright, there are cameras hidden on either side of you and a crew at the top of the steps. You're going to walk up there, introduce yourself, and he'll walk you inside." Jose places his hand on the small of my back, urging me forward. I take slow steps up the stairs, a million things firing off in my brain at once. I'm wearing the floor length black dress I borrowed from Ryan, it's sleeveless with a low cut back. Thank God for strapless push-up bras. The click clack of my heels seems to echo in the silence as I make my way up.

Finally, I reach the top of the staircase and waiting, with his hands in his pockets dressed in a black suit that was very obviously custom made for him with the way it hugs his biceps, is the man of the hour with his back turned to me. He's lean with broad shoulders and loosely coiled hair. He looks to be a bit taller than River, who stands at an even six feet.

Slapping a smile on my face, I push my breasts forward and run my fingers through my braids. At the sound of my approach, he turns. His dark eyes light up with recognition, his mouth sliding into a cocky grin.

My mind goes blank, and I stumble to a halt.

"You gotta be fucking kidding me."

# Chapter Nine

Standing before me is the man who crashed the casting call. The crew behind the asshole drop their cameras and look at each other. A man with an obvious air of importance bulldozes his way to the front. It takes a moment, but I recognize him from my interview as well. Noah's eyes narrow into slits as he rounds on me, still dripped out in designer.

"Which one is this?" He jabs his finger at me. Jose runs up beside him.

"Number ten, Indigo Johnson." Jose supplies.

"Want to explain that reaction number ten?"

"He took me by surprise is all." Throwing my shoulders back, I look Noah in the eye.

He sneers at me and shakes his head. "I knew you'd be a mistake. As far as the world knows, you've never seen him before. Lopez." Noah yells, even though Jose's literally right next to him.

"Take number ten back down so we can reshoot." Noah makes it back behind the camera crew even with the stick up his ass. Jose hooks his arm around my elbow, dragging me back down the steps.

"I thought this was reality TV?" I say into Jose's ear.

"Honey, reality's what we make it. That man is Noah Anderson and he's got more pull around here than I do. So avoid getting on his bad side, please. If you look good, I look good." Jose turns me toward the steps again and uses a tissue to blot the sweat off my nose.

"Alright remember, this is possibly your future man."

"Doubtful." I mumble under my breath.

He gives me a thumbs up before talking into his radio and gesturing for me to go.

Second time's the charm. Now that I know what's waiting for me my nerves have subsided. What game's this guy playing? When I reach the top of the steps, he's got that shit-eating grin plastered on his face. He's loving that I don't know what's going on. Out of the corner of my eye I see Jose doing a dramatic swoon, I guess he's trying to tell me to put on a show. I physically force my eyes not to roll and pull the corners of my mouth up.

"You're absolutely stunning." He reaches for my hand and presses a kiss to the back of it. I'll give it to him. The jerk's voice is smooth as silk, deep and clear. He looks at me through his lashes and winks.

Oh. He's good.

"Thank you. You don't look too bad yourself." I attempt to pull my hand free and fail. A smile plays at his lips, but he fights it.

"May I know your name?" He asks.

"Indigo Johnson."

He finally lets the smile win and I hate that it enhances his features.

"A woman of few words. Don't you want to know mine?"

No, not really.

"Yes, of course."

He laughs under his breath, as if he knows exactly what I'm thinking. "My name's Kade Ikeda, and it's a pleasure to meet you, Indigo." I try again to remove my hand from his, but he's got an iron grip. His eyes disappear into his smile as it deepens. The asshole thinks he's funny.

"Shall we go inside?"

"Sure, let's do it." I smile and let him pull me to his side and toward the open doors of the mansion. The jerk smells good too. Like whiskey and spice.

"You ready love?" He asks in a low whisper.

"What exactly are you planning?" I whisper back.

"I have nothing but honest intentions." He uses his free hand to cross his heart.

"Look alive, beautiful." He mutters as we reach the wide double doors.

The mansion is large, open and perfectly decorated. The cream tiled floors are so clean I can see my reflection in them. It's mostly empty in the foyer, with a dazzling chandelier hanging overhead. Off to the left is a sitting area with luxurious couches that look like they cost more than my rent. There's a wide hall off to the right that appears to have a few bedrooms and a curved staircase that leads to the second floor. Before I can take in my surroundings, the girls crowd Kade and I'm effectively shoved to the back of the mob.

"Kade, can I get a moment with you?"

"Kade, I see there's a piano. I am classically trained and would love to play for you."

"Kade, what would you like for breakfast in the morning?"

"The vultures are circling." Gabby mumbles, shaking her head. She and Cameron have found themselves in the back with me. Kade continues to be bombarded. He smiles politely, but it doesn't reach his eyes. I almost feel bad for the guy.

Almost.

A woman with long lilac colored hair that falls in perfect waves, and lightly bronzed skin pushes her way to the front. Her eyes are large and unblinking, and she stares at Kade with an unfiltered admiration.

"I'm so happy that we're finally together." She says breathlessly as she digs her nails into his forearm.

Kade peels her fingers off him. "Serenity, right?"

"Yeah, I—"

The havoc's silenced by two sharp claps. A woman with platinum blond hair, ivory skin and a tight red dress stands before us.

"Hello ladies, I'm Marissa Love and I'll be your host during your stay here. I hope you've enjoyed your time thus far." She smiles widely and slowly rakes her eyes over us. A few girls squeal at the sight of her. "You've all come for a whirlwind romance with our bachelor, but being with someone with so much notoriety isn't easy." She turns her body toward the large camera behind us. "Can you handle the pressure? Or will you have a meltdown?" She leans forward, pointing at the camera.

"Got it." One cameraman shouts. Marissa's shoulders drop and a bored expression replaces the excited one that was there a moment ago.

"Alright ladies, all of you come to the center." Jose shouts. We do as we're told. The staff moves us into position, two rows of five. I'm placed in the back, likely because of my height. At 5'8 I'm taller than a lot of the girls here. I notice River standing behind Jose. His arms folded over his chest as he says something to the crew member beside him. Marissa takes a swig of her water bottle before standing in front of us, Kade at her side.

"We're rolling." A staff member behind us shouts.

"You're about to find out how important first impressions are. Kade, please choose three girls for one-on-one conversations." Marissa takes a step back.

"With so many beautiful women here tonight, this wasn't easy." Kade pauses for dramatic effect. His eyes flit from one girl to another.

"Nervous, Kade?" Marissa smiles, causing a smattering of laughter.

"Never." He tilts his head.

"Sabrina, Gabby and Indigo, I hope you'll join me tonight." His eyes meet mine before he turns his attention on Marissa.

"The rest of you will be shown to your rooms, so rest up."

"This isn't fair." Serenity hisses and stomps away.

"Follow me, please. All your rooms will be on the first floor." A crew member leads the remaining girls away.

"I'll go first." Sabrina flips her hair over her shoulder.

"That's fine. Better to save the best for last." Gabby taunts.

Sabrina laughs and looks at Gabby from head to toe, "Whatever makes you feel better."

Gabby's nostrils flare and her lips part, but Kade approaches and her mouth snaps shut. "Ladies." He gives a small bow of his head. Sabrina rushes toward him, wrapping her arm around his.

"I'm excited to get to know you more." She leans in close, pressing her breasts into his arm. "I think we may have a lot in common. My family is from Korea, but we visit Japan often." She continues.

"Japan's always a good time. I grew up in Georgia since that's my mom's hometown." Kade pulls her away.

A camera nearby zooms in on my face as Jose comes to my side. "We're going to use this time to get your thoughts on Kade and being chosen." He blots at my face again and offers me a small cup of water. Another producer pulls Gabby to do more of the same. The moment I take a sip, the cup's being pulled away by Jose and he's turning my body toward the camera. "Alright, Indigo. How did you feel when you saw it was Kade Ikeda waiting for you tonight?"

I'm unprepared for the question because, as it stands, I still don't know *who* he is. "I was honestly overwhelmed. Kade's a lot to take in."

"What about being chosen as one of the girls he clearly has his eye on. How does that make you feel?"

"Um," I'm not sure how I feel about it. Confused mostly. "I'm happy to know Kade has taste."

Jose releases a hearty laugh. "That's all we have for you right now. When Kade comes for you, the cameras will follow." Jose presses his hand to his mic and then leaves without another word.

"Jose's not your friend." River stops at my side.

"Do I know you?" I scrunch my face and can't help the smile that breaks free.

"I'm being serious. Jose's nice enough, but he'll push you into situations that benefit him."

Gabby steps in front of us, looking from me to River. "Am I interrupting something?"

"Kade will come for you next." River takes off not acknowledging Gabby at all.

"What's up with him?" She takes a drink of her water bottle.

"Who knows? By the way, who is Kade? Like, what makes him famous?"

"Kade acts. He used to get a lot of work, but then he started getting in trouble. His team put him on lockdown, and we haven't heard much from him in the last year."

"What kind of trouble?"

"The girl kind. Guy's a serial dater. He isn't known for taking relationships seriously. He's also known to be hot head; he's had his fair share of arguments hit the blogs." She shrugs.

"What made him do a show like this, then?"

"Who knows, maybe he's matured." She gives me a wry smile. "We're two for two on the hot mess express though, because the host isn't much better."

"Why's that?"

"Her name's been in the blogs a thousand times for one scandal or another. The most recent news is about her messy divorce. She was exposed for cheating." We both look up at Marissa, who's fussing over her hair.

"Excuse me." Kade returns with Sabrina no longer attached to his arm.

"May I steal Indigo from you?"

"Of course." Gabby smiles and Kade captures my hand in his. The camera crew swivels around us, following Kade's lead to a back door past the staircase. We end up in a garden filled with flowers. He stops at a bench and takes a seat, so I follow suit.

"So, tell me about yourself. Who is Indigo Johnson?" He leans back on both his elbows and tilts his head. Kade Ikeda has been toying with me all night, and I'm going to beat him at his own game. A few stray strands have fallen from his perfectly styled hair. So, I lean forward to push them back and use my free hand to trace his jawline, his stubble grates against my fingers.

"I specialize in beauty; I enhance what's already there."

"Ah, makeup, I thought you did all this for me." He grabs my wrist, and his eyes travel across my face.

"Women don't wear makeup for men."

"Then who's it for?"

"Maybe I just want to look good, Kade."

His eyes move to my lips. "You didn't get ready today with me in mind?"

Encroaching upon his space, I bring my lips to his ear, trailing my fingers up his forearm. "Do you want me to have you on my mind only when I get ready, or should I think of you tonight, too?" I breathe in his ear and an honest to God shiver runs through him. I pull away in surprise and then laughter bursts from my lips.

"You have an obnoxious laugh." He glares at me as he straightens his suit coat, a slight flush coloring his tawny skin.

"Hey now. I've been made fun of my whole life about my laugh."

"You're cackling like a witch." He gives me a half-smile.

I clutch my invisible pearls. "No, you didn't." I cluck my tongue and shake my head. "I'll let it slide this time."

"So, what's your plan?" He asks.

"What plan?" For a moment, I think he realizes I have ulterior motives for coming here, but then he smiles.

"The one that makes me fall for you."

"There may be nine other girls here, but you're the one with something to prove."

He pauses, considering my words, but then the sound of muffled speaking comes from his earpiece and he's listening to whoever's speaking on the other end.

"It seems our time's up." He stands and offers me his hand. I hesitate, but he grabs me anyway, pulling me to my feet. We reach the door leading back into the main room and he leans down, whispering into my ear, "If you want to think of me tonight, I wouldn't be opposed."

My head swings in his direction, but he's already moving toward Gabby.

"You're better at this than I thought you'd be. If I didn't know better, I'd think you were into him." River moves from behind the cameras and approaches me.

"Well, you do know better."

"Right."

"You gonna show me to my room?" I use my hand to gesture toward the hall the girls traveled through earlier.

He sighs, leading the way. "Your room's going to be to the right." We pass a few doors before we arrive at one near the end. "This one's yours. You share it with two other girls."

"Thank you, sir." I reach for the door, but he drops his hand on my shoulder.

"I know I told you to keep your distance, but come to me if you need to. These shows don't have the best intentions." He lets his hand drop. "Don't go falling for Kade."

"I know what I came for, and Kade isn't even on the list." I'm here for the weekly deposits, and to boost my following. He doesn't look totally convinced, but he doesn't push it.

"Get some rest." Chatter emits from his radio, and he nods before turning his back on me.

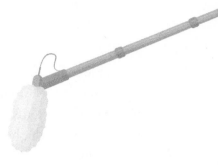

# Chapter Ten

*I*'m not sure how to feel when I find that Cameron's one of my roommates. She gives me mixed vibes after how our conversation ended, but luckily my other roommate, Jasmine's a talker. She left no room for awkward silences. Jasmine's tall and full figured with copper colored skin and waist length brown hair that falls in waves at her side, a beauty like all the other women here. They were still unpacking when I made it to the room last night.

This morning, I am struggling with the 7 a.m. start time. Jasmine, Cameron and I are the last ones to make it downstairs. The camera crew runs circles around us, and Marissa stands in the center, an assistant applying blush to her cheeks.

Jose waltzes over with a clipboard in hand, "Good morning, don't you all look gorgeous this bright and early."

Cameron shoots a nasty look in his direction.

"Hey, I don't choose the schedule. You'll be in group one. Stand with the women to the right until Marissa's ready." He points and takes off.

"Is Jose your producer too?" Cameron asks, turning to look at

Jasmine and I.

"Sure is. He's cute." Jasmine nudges us.

"Uh girl, you know he's not straight?" Cameron laughs.

"So? I may be here for Kade, but I'm not blind. The one over there can get it, too." She angles her head to the side, and I turn to see who she's referring to. River's talking with Sabrina. He's leaning over her, helping adjust the cords to her mic, and she brushes her fingers against his arm, smiling at him coyly. His curls fall over his eyes, but they don't hide the smile he gives her in return. Biting the inside of my cheek, I turn away.

Jasmine elbows my side. "What? He not your cup of tea?"

"Even I have to say he's nice to look at." Cameron lets out a low whistle as her eyes travel over River and my irritation spikes.

"What? No, just—eyes on the prize, right? We're here for Kade." They share a look and my eyes drift back to River. Sabrina's still speaking to him, her hand tugging on the bottom of his shirt. I haven't had to watch River hit on anyone in years and I'm not going to start now.

Ignoring it is easier said than done though. I fight the urge to remind him he's at work when Kade finally joins Marissa. They hug and she whispers something in his ear. Unfortunately, he's handsome as always. His hair tied back into an effortless bun at the nape of his neck. He's wearing gray sweats and his white tee hugs his form. He rubs the stubble sprinkled along his strong jaw as he speaks to her. The crew is finally in place and Marissa turns on that megawatt smile.

"We have a lot planned today. Each group will do some promo work for the show, along with Kade." She pauses, clasping her hands together. The girls cheer in excitement and she smiles, appeased by the response.

"Group one will go to a photo shoot promoting this season of *The Love Meltdown*. Staff will take care of your hair, makeup and clothes on site. Talk about princess treatment." My group squeals with excitement. "Group two will do a radio interview with Kade this afternoon, so take time this morning to get ready. We have a limo for the first group right outside. Remember, this is a chance to get to know Kade. Make it count." She points an earnest smile in our direction, but as soon as Jose signals for the cameras to stop rolling, her face drops. "Somebody turn the air up. My face is practically melting." Marissa complains to whoever's closest.

"Ready?" Kade asks and Bethany and Serenity each grab one of his arms, practically dragging him out the door. The drive, thankfully, isn't long. The girls fight to dominate the conversation while Kade, to his credit, attempts to spread his attention evenly. I decide not to add to his stress by sitting back and allowing the other girls to have their moment. When we reach our destination we're ushered into a studio with bright white walls and a backdrop placed in the center. Cameras and lights are set up and the staff is already prepping the makeup stations.

A woman approaches our group, smiling brightly and carrying a large camera in her hands. "Good morning. I'll be taking your photos. If there's anything I can do to make you more comfortable, please let me know."

Kade offers his hand, and she shakes it enthusiastically. He introduces himself with one of his signature devastating smiles. She turns a light shade of pink before tapping her chest. "Elizabeth. You guys can call me Liz, though. This morning, we'll start with Kade and Bethany."

A staff member steps up next, he points to a few buffet tables lined at the back wall, "We have food on the back tables and an omelet station if you're hungry. After you grab food, if you haven't been called, please change into your clothes. There are garment bags with your names on them against the wall." He points to a rack beside the buffet tables.

"You're Cameron, right? We need you in hair and makeup. Follow me."
Cameron obliges.

"Are you nervous?" Jasmine asks as everyone disperses.

"Not really. I've gotten to help with a few shoots before and I love
the energy."

"Model?"

"Makeup artist," I grin. "I want to ask if I can do my own face."
Promoting myself is the main prerogative, and this is an opportunity
to do just that. I don't miss the cameras filming our conversation either.
Every chance to put myself out there, I'm going to take.

I leave Jasmine at the buffet and head toward the garment bags. A
few other girls are also grabbing theirs and undressing in the middle of
the room. So, I take their lead. Unzipping the bag with my name reveals
a white dress, which appears to be the theme for today's shoot. My dress
has a corset as the bodice that pushes my breasts to the forefront. The
skirt flares and drapes nicely, stopping mid-thigh. The sleeves fall off
my shoulder; and the ruffles look like small clouds wrapped around my
arms and stop just past my wrists. I fumble through the straps on my
heels before looking for who might be in charge. It's not hard to figure
out who's the boss. A woman barks orders while applying lipstick on
the girl in her chair. She doesn't look up from her work, but grunts in
acknowledgment when I stop in front of her.

"Is it okay if I do my own makeup?"

"Be my guest. We're on a tight schedule. If your makeup doesn't
translate well on camera, don't come crying to me." She points to an
empty station. "You can use that area. Someone will be over to help
with your hair." She goes back to ignoring me and I get to work.

One look in the mirror and I have to admit the dress accentuates all
of my body's dips and curves in the best way. My breasts have never been
big, not small, but nothing to write home about. They look amazing

in this dress though, and the corset cinches my waist, emphasizing the expanse of my hips. Going with neutral tones on my eyes, I add a mauve to my lid and a deep purple color on the outer corner for depth. I played up the white by adding a shimmering silver color to my inner corner and a matching highlight to my nose. The drawer is stocked with a few small crystals. I apply them along the crease of my lids before finishing with a sharp black wing liner. To complete the look, I swipe a nude color to my lips and top it with a shimmery gloss.

As promised, the hair stylist made her way to me. She makes quick work, consolidating my braids into two thick French braids and knots a lace bow to each. One of the assistants hands out cups of water and I take one gratefully before moving to watch Cameron and Kade. They're facing each other and she looks nervous. Kade smiles down at her, gently taking her elbow in his hand and guiding her by the small of her back with his other until she's pressed against him—head resting against his broad chest. She smiles at the camera, and he rests his chin on her head.

I hadn't realized how intimate the photos would be. The thought of being pressed up against Kade has a tingle crawling down my spine. I shake my head and pat my cheeks. Focus. The money makes this worth it. Every week my bank account gets fatter and now's my chance to show off some skill.

The photographer dismisses Cameron and turns to our group. "Jasmine Martinez." She calls and Jasmine takes her spot next to Kade. By now, everyone's finished getting ready and has stopped to watch. Jasmine doesn't seem bothered, though. She confidently leads Kade at her pace. Moving him into her, adjusting their positions. His hand lands just below her hips and she turns to him and giggles, "You trying to cop a feel?" They both laugh as the camera clicks.

"Do you think she's his type?" Bethany frowns.

Jasmine is easily one of the most beautiful girls here. From her naturally bronzed skin to her curvy shape.

"I think she's cute." A petite woman beside her shrugs. I haven't gotten to meet everyone yet, but at least this one isn't rude.

"Her face isn't bad, but he'll never pick her. She's here for," Bethany lifts her hand and does air quotes, "Diversity." At her last words, her eyes flash in my direction.

"No, that bitch didn't." Cameron pops up at my side.

"Who're you calling a bitch, home girl?" The blond rolls her neck and smacks her lips, and my mouth falls open.

"Don't do that, because when I come for you, you're going to be crying and I'm the bad guy." Cameron grits out.

I step in front of Cameron and let my eyes crawl over Bethany. "There's nothing special about you. You're boring. I'd be mad too if I was forgettable. How much do you want to bet Kade doesn't know your name? I can guarantee he knows ours. He definitely knows Jasmine's. But you...?"

By now she's red as a tomato and her hands curl into fists. She looks like she's fixing her mouth to yell, but then she bursts into tears.

"Oh god why do the ones that start it always cry?" Cameron throws her hands up.

My lips turn down in disgust. At the sound of the girls wailing Kade comes over. He looks between Cameron and I and then settles on Bethany who's in tears.

"Are you okay?" He asks.

Bethany tearfully shakes her head. She reaches for him and points a glare in my direction. Ugh of course he thinks we're the problem. Somebody get this girl an Academy Award. "Those two are behaving like bullies. They jumped in my conversation and began attacking me." She shakes like a leaf, but he wraps his fingers around her wrist, prying her off.

"I'm sorry, but can you tell me your name again?"

She pauses and her tears stop falling.

"Bethany." She practically whines, stomping her foot. It takes everything in me not to laugh at the display.

"Ah, well, I'm sure this is something you can handle as an adult. My cousin is four and can have a discussion without crying to get her point across. Can I ask you to do the same?"

Bethany blinks up at him, and her face becomes redder than I thought possible. "You're not even listening to me. I'm the one being ganged up on and you're being rude." She crosses her arms over her chest.

"It sounds like I'm not your type. You're definitely not mine. So let's not waste each other's time." Kade dismisses Bethany by turning his back on her to face me. "You ready Indigo?" He pulls me forward before looking over his shoulder.

"Brittany, security will take you back so you can grab your things before leaving." I hear Bethany gasp and then the sound of her heels slamming against the floor as she walks away. It takes everything I have to stifle my laughter. Liz smiles at Kade and I once we settle in front of her. "Forget I'm here. I'll capture the moments that matter, so do what feels right."

Despite my bravado a moment ago, this is awkward.

"Nervous?" Kade's arms slide around my waist as he positions himself behind me. I angle my head toward his and come face to face with his dark eyes piercing into mine.

"Not at all." I lie. My heart knocks against my chest at his proximity. Liz kneels in front of us, and I find I don't know what to do with my hands. Or my legs. Or any part of my body really, I'm not used to being the one in front of the camera. Kade hums a melodic tone. The action causes a slight tremor to travel through me.

"You're allowed to touch me, you know." His breath fans across the shell of my ear and my face warms. One of his hands makes its descent toward the inside of my thigh. My breath catches in my throat, and I cover his hand in mine—ending his exploration. He removes his other free hand from my waist and trails the pads of his fingers along my spine, causing me to arch into him. He continues until he lands at the nape of my neck. Reaching with my remaining hand, I grab him, but he encircles my wrist first, pulling my hand behind his head so that we're tangled in each other. Liz clicks the camera furiously as she moves around us.

"Your makeup is beautiful. You're definitely talented." Kade mumbles.

"How'd you know I did it?"

"You stand out."

Pride swells in my chest. I still hold his hand on my lower thigh captive as his fingers flex and then he rolls the fabric of my skirt between them, causing the material to rise. I gasp and pull at his hair in response. He releases a soft groan and I bite my lip.

Liz averts her gaze. I release Kade and attempt to step out of his trap, but he hauls me back into him. "Pay back for your teasing in the garden." His mouth's on my ear and my cheeks are blazing now. He tilts his head to the side and returns my irritation with a breathy laugh.

"Um, I think I got the shot. You guys have real chemistry. Felt like I was intruding." She tugs a few stray strands of hair behind her ear. "All we need now is a group photo." She gives us a smile and the staff starts rounding everyone up.

I attempt to move to the back, but Kade holds me at his side. This may be more than I bargained for.

# Chapter Eleven

C an I sue production if I break an ankle? Today's group date is roller skating and I'm scooting around like a toddler. It doesn't help that they've brought us here on a Saturday and it's full of people who know what they're doing speeding past me. River laughs and I shoot a nasty glare his way. He's standing with the rest of the camera crew, watching me embarrass myself on national television.

One of the other girls brushes against me and that's all it takes to lose my footing. My body rocks forward and my skates slide in opposite directions. My hands reach for the nearest person, and I pull myself into an upright position.

"Watch it." The girl shakes me off, and my embarrassment is overwhelming.

"Sorry." My irritation increases when she rolls her eyes in response. I haven't had the pleasure of meeting this bag of sunshine yet. She has pale skin, burgundy hair and a multitude of piercings with earrings that dangle as she shakes her head. I'm still wobbling on my skates when a small blond skates to my side with ease. Her hair falls in loose waves that graze her shoulders.

"You look like a baby giraffe girl." She hooks her arm around mine and smiles, easing my nerves.

"Don't mind Nicole, her attitude doesn't have an off switch." She waves her hand dismissively. "My name's Hanna."

"Indigo." I let Hanna take the lead, guiding me back on to the carpeted area. "There are a lot of interesting personalities here." I look pointedly at Sabrina gliding along the edge of the skating rink with Kade holding her hand. Hanna follows my gaze and laughs.

"Sabrina's not so bad. We share a room, and I struggled the first night. I came here thinking it'd be a cool way to find love if it works. The first night, my nerves were getting to me and I had a small freak out session after filming. I got stuck with Nicole as my second roommate and she doesn't sugarcoat anything." Hanna wrinkles her nose and glances at the pierced vixen. "Sabrina told her to shut up and took the heat off me, so I guess I'm grateful."

"You sure she doesn't just like to argue?"

She giggles and slaps my arm as if I'm being ridiculous. We watch the others do laps and I feel guilty she's stuck keeping me company. Before I can suggest Hanna leave me behind, Kade stops in front of us. He helps Sabrina off the rink, and she leans into him even though she has no trouble keeping her balance.

Cameron and Nicole both race to get to Kade first. They almost collide, but they slide to a stop before impact.

"Do you mind doing a lap with me?" Nicole asks, hip checks Cameron and offers Kade her hand. Nicole may have a stank attitude, but even I know she is beautiful and by the looks of it, Kade knows it too. His eyes wander over her appreciatively, and she takes that as a green light, dragging him back onto the floor.

"It's the same girls getting time with him." Cameron puts her hands on her hips.

"I'm sure he'll go with everyone at least once, dates not over." I pat her shoulder.

"Or he only has time for a few, and you won't make the cut." Sabrina shrugs.

"Oh, he'll have time." Cameron waves her off.

"We'll see." Sabrina sings.

"Not that bad, huh?" I whisper to Hanna.

"Deeeeeep down, she's good." She nods as if trying to convince herself.

We chat while Kade and Nicole do a few laps, joining us again when they finish. Before Cameron can ambush him, a radio beeps and I look over my shoulder to see River approaching.

"Lunch is ready. Be aware that we're still filming." He jerks his head to a sectioned off table away from the rest of the customers.

"Will you be joining us?" Sabrina throws a coy smile at River.

"I'll be nearby if anyone needs anything."

"Anything?" She skates to his side and runs her hand down his arm.

"Anything related to filming." He shakes his head, smiling.

He tells me to keep my distance, but openly flirts? The urge to wipe that stupid smile off his face is strong. Instead, I grit my teeth and scoot my skates toward the food. Cameron and Hanna sit on either side of me while Sabrina and Nicole snagged the seats on either side of Kade. Conversation flows smoothly even with the cameras jammed in our faces. Hanna's apparently a veterinarian, Nicole manages her father's store, Sabrina travels... whatever that means. Cameron mentions a gala she has in the works and name drops all the people that are going to be there while simultaneously inviting Kade. He smiles politely, but looks uninterested. Not that Cameron notices, she's just happy to have his ear.

They seem to have it all together. Seeing the passion as they talk about what they do only motivates me more. I came here to make myself known. That means playing into this like everyone else. Kade seems to be done eating, so when there's a pause in the conversation, I take my chance.

"Do you want to hit the rink?" I hook my thumb behind me and catch River frowning. He knows my ass can't skate. Kade's mouth lifts in a slow smile and I can feel Cameron glaring at me. Sorry girl, you snooze, you lose.

"Of course." He stands, grabbing my hand. Taking the lead, he pulls me behind him. The DJ's playing a hip-hop track and the lights dim. Cosmic lighting dances across our skin and Kade's smooth with it, bouncing his shoulders while swaying to the beat. He gets ahead of me and spins so he's facing me.

"You too good to dance with me?" He calls over the music.

Rolling my eyes, I shake my head. All the spinning lights make it harder to keep my balance and I trip forward into Kade's arms.

"Now, aren't I supposed to be falling for you?" He asks as he steadies me and takes hold of both my hands, still skating backwards effortlessly.

"Ha, ha, hilarious." Every stray skater that breezes by makes me flinch with the anticipation of being knocked over. Kade releases my hands and grips my waist, and then spins us around. He holds me steady, but I cling to him anyway, holding my breath. I press my head to his chest, and I feel his laughter rumble through him.

"Do you have a skate related trauma I should know about?"

"Never learned." I shrug.

Kade clucks his tongue. "Lesson One: loosen up. Being stiff like that's going to tire you out." He maintains his hold of one of my hands and skates behind me. He rests his free hand on my upper back and presses softly. "Straighten your back, stop slouching so much."

"I'm scared I'll fall."

"And that's exactly why you'll fall. Relax." He removes his hand from my back, but I feel it reappear on my upper thigh and trail down to my knee, and my entire body tingles in response to his touch. "Keep these shoulder width apart." He taps my knee and I do as he says. Both his hands land on my waist and he applies pressure, forcing me to bend. "Stay in a small squat. It'll help your balance. Small steps. Propel yourself forward and glide."

I try to relax. My steps are more confident, and I do my best to ignore everyone around us.

He slides his hands into my front pockets and pulls himself closer. "Just like that." He whispers into my ear, and I feel my face warm. "I'm going to let you go now, okay?"

When I turn to look at him, he's not smiling. He looks genuinely concerned. "I can do it." Even though I've picked up more speed than I meant to, I smile to ease my nerves. I know he's left me when his warmth disappears too. He passes me easily and spins so we're facing each other. Picking up the pace, I take longer strides to keep up with him and I realize I'm cheesing. Big ol' grin on my face.

"I'm doing it." Yelling over the music, I point at my feet.

"You are." Kade laughs, shaking his head. He slows down and takes my hand, skating at my side. "Come on beautiful girl." He sways with the music. It's switched to a slow R&B track and the DJ calls for couples only. I move toward the exit, and he pulls me back to him.

"Where you running off to?" He asks as we breeze past it.

"I wasn't running, thought maybe you'd want to switch out. You have other women waiting on you."

He grins down at me. "You not having fun with me?"

"I'm trying to be mindful of the others."

"I want to spend more time with you."

My eyes connect with his, and he gives my hand a squeeze, making my heart rate tick up. Aw crap, that's not supposed to be happening. My resolve's stronger than a handsome face and one good date. Kade's charming, better at this than I thought. Shaking my head, I remind myself that he probably spits the same lines on all his dates. He's just as aware of the cameras as I am. Instinctively I look for them, and there are a few floating around us on the rink, while the rest of the crew films from the carpeted area. River stands among them, and his eyes are locked on Kade and I, our hands still laced together.

Without thinking, I snatch my hand away and jerk back, knocking into a couple beside us. I over correct and accidentally cross my feet and trip over myself, landing hard. My hip burns from the impact and my right ankle throbs. Moving it makes me hiss in pain.

"Are you okay?" Kade bends over me.

"I'm fine." I bite back a groan as I attempt to stand and give up.

River's made it over and by now the crew has made a wall around us and my embarrassment sky rockets. "Don't try to stand."

"I said I'm fine."

River ignores me and takes my ankle in his hand, gingerly applying pressure, and I suck in a breath. "I'm taking you to have this checked out." He presses his hand to his ear and says something into his mic.

"Don't we have an onsite medic? It's not that serious." I sigh, knowing this isn't a battle I'll win.

"They don't have the equipment to see what damage you did." He turns his icy stare on Kade, who gives him the same energy back. "You can continue with the date, filming's still ongoing." River is already draping my arm around his shoulders and lifting me up. I do my best to avoid putting weight on my bad side, but even standing hurts.

"Nah, I'll go with her." Kade steps toward me.

Noah's made his way onto the rink and looks pissed about having to be bothered with me. "You won't. There isn't enough footage for the day."

"I don't care about the footage. She fell on my watch." Kade's frown deepens.

"That's on her," Noah turns his frustration on me, "You signed waivers, by the way."

I snap my fingers to get Kade's attention. "It's my fault. I'm fine going by myself. Continue your date." I nod at River, and he takes that as his cue to haul me off.

Noah calls after River, "Make sure you update us on her status. I don't want any snags in filming because of this."

What an ass. "Is Noah your boss?" River's determined to get us out of here and I struggle to maintain a good pace, gritting my teeth every time my bad ankle makes contact with the ground.

"Yes, and no. He's Kade's publicist. I'm not sure what kind of contract his management team set up, but Noah has a lot of control over what goes down here. Noah asked me to work this gig with him as a favor."

"You've worked with him before?"

"Not this closely, so I don't know the guy, but he has the connections I need." River pushes the doors open and we make our way to his truck. He has to practically lift me up into the passenger seat, and it takes everything in me not to yell when my ankle bounces with the movement.

"I'm sorry for causing trouble." I promised when I decided to do the show I'd lay low and now we're headed to the ER.

River buckles in and kicks the engine on. "Don't worry about it. I'm sorry your date was interrupted. Looked like you were into him." He doesn't look at me as he pulls off.

His words make my chest tighten because, if I'm honest, I did enjoy it.

# Chapter Twelve

*H*ours of sitting in a frigid waiting room to be told I have a low-grade sprain. One week for the swelling to go down, another two to be completely healed, and an undetermined amount of time to get over the embarrassment of the whole situation. "What are the odds they air me face planting?"

River sticks the key in the ignition and cracks the first smile since bringing me here. "Highly likely." He'd been tense until they confirmed nothing was broken.

I throw myself back in my seat and sigh. "That's funny to you?"

"You getting hurt isn't funny." He frowns, but then turns to me with a lopsided smile, "You falling kinda was though. Wait until you see the face you made on the way down."

"Ugh." I slide my hands down my face.

"Why'd you go out there when you know you can't skate?" He asks as we pull off.

"Screen time." Technically, my mission was accomplished. If biting the dust gets people to look me up online, maybe it's worth it.

"Was that all?" He keeps his eyes on the road and the same tension

I felt when we first headed to the hospital's back.

"What else would it be?"

"Just like you have your own agenda, Kade has his. You said you didn't come here for—"

"I didn't." The date with Kade was fun, but that's all it was. River making up scenarios in his head is beyond frustrating.

"I'm not used to seeing you... This is harder for me than I thought it'd be." He holds tension in his shoulders and leans forward in his seat.

"Keep yourself busy then. Sabrina seems to hold your attention." I'm being petty. I shouldn't, but I'm tired and it's apparently bothering me more than I thought.

"Why are you bringing her up?" He glances at me.

"The same reason you're bringing Kade up."

"Is it?" We're at a red light and now he's looking at me full on and I squirm in my seat. "Are you jealous?" He pushes.

"If I said yes, would it change anything?" I laugh.

"It would." There's no amusement in his tone. His eyes move across my body and every part of me ignites. His mouth parts, but before he can say anything, the light turns green and I relax when he finally faces the road. Taking a deep breath, I rest my head against the cool glass of the window. I hear him chuckle beside me and I glare in his direction. I feel him look at me from time to time, but I'm too annoyed with him to acknowledge it. It's embarrassing the way my body reacts to his teasing. We stop at the pharmacy, pick up my meds and River fills the silence the rest of the way to the mansion. He lets me know Ryan calls to check on me every day. His mom brings up visiting after this is over any chance she gets and my mother isn't happy I didn't call her before leaving. I feel kind of bad about the last bit.

"You going to keep ignoring me?" He puts the truck in park, and I shrug. I can feel my ankle burn just thinking about walking up the steps of the mansion. Gritting my teeth, I scoot out of my seat and slam the door behind me. The first step stings, the second makes my eyes water. I'm bracing myself for the third when River takes my hand and throws my arm over his shoulders, slipping one arm behind my knees and the other around my waist. My feet leave the ground, and he presses me against his chest. "I'm not letting you make your injury worse because you're pissed at me."

"Do what you want." I mumble and he holds me tighter, but we don't move. "What are you waiting for?"

"What are you mad about?"

"I'm not mad." My tone says otherwise.

"Then look at me." He's silent, patiently waiting. I blow out a frustrated breath and do as he asks. "It's not like that between Sabrina and me."

"Yeah, okay, like I said. Do what you want."

He laughs but starts ascending the steps. "I'm too busy looking after you for all that."

I'm still annoyed, but I can't help smiling. River's muscles flex, as he adjusts my weight and the same fire I felt earlier burns everywhere his skin meets mine. Is it crossing a line to be this attracted to your friend? I mean, I'm not blind. Chewing my lip, I look up and he's completely unbothered. Racking my brain, I think back to the girls he's dated. I'm not sure if he has a type, but clearly I'm not it. Not going to lie, my pride takes a hit.

"What kind of women do you like?" We've never discussed this type of thing before, mostly because I don't enjoying hearing about it.

"Why?"

"Curious. What gets you going?"

"You planning on setting me up?"

"Maybe." I shrug, but the idea doesn't sit well with me. Thinking about River dating always makes my stomach twist. Part of me is scared he'll do what I did and leave me behind. I guess I'd deserve it.

"I'm not looking."

"You already have someone in mind?"

"Working on it." We reach the top of the steps, and he sets me down. This revelation has my head spinning. Hurt follows behind the shock because he didn't tell me he was talking to anyone. The rational part of my brain understands that I pulled away from our friendship first and this isn't a topic we usually discuss, but I feel the sting anyway. He opens the door and I stomp past him, forgetting about my busted ankle, and wince at the pain.

"Woah, take it easy." He reaches for my hand, but I shake him off.

"I got it from here." I walk past him but then pause because I feel bad for snapping, "Thank you for taking care of me." He easily keeps up with my pace as I hobble pathetically toward my room. He doesn't say anything more, but I side eye him and catch the corners of his lips twitching. "You know, if you like this girl, you should tell her."

"Is that right?"

"Yeah. Also, asking me to sleep in bed with you when you have someone you like probably wasn't a good idea."

"Anything else?" He hands me my meds and we stop in front of my door.

"How much do you like this girl?"

He skims his fingers along his chin. "This is something I should be telling her, isn't it?"

"I'm trying to help." I turn away from him and open the door. River's arm juts out, and the handle flies out of my hand as he pushes it back closed. When I look over my shoulder, he's inches away from my face.

"You're right. I've been holding back." He tucks a few of my braids behind my ear. His touch lingers and everything in me stills. River's fingers trail down my neck and along my collarbone. "I've wasted so much time." His touch sends rivulets of pleasure through me. I press back against the wall, but he comes closer. "I hope she's ready." His smile's downright sinful. He reaches past me, opening the door. "Good night, Indigo."

He turns his back on me, and I stumble into my room and shut the door just as my knees give out. Poor girl doesn't stand a chance.

# Chapter Thirteen

After a week, my ankle's mostly healed. Other than a group hiking trip, I've been able to keep up with everyone else. I thought being on reality TV would be fun but time crawls here, and outside of scheduled activities there isn't much to do. Everyone is getting a solo date this week and I've been dying for my turn just to get out of the house. Production ushered Kade and me into a limo and even taking a drive feels nice.

"What do you have planned?" I ask as I try to find anything familiar outside the window.

"You'll see." Kades eyes flick toward the cameras positioned throughout the limo, then travel down my body before he takes my hand. Is everything he does calculated?

"Is this one of your moves?" I hold our hands up.

"One of us has to make one. Or is making me impatient a part of your plan?"

I wave my hand dismissively. "From what I hear, you get more than enough attention." Kade doesn't seem like the type looking to commit.

"Oh? Are we going by what others say? I heard a lot about you before

too, but I don't think any of it's true." My mouth pinches together at the thought of him seeing all the nasty things said about me online. "When relationships don't work out, sometimes the story becomes twisted." He holds his hand in between us. "Start over?"

He's saying he won't judge me, even after I've judged him. What a hypocrite I've been. It's true that even though we didn't start off on the right foot, he's been decent to me since I've gotten here. I may not be here to date him, but that doesn't mean we can't get along.

"Start over." I agree, taking his hand in mine.

He smiles, but there's no warmth behind it, "I didn't say that to get you to let your guard down. You should still be careful."

"Of you?"

His smile widens, and this time, it feels real.

Kade makes small talk. He's good at putting people at ease. I can see how he may have gotten the reputation he has with women. If I didn't know better, I might've fallen victim.

But I do.

The limo rolls to a stop. Kade opens the door, stepping outside and offers me his hand. As I get out of the car his other hand goes to the small of my back. The camera crew maneuvers around us, dangling mics above our heads as we enter a restaurant. A few tables are placed throughout the room, but one's decorated with beautiful flowers, small unlit candles and a decorative lace tablecloth. We're greeted by a petite older woman with jet black hair pulled into a sleek bun. She smiles politely and does a small bow as we approach. Kade reciprocates the gesture, so I do the same. Her smile broadens at my attempt.

"Hello, My name's Yua Ito. I'll be helping you prepare your meal for the afternoon." Her words are heavily accented, but she speaks slowly for clarity.

I look to Kade in surprise. "You cook?"

"I'm more than a pretty face."

"That's not what I meant, obviously you're more than that I-"

"So you think I'm pretty?" He asks, thrusting out his chest. My lips twist and he laughs.

"Leave the poor girl alone." Yua chides Kade as she hands us aprons and hair nets. She leads us to a pristine kitchen in the back of the restaurant with stainless steel everything.

"Cooking is putting your heart on a plate." She smiles, placing a small tray of boneless chicken thighs already chopped into nuggets.

"Kade, why don't you tell her what you'll be making today?" She beams.

"My father's karaage chicken was a staple growing up and my mom's famous for her mac. I thought this could be a way to share a bit of who I am." Kade smiles softly.

"I've never had karaage, I'm excited to try it." I give his hand a squeeze.

"Before we start, Kade insists you wash the chicken. I will set out the seasonings for you while you do so."

"Mom never let us cook without washing the meat." Kade moves to the sink.

I give him a knowing look. "Smart woman."

We start rinsing the chicken, patting it dry while our fingers and elbows bump into each other. I attempt to make room between us, but he actively closes the gap. We season everything generously, letting it sit so it can absorb into the meat while Yua instructs us on how to start the mac.

"I make a mean macaroni." I reach for a block of cheese and begin grating.

"Do you now?" Kade's words drip in sarcasm. It doesn't take long for me to feel the strain in my arm. I need to get in shape. "You tired already?" Kade leans forward, elbows resting on the counter.

"Between grating the cheese and boiling the noodles, who's job's harder?"

"If you need help, all you have to do is ask."

"A gentleman wouldn't wait until asked. He'd just do it."

"I never said I was a one." A sly smile spreads across his face. "Maybe I like to see you sweat." I can feel my face heat under his gaze.

"Keep watching, because you won't be touching." I warn.

"Is that right?" He moves closer, placing his hands on either side of me. His breath warms my neck.

"What are you doing?"

"Not touching you." He murmurs, "Even though I'd much rather be doing just that."

Kade Ikeda's dangerous. He has a way of making me want what I shouldn't. Twisting my neck to look at him is a mistake, because now we're nose to nose. He has a hungry look in his eyes and my breath catches. Kade's pure temptation. Heat flows through me and I squeeze my thighs together. If this is him not touching me, then…

I clear my throat. "Not happening."

"I've never been one for rules. I think you're setting them just to entice me."

"In your dreams."

Kade reaches around my waist, his touch feels like small sparks of electricity against my skin. He takes the cheese grater and moves to my side, taking care of the rest while I watch and that's definitely more my speed. When we get the mac in the oven, Kade begins cleaning up, wiping down counters and rinsing dishes.

"Need help?"

"Nah, isn't this what those gentlemen you like so much would do?"

I size him up. "Doesn't feel very Kade. I'll dry while you wash."

He hands me a towel but doesn't let go. "How would you know what I feel like?" A slow grin breaks across his face.

"That's not what I meant." I tug the towel from his hands. He hands me a dripping pot and I work to dry it.

Kade's a lot different than I imagined. Getting a pulse on what he is after is difficult. When we finish cleaning, we move back to frying the chicken until the nuggets are nice and golden. The mac finishes shortly after.

"It smells amazing." Yua looks over the food. She snaps her fingers and a staff member takes our aprons and guides us to our table. The candles between us are lit and the flowers in the center are beautiful. The server fills our glasses with wine and sets down two plates of vibrant leafy greens before we're left alone.

"So what does Kade Ikeda like to get into?" I ask before taking a bite of my salad.

"I enjoy working with my hands."

Pausing mid bite, I look him over. That's one of the last things I expected. If I had to categorize Kade, I'd say he was beautiful, not exactly the rugged type. He has delicate features and even though his body is riddled with muscles, he's more lean than bulk. He's always so well put together. I figured he was a pretty boy who cared more about how he looked than I did.

Imagining him in the sun, sweaty... and dirty—you know what? Never mind. Let's not imagine that because the mental image is doing something to me, "What's something you've made?"

"I recently helped a nonprofit rebuild homes after some flooding, but before that I made a rocking chair." He shrugs, pushing the food around his plate. He's brushing it off like it's no big deal, but he's obviously proud. Also, imagining Kade in a rocking chair is ridiculously adorable.

"I like the feel of community. My mom's military, so we moved a lot as a kid, and I never got to settle."

I'm trying to process this new information. I've known for a while now that he's not exactly the asshole I thought he was, but to imagine him helping others in his free time makes me realize I have no idea who this man is. It also makes me realize I want to change that. I want to know Kade.

"Shouldn't that be well known information? If Kade Ikeda, notorious bad boy, is out building homes for people and relaxing in rocking chairs on his free time, you'd think that info would be blasted."

"That's not what they want to see, and I like my privacy." The way he says it sounds sad.

"What about friends?"

He looks at me and there it is again, that bitter smile of his. I've never met someone who smiles so much but hardly ever means it. "I have a hard time with people."

"You're doing well here."

He sips his wine, ignoring me.

"Most of the girls just want to breath your air, you don't have to try that hard." It's perplexing to think that Kade, of all people, is a loner.

"And what do you want from me?" his eyes catch mine with unwavering focus. My heart feels off beat, but I hold his gaze. I've learned that Kade likes to see me flustered.

"Just be you. If you're not what they portray you to be, then stop pretending you are."

He blinks at me, then a real smile breaks through. "You don't even know what you're asking for." He says just as the server returns with two plates of the karaage and mac. My mouth waters as the smell wafts from my plate.

"What's this?" I point to a small sauce tin filled with a yellow mixture with red seasoning on top.

"Japanese mayo with togarashi, it's to dip your chicken in." He grabs a nugget off of his plate, dips it in the mayo, extending it toward me. Hesitating, I look from him to the chicken. I've never been fed before, but it would be awkward to refuse him in front of the cameras, right? I scoot to the edge of my seat, leaning forward and take a bite. My lips brush against his fingers and I feel heat creep up my neck.

Kade places the rest into his mouth and licks his fingers, the same ones my lips grazed. Suddenly it feels warm in here and I fan myself.

"It's good, right?" He swipes his tongue across his lips and I drop my gaze because I can't be held accountable for the direction my thoughts go in if he keeps eating like *that*. The flavors go so well together. The heat from the seasoning on the mayo and the creamy texture pairs perfectly with the savory chicken.

"Oh man, that's great. It's juicy too."

He nods in agreement.

"So what about acting? Do you not do it anymore?" I ask before dipping another nugget and taking a bite.

"I do it every day." Kade's eyes latch to mine. "I have a project I'll be working on once this wraps up." He sets his fork down and tilts his head. "How does Indigo Johnson like to fill her time?"

"Horror movies. Specifically, the really cheesy kind. If it has bad acting and gore, I'm there. I wish the mansion had a TV, talking about you with the others all day's a drag." I roll my eyes for emphasis, fighting a smile.

"Is that right? I think I'm rather interesting. I can give you some new material, make it less boring." His knees knock against mine under the table and my lips pinch together.

"I think I'll manage. Now if you sneak in a TV and some DVDs let me know."

"I'll keep an eye out."

We spend the rest of our dinner discussing my favorite movies and the things Kade's built. The list is long. From tables to shelving and even a bird house he seemed embarrassed to talk about. When he speaks of what he's created, his eyes light up and he speaks in a fevered tone. Seeing the passion in him is jarring. Every time he realizes he's opening up, he backtracks and tries to make it seem like the things he cares about aren't that important.

"You're cuter like this." I say, pushing away from the table and resting my hands on my belly. Which, by the way, feels as though it's ready to burst at the seams.

"Like what?"

"Being nerdy about your woodworking."

"Nerdy? You just told me your favorite movie is about killer rabbits."

"You'd be surprised how violent they are. Millions suffer every year."

"How was Easter for you in your childhood?" He legitimately looks concerned.

"Hey guys." Jose approaches our table. "Times up." He taps his watch.

My smile falters and I look to Kade, and he gives me a half-hearted one in return. We both stand and he takes my hand, and I'm surprised by the jolt of energy I feel at the contact. His fingers tighten around mine and I find myself leaning into him. When we get inside the limo, Kade reaches for one of the cameras I spotted on the way here.

"What are you doing?"

"Giving us some privacy." He says as he presses a small button on the side. He does the same to three more before he's satisfied that he's found them all.

"Are you allowed to do that?"

"Ask for forgiveness, not permission." He quips as he reaches his hand under his shirt and unclips his mic.

"Turn yours off too."

"Why?"

"Didn't you want to know why I picked you?" He gestures to the mic clipped to my chest. Curiosity wins, and I flick the switch.

"So why am I here? You clearly didn't like me at the casting call."

"You didn't like me. I liked you a lot. I thought you were one of Noah's picks, so I tried to piss you off because Noah chooses girls like Bethany."

"Why keep him around, then?"

Kade's expression hardens. For a moment, I think I've offended him, but then he relaxes and runs his hands through his hair. "I don't agree with his methods, but they work. This show was his idea." He moves from his seat to sit beside me. "I had little say in the decision making process, so when they were going to pass on you, I told them you were my pick."

"You chose me to defy them?"

"You were my one choice. The one thing I had a say in."

"Why are you here if you don't want to be?" I've been thinking of Kade as this untouchable celebrity with an inflated ego and an attitude problem, but the Kade with me now is the opposite of that.

"I don't think you want to do this either." He says, turning his dark eyes on me.

"I didn't. Not really. Then, I thought I could turn a bad thing that happened into an opportunity."

He nods as if he understands, and maybe he does. Again, I'm reminded I know nothing about him.

He continues, his shoulders dropping a little. "Do you remember what you said? About controlling the narrative and people forcing their idea of you down your throat? People have done that to me my entire career. Everything about this life's manufactured. From my image to the people I surround myself with." He tilts his head toward me. "You said you wanted to change the narrative. I saw what people posted about you and it didn't seem to shake you." He laughs and folds his arms over his chest. "I was impressed." He shrugs.

"You cyber stalked me?" A smile breaks across my face.

"Don't get a big head. I wanted to make an informed decision."

"And? What made you decide?"

"Your ex made a post calling you a crazy bitch for taking his stuff and throwing it out the window, and you reposted it with the caption *"use code CRAZYBITCH when booking for 20% off your service."*

We both look at each other before bursting into laughter.

"Allegedly. He never had any proof. Also, I know it's going to make me sound guilty, but it really wasn't me."

Kade's still laughing and I realize that it's the most, honest unfiltered emotion he's shown all day. Joy looks good on him.

"What do they have on you?"

He takes one of my braids, rolling it between his fingers. "Why? You going to save me?"

We stare at each other because now I know this arrogant persona's a façade. Underneath all that bravado, I think Kade is hurting.

"I have a proposition for you." He straightens in his seat. "You didn't come here for me."

Guilt makes a reappearance. Before I can apologize, he cuts me off.

"Don't. It's okay, you aren't the only one. I got myself in a bind and this was my way out."

"What do you want from me, then?"

"An ally. I'll help you. I have connections you need and I get someone here not trying to get something out of me."

"Wouldn't I be doing exactly that?"

"You'd be doing me a favor in return."

He drops his arm around my shoulders, "I'd be using you too. I need a buffer."

"What would that entail?" I knock his arm off my shoulders.

"Sometimes I just need to get away. Having nine women might have been my younger self's dream, but it's my current self's nightmare."

"So you want me to cock-block you?"

His head falls back, and laughter fills the limo. "Essentially, yes. That's exactly what I want."

I chew my lip. He and I may not have come here intending to find love, but not everyone's so callous. "There are girls here that want to get to know you."

"I know."

"You'll have to pick someone."

"Why not you?"

Winning would boost my following while also creating paid opportunities. I'd be able to stand on my own, but if he chooses me, it won't end there. "People would expect us to be with each other even when the cameras stop."

"Being with me wouldn't be all bad."

"While tempting, I'm trying to start a business. The busiest time will be once this ends."

"Until the finale then, you'll get your exposure and I'll double your weekly stipend."

It doesn't feel great to take money from him, but I need the cash and he doesn't seem bothered. Thrusting my hand between us, I make a decision.

"Final two."

He smiles and grasps my hand. "Final two."

While still holding tight, he pulls me closer. "One last thing. Make sure you don't fall for me."

I snort, "I should be telling you that." I've got this nagging sensation that this is a bad idea, but how can I turn down a deal like that?

"You have nothing to worry about on my end. I'm not capable of that."

# Chapter Fourteen

"**Y**ou cut your mics?" Noah's nostrils flare as he rounds on us.

"It was an accident." Kade feigns innocence.

"And the cameras?"

"Whoops." He slides his hands in his pockets.

Noah turns his anger on me, "Getting in his pants won't keep you here longer. You'd have better luck coming to me if you're that desperate."

My face flames at the suggestion that we cut the cameras to have sex in the back of the limo.

"It was my idea. I didn't give her a choice." Kade steps in front of me.

"Don't let it happen again." Noah narrows his gaze. They stare each other down until Noah concedes. His eyes land on me, and I flip him off. The vein in his neck pulses and he turns on his heel.

"Even I have a watchdog." Kade sighs.

Serenity approaches from the front doors of the mansion. She smiles when she sees Kade and rushes to cling to his arm, "Can I steal

you?"

Kade looks at me for approval. Or maybe it's a call for help. Serenity's intense.

"Go ahead." I wave him off and he frowns, but allows her to tow him away. We never said the deal started today.

Jose jogs down the steps with a camera crew, "Hey babe. I'll make this as painless as possible, I promise."

Sighing, I nod as the crew surrounds me. Out of the corner of my eye, I notice River standing off to the side of the mansion. He's talking with Sabrina and she looks upset, her hands waving frantically as she speaks. He places his hands on her shoulders and she flings herself into his arms. River shocks me by responding to her touch. Holding her and messaging circles against her back. I feel a tight pain in my chest as I watch. Her shoulders tremble and she buries her face into his chest, and he just lets her.

"Indigo?"

My attention snaps back to Jose.

"You alright?"

"Yeah. Sorry, what do you need?"

"Just a few questions and you're off the hook. This was your first proper date. Do you feel yourself falling for Kade?"

My brain is slow to comprehend because my attention is split between this conversation and River. "I'm always surprised by what I learn when I'm with him. How can my feelings not grow?" It feels weird to paint our relationship as more than what it is, especially when I know Kade's not interested, but it's what we agreed on.

"Do you feel confident about the upcoming elimination?"

"No way. Just because we had a date doesn't mean he'll choose me." How pointless can these questions get?

"How would you feel if he sent you home?"

"Devastated." My voice is monotone and Jose pauses, searching my eyes before continuing.

"Kade's known for his playboy style. Do you think you're the woman to tame him?"

My irritation flares. I'm dying to pull Sabrina and River apart and I'm frustrated that production's pushing this narrative. From what I've seen, that doesn't appear to be who he is at all.

"I don't think Kade needs taming. Anyone thinking they need to change him doesn't deserve him."

"I guess you do like him, huh?" Jose signals for the camera crew to disperse. "I don't mean to be annoying; these are questions I'm told to ask. I know Noah got on to you about the mics and cameras, but don't let it get to you."

"How'd you know?" Word spreads faster around here than I thought.

"The star of the show goes ghost and all our feeds cut out. Hard not to notice."

"You're not going to ask what happened?"

"Do I need to? Kade doesn't like following the rules. I'm surprised this didn't happen sooner. Besides, you don't seem the type to use those methods."

Jose's blind faith in me helps soothe the burn I felt from Noah's shady comment earlier.

"Alright hun, get some rest." He mumbles something into his mic as he leaves.

Instead of heading inside, I move along the side of the building, using the bushes as cover while straining to hear what River and Sabrina are saying.

"No one has to know. I'll be on your side." River's speaking. I'm itching to take a peek, but fear of being caught holds me in place.

"Because it's your job." Sabrina sounds weak, the total opposite of what I've known her to be.

"I'll support you because you need it, and because I want to." There's a pause before Sabrina breaks the silence.

"I don't know why I did that." Her voice is quiet.

"I'm not here to judge."

"What'll happen if someone finds out?"

"They won't. I won't let this hurt you. We'll figure it out."

"What the heck." I breathe. Curiosity claws at me and I have to look. So I peer over the shrubs and attempt to get closer for a better view and lose my footing. I fall into the foliage, letting out a squeal on the way down. My arms scrape along the branches as I try to wrestle my way out of them. Finally, I untangle myself only to see they've made their way over. I brush the leaves off my shirt and scowl at River, who looks like he's fighting back a laugh.

Sabrina's pissed, but there's fear there. Maybe she thinks I'll report what I heard. As much as seeing them together pisses me off, I wouldn't do that to River.

"Don't for a second think you can use what you heard against me. You don't want to make me your enemy." She steps in front of River as if she has to protect him from me.

"Are you threatening me? I don't care about whatever you guys have going on." My eyes jump to River and for some reason, I feel betrayed. I wonder if he can hear the lie in my words, because I do care. I care a lot.

They share a look and confusion colors her features before her lips curve into a wicked smile. "You cared enough to hide and watch us." She shoulder checks me hard and stomps off.

"Real mature." I mumble.

River takes a step toward me, and I step back, shaking my head. "What was that about?"

"Nothing." He looks away from me.

Hurt stabs at my chest. He's lying, and not even doing a good job at it. We never lie to each other.

"She's just one of the girls I'm assigned to. Like Jose's assigned to you."

"No. This wasn't anything like me and Jose. Jose doesn't hold me like that."

"Why does it matter to you how I treat her? From where I'm standing, Kade has you wrapped around his finger. You said you wouldn't fall for him, but he was holding you when you stepped out of that limo. He's constantly touching you and you let him. Why's that?"

"Don't try to turn this on me." We've never gotten this heated before. It feels like this is snowballing into something bigger and I don't know how to stop it.

"What happened in the limo when the cameras were out?" There's a note of desperation in his voice that I've never heard before.

"Nothing."

We stare at each other long and hard. I've never hidden anything from him before, but he's clearly hiding something from me. I know it's childish, but I can't help being petty back.

"We're arguing over nothing because apparently that's all that's going on between you and Sabrina and that's all that's going on between Kade and me. I'm surprised you even paid attention to anything going on with me when you've been so caught up with her."

"I can never not pay attention to you." He runs his hands through his hair and his jaw sets into a hard line. He moves closer, grabbing my forearm and pulling me toward him.

"Seeing you with Kade drives me crazy."

That familiar fire dances along my skin at his touch. "Why?"

"Why do you think?"

My heart hammers against my chest. I need him to say it, to be clear. Too many times have his words and actions ballooned hope only for me to have misinterpreted the situation.

"Kade isn't a good guy. Javi just crushed you. I won't watch Kade do the same."

Just like that, everything in me deflates. He's being overprotective, and I can't stand it. "You don't know him at all. He's extremely considerate and the things he does for others… you have him all wrong."

"You do like him."

"Why's it your business? The idea of me coming here bothered you before you knew it'd be Kade. Is he the problem? If I leave the show and find someone else, would you be okay with it?" My hands are shaking, and I have to fight to keep my voice even. I'm scared I've given River the opportunity to hurt me. That me asking for clarity is going to be painful, but I need to fully let go. The line needs to be drawn.

"It's not just Kade. I don't want you with anyone else." His eyes don't waver from mine.

"Why River? I need to hear you say why."

"Because when you were with Javi I thought I'd lost you for good. Because when he fumbled I was angry for you but happy for me. Because when I see you with Kade, see the way he watches you and the way he hovers around you. I want to lose control. I want to shut this entire fucking show down to keep him away from you." He closes the distance between us and places his hands on either side of my face. "Because I think you belong with me." He presses his forehead against mine.

River Beck's saying words I've dreamed of. My body reacts to his touch, and I want to run my fingers down his chest and pull him impossibly closer. I want to know what it's like to give in, to have what I've felt reciprocated, but I don't. I press my hands against his chest, but he holds firm.

He's waiting for me to respond, but I'm hesitating. All of this feels sudden. I feel guilty for thinking it, but what if he wants me in this moment because he isn't supposed to have me? He claims he wanted me when I was with Javi, but he said nothing after we broke up. Now he wants me because Kade looks my way. What if I cave and his feelings are fleeting? Our friendship would be ruined. To my knowledge, River's never looked at me like a man looks at a woman. Can he change our dynamic?

"I don't think you understand the gravity of what you're doing right now. Can you handle the consequences?"

The corner of his mouth lifts. "Are you asking if I can handle you?"

I pull his hands from my face. "I'm being serious. Can you handle being together? We'd be different." I take a step toward him, placing my hand on his shoulder, then trailing my fingers up his neck, cupping his face. I run my other hand down his chest and tug the bottom of his shirt, bringing him closer.

"Can you cross the line? Can you do what lovers do with me? Can you see yourself holding me?" I remove my hand from his cheek and wrap my arm around his neck, pulling him even closer, pressing my chest against his. "Can you picture yourself kissing me?" I use my other hand to pull the collar of his shirt, drawing his face toward mine, but before our lips touch, I move my mouth to his ear. "You think you want me River, but if we cross those lines, we can't go back." Releasing my hold on him, I put some distance between us. "When we were younger, you told me you didn't like me romantically and that we shouldn't ruin what we have. You were right then. I don't think you want me. I think seeing me here makes you think you do. Friends get jealous of friends too; we've always been so involved… it's easy for the lines to get muddy. Whatever's going on with you and Sabrina… I'll stay out of it."

River steps toward me and opens his mouth, but the sound of

footsteps kills whatever he was going to say.

"Is everything okay?"

I look over my shoulder to see Kade with Serenity on his arm. He looks at River before turning his attention back to me. Serenity is clearly unhappy with the interruption, pouting and glaring daggers in my direction.

"Are you doing alright here?" Kade asks again. My nerves tense. I'm unsure how much they overheard.

"I'm fine. I had questions about our schedule and he was trying to answer them."

Kade looks over my shoulder and I don't know what face Rivers' making but Kade's mouth tilts downward.

"Are you guys heading inside? I was about to go in." I hope Kade can't tell how badly I want to get them away from each other. If he does, he doesn't mention it, just offers me his other arm.

"We just finished our walk." He moves to take us toward the mansion doors, and I fight the urge to look behind me.

# Chapter Fifteen

oday requires concealer. I apply a generous amount to cover the dark circles I've developed. River freaking Beck has consumed my thoughts all week. To be fair, I don't have an outstanding track record with men, but he's letting his incessant need to protect me from myself confuse the situation. A tiny part of me feels guilty for snapping at him. I know he cares. It doesn't help that any time my brain has strayed from thoughts of him, Kade plagues me instead.

"The next couple of weeks are going to be long." I mumble.

"Dang, am I that bad of a roommate?" Jasmine plops down on my bed, jostling all my makeup.

"Of course not. You're perfect."

"I am," she agrees, inspecting her fingernails.

After applying a little color to my lids, some mascara and blush, I pack everything away.

"How are you guys not nervous? I'm freaking out." Cameron asks from her bed.

"Oh, I am. We haven't had much time with Kade and now we're going into an elimination." Jasmine slips on her heels.

"What about you Indie? How do you feel?" Cameron nods in my direction.

"I try not to think about it. If he doesn't choose me, then it wasn't meant to be."

"I guess you wouldn't feel like us. He keeps pulling you away for chats." Cameron smiles, but it looks forced. Unfortunately, I can't completely deny what's she's saying. Per our agreement, I've effectively held up my end of the deal. I cling to his side, and he picks me for solo conversations anytime he has a choice. She's not the only one fed up with me. Serenity looks like she wants to strangle me every time I open my mouth and River hasn't spoken to me since our blow up.

"That's not it." I speak slowly.

"How into him are you?" Jasmine asks, but I don't sense any of the malice I'm getting from Cameron.

"I mean, we just got here." I clip my mic on and slip on my heels, ready to exit this conversation.

"So, you don't even know if you like him?" Cameron leans back on her hands.

She's trying to force an answer out of me. "If you're asking If I'm in love with the guy, the answer's no."

Jasmine looks between us and cuts in. "That's valid. Arguing about it doesn't change the fact that it's Kade's decision. Indie's not forcing him to choose her."

Cameron looks like she still has more to say but decides against it. We head downstairs and when we reach the foyer, Marissa's front and center. She smiles brightly with Kade at her side, leaning into him and fluttering her lashes. You'd think she was a contestant. We get into formation and Jose gestures for us to smile before signaling to Marissa that we're good to go.

"We have a busy day planned. However, before that, we need to get the less fun part out of the way." She lays a light touch on Kade's shoulder.

"The woman I'm sending home, I feel I haven't been able to connect with. Aashvi, I'd be doing you a disservice by keeping you any longer."

He's so dry, we gotta work on his delivery. I don't recognize the name, but the small gasp one girl makes signals who he's referring to. After Bethany's dramatics this girl's calm, albeit a little teary eyed. She breaks formation, saying her goodbyes before production takes her away.

Marissa takes her place back at the front. "Since we're amid spooky season, we have some ghastly dates planned. Will today be a nightmare? Or a dream?" She taps her chin and looks at us curiously.

"Group one will go to an escape room this afternoon and Group two will visit a haunted house this evening."

If it's one thing I love, it's a good Halloween themed event.

---

I needed to get out of the house. Staying inside to avoid River because I don't know what to say to him is exhausting. Turns out that the universe has some type of vendetta against me because Sabrina's in my group for the haunted house, which means River's a part of our production team.

Serenity sits across from me while Sabrina and Hanna sit at the back of the limo. When Hanna catches me staring, she smiles and gives me a small wave. Sabrina tracks the movement and narrows her eyes at me. I don't know if I'll ever understand how someone who acts like they breathe sunshine and rainbows like Hanna can be so content next to someone like Sabrina.

"Do you like haunted houses?" Attempting small talk with Serenity is like pulling teeth. Her eyes jump to mine but don't really focus. She never seems interested in anyone other than Kade.

"Kade doesn't like them, so why would I?" She shrugs and looks back out the window.

"He doesn't?"

She sighs like I've asked a stupid question. "He did an interview a while back, saying this type of thing doesn't interest him."

"Oh, must have missed it." I shrug.

"None of you know him." She mumbles.

"And you do?"

"Yes." She scoffs.

Okaaaay. This time, I let the conversation drop. We finally arrive at our destination and Jose preps Serenity and me for filming. Sabrina and Hanna linger by the limo. River responds to something Sabrina says and allows her to lean in and brush her hand against his arm. Turning away from them, I remind myself that it's none of my business. However, it doesn't mean that it's not becoming increasingly annoying.

Jose went over the rules before leaving, but he feels the need to repeat them now that we're here. "As always, make sure your mics are on. The staff has requested I ask that you guys remember that no matter how scared you get, do not touch the actors."

"Are they allowed to touch us?" Hanna raises her hand as she and Sabrina join us.

"No. They will chase you, though."

"Everyone ready?" River asks Jose.

"Yeah, just waiting on Noah to get here with Kade." Jose glances at his phone.

River looks at all of us, but he stealthily avoids eye contact with me. Even though I've evaded him, knowing he's doing the same is irritating. I'm not sure how to stop the distance that's growing between us, and this is exactly why we should keep things the same.

River checks his watch before speaking. "The venue's a bit of a maze, so try not to fall behind. If you find yourself lost, look for exit signs or one of us will come find you, eventually."

A car pulls into the slot behind ours. Kade looks effortlessly handsome. Hair tied in the usual knot at the nape of his neck. He's wearing a graphic tee with a plaid button up over it and loose-fitting jeans.

"I'm serious. Don't try anything today." Noah comes to a halt in front of us.

Kade ignores him, "Ladies." He tilts his head and gives a two-finger salute.

"Alright. Cameras are ready, you guys can head in. Once you complete the maze, we'll meet you at the other end." Jose pats Kade on the back, urging him forward.

"You ready?" Kade offers me his hand and I can feel Serenity burn a hole in my back with her eyes.

"Nope." Noah grabs Kade's hand and turns him to Hanna.

"Hanna will enter with Kade."

"Are my dates going to be micromanaged, too?" Kade's jaw clenches.

"Don't act like you haven't done anything to deserve it." Noah sneers. Kade stares at Noah before sighing and offering his hand to Hanna. She's unbothered by his reluctance and takes it happily.

River stands behind Noah and Kade with his arms folded over his chest. He doesn't avoid me this time. The intensity of his stare makes me feel bare. I'm doing the right thing. Ruining our friendship over temporary emotions would be stupid. A failed relationship with River would be a domino effect. Our lives are too entwined for a nasty breakup.

"Alright, have a good time." Jose dismisses us and I trail at the back of the group. An employee standing at the door greets us.

"I'm glad you made it. In order to be completely safe, you have to get to the compound with the rest of the survivors, it's just past the graveyard. I've received reports of the dead breaking free. I wouldn't worry though." She smiles brightly after her spiel, pushing the door open. "Follow the lights to find your way."

The fog filling the room makes it difficult to see. There's a string of lights hanging from the ceiling along two paths. One is lit with yellow lights while the other is lit with red. There's a soft haunting melody that plays, broken up by the sound of recorded screams.

"Which way should we go?" Hanna asks as she takes hold of Kade's arm.

He looks between both paths. "This way." Kade takes us down the red path.

We creep forward entering a dark corridor and a woman jumps out from a hidden door, wailing before disappearing back behind it. Hanna screams and Kade freezes.

Laughing, I pat Kade's shoulder. "You guys, okay?"

They shoot me annoyed looks and we press forward and come to the end of the hall where we must choose between two doors.

"Left." Sabrina demands and we all turn to her.

"Left feels lucky." She shrugs and Kade's lips press into a thin line. Maybe Serenity was right. He looks like he wants to be anywhere but here. He gives a subtle nod and opens the door, its pitch-black inside. Like can't-see-in-front-of-your-face dark. Further ahead is a single flashing light bulb and a lot of the noise from before is muffled once the door shuts behind us.

Everyone's silent as we stalk forward, and my nerves are on high alert. The quiet seeps into my bones. We're slowly getting closer to the blinking light when I feel a large hand wrap around my mouth and an arm tighten around my middle, pinning my arms to my side and dragging me back. My scream is muffled and when I attempt to kick, my assailant bends backward, lifting me off the ground.

We were told the actors wouldn't touch us; this isn't an employee. Terror makes my mind go blank. I'm being taken further from the group, to the right side of the room. Whoever has their hold on me finally puts me down, but doesn't let go.

"Don't scream." River whispers and everything in me relaxes. I feel his hand reach for the wires under my shirt, ripping the mic off before I can stop him.

The hell? Reaching behind me, I punch him in his chest. "What was that for?" He pulls me forward, and I hear a door open. A light clicks on and we're inside a small supply closet.

"River, what are we doing here? Are you trying to lose your job? This whole thing's being filmed." I'm whisper shouting now.

"It's too dark for them to film in that room."

"So, you planned this?"

He steps toward me, and I flatten my back against the door. That doesn't stop him from advancing, he places both hands on either side of me and leans in close.

"River, what are you thinking?"

He presses his head against my shoulder and breathes in deep.

"Are you okay?"

"No. Blue, I'm not okay."

My pulse speeds up at the sound of my old nickname on his tongue. "What's going on with you?"

He pushes away from my shoulder and stares directly at me. I don't know what face to make or how to react with him so close. He removes his right hand from the wall and gently tucks my braids behind my ear, causing my stomach to do somersaults.

"This could ruin everything." My words don't hold the same confidence they did before.

"I'm already ruined." He moves his hand from my hair and traces a line of fire down my arm. "You asked me if I could hold you." Both his hands go to my waist. He slips them under my shirt and grips my hips, kneading my skin with his thumbs and boy, is it doing things to me.

"River."

"You asked me if I could kiss you." He closes the distance between us and places a soft kiss to my neck. It's like air brushing against my skin, but then I feel his tongue graze from the base of my neck to the shell of my ear, sending waves of pleasure through me. "Is this what friends do, Blue?" His mouth is still on my ear and any resistance I'm clinging to is fading.

"What are you doing?"

"Crossing the line."

His mouth's on mine, and everything about this kiss is raw emotion that's been held back for too long. His tongue glides against the seam of my lips, asking for permission, and I let him in. My hands go to his hair, and he presses his knee between my legs.

His hands travel higher, lifting my shirt. The cold air caresses my skin and I moan into his mouth. All my nerves come alive. I want to touch him too, explore his body. Working my hands under his shirt, my fingers meet with the solid planes of his chest. His mouth leaves mine and his tongue revisits my ear.

Before I can stop myself, I'm moaning his name, and this only emboldens him. His hands stop their climb toward my chest and make their way back down. His fingers flex before gripping my ass, as his teeth pinch at the skin at the base of my neck. River's name is on my lips again because I'm falling apart and I want him to know he's the one doing it to me.

"You're so beautiful." He tightens his grip on me, and his words send warmth crashing through me. Before I can process what we've done, what we're doing—the sound of muffled yelling on the other side of the door makes me freeze. I'm panting, and my heart is knocking against my chest. River doesn't let me go, but he stops to listen.

"Indigo, where you at girl?" That's Hanna.

"Production said they would come for any idiots that got lost." That's Sabrina.

"Kade won't finish the maze without her." Serenity sounds close and irritated.

"River, I have to leave before they try this door."

"I don't want to go back to before." His words come out in a harsh whisper.

What we did felt right in the moment, but as I come down from the high and back to reality, I'm realizing what a mistake we made. "We have to try. This messes everything up."

"I won't let it."

"You can't make that promise. If it doesn't work, I don't know that I could still be around you. I'm not okay with taking the chance of losing you."

River's hair's a mess of tangled curls, and my lipstick stains his skin.

"Indigo, are you in this room?" I hear Kade shout from the other side of the door and guilt finds its way into my heart. I feel like I'm betraying him, which is ridiculous. We have a deal—a transaction. Not a relationship. My eyes flick toward the door and River's jaw ticks.

I don't like Kade. Not like that.

But I did promise I'd be there for him and I'm not holding up my end of the bargain. Sneaking around with River could mean losing what I came here for and Rivers job would be on the line.

"I have to go." Making up my mind, I readjust my clothes. The footsteps on the other side of the door move further away and I feel myself relax.

"Look at me and tell me you can act like nothing happened. Tell me there's no part of you that wants this. You're so focused on the possibility of us failing, you can't see how much potential we have to be everything."

I bite my lip because I can't tell him I don't want this, and he knows it. Finally, I look into his eyes and he gives me a half smile.

"If at any point you decide you don't want me, tell me and I'll stop. Not that you don't want to ruin what we have—me. If I'm not what you want, you tell me, and I'll back off."

All I can manage is a small nod before I exit the closet, closing the door as quietly as possible behind me.

# Chapter Sixteen

"**D**idn't sleep well?" Jasmine hands me a mug of warm coffee before sitting on her bed across from me.

"That's an understatement." I mumble over the warm drink, taking in the scent of the coffee beans and vanilla creamer. Thoughts of River kept me up at night and it didn't help that when I drifted off, I dreamt of his hands on me—his lips traveling across my body. When I woke up and realized it wasn't happening, I was frustrated for *other* reasons.

"Your makeup's always so cute." Jasmine comments.

Unsurprisingly, I was chosen for a date later this evening. While most of the girls opt to take advantage of the hair and makeup team, I always do my own. Got to take advantage of the free advertisement. So even though my date isn't for hours, you best believe I'm going to walk around with my face beat for the cameras all day.

"You have to let me do yours next time." Today I went with a more colorful look. Deep shades of orange and gold with a sharp eyeliner in a bright yellow. I paired it with a taupe ribbed tank dress and nude heels for balance.

There's a knock at the door and Jasmine hops off the bed to answer. She runs her hands through her hair at the sight of whoever's on the other side.

"Hello, I came to grab Indie." Kade's voice reaches my ears and Jasmine steps to the side, looking disappointed.

"Our dates not until later tonight." I look at the clock, it's just past 8 a.m.

"I know." He shrugs.

I'm learning to roll with Kade's spontaneity. I get up and follow him down the hallway. He's dressed nicely. Curls freshly moisturized, a light cologne, mic clipped and ready to go.

"Don't you have a date this morning?"

"I do. But I wanted to see you."

I side eye him as we make it to the foyer. "What for?"

"All the time we've spent together lately, and you don't like me yet?"

"It's not that. I just want to be in the know."

"Just know that you can trust me." He stops and offers me his hand, so I take it. Because I do trust him.

"Alright *Aladdin* is there a magic carpet up here or something?"

He laughs and heads up the stairs. All our rooms are on the first floor, so I haven't had the chance to see the second. When we reach the top, the walls are lined with floor to ceiling windows. There's a sitting area in the center and a hallway on either side lined with rooms just like the bottom floor. Kade moves to the right, and we approach an open door. He peers inside, and curiosity gets the better of me. When I look past him, Cameron's sitting at what looks like a vanity. Makeup's spread across the counters and a woman stands tapping her foot and typing furiously on her phone with one hand, while the other's hung in a sling.

"What Kade?" She snaps, looking up from her phone. She's model pretty. Tall with long legs that don't quit, jet black hair parted down the middle, stopping at her waist and skin as vibrant as the night, with warm purple undertones. Her lips are twisted into a scowl, and she slams her phone on the counter, making Cameron jump.

Kade ignores the clear *fuck off* vibes this girl's dishing and waltzes inside. "I was looking for Noah. Everything okay?"

She turns on him and points at Cameron. "What do you think? Ya'll are filming in forty minutes and she's still bare. The twins are stuck in traffic, and I can't work with my left hand."

Her eyes fall on me and she shakes her head, "Nope, not happening."

"What's the plan then, Drew? I think Cameron's beautiful as is, but I wouldn't want you to get in trouble."

"Shut up Kade, you don't care about me. This is about her." She nods her head in my direction.

"We were passing by. If you've got it handled, then…" He turns to leave.

"Wait." Drew calls and I see the corners of Kade's mouth lift. She catches the smile he's trying to hide too and flips him off as she grabs my arm.

"Let me see what you can do." She gestures to the makeup on display and smacks her gum.

"What?" I'm beyond confused. Kade pushes me forward and Cameron looks uncertain.

"You do makeup, right? This one won't shut up about how much talent you got." She glares at Kade, "I jacked up my arm and my assistants are no shows this morning. As pretty as this one is, if I send her out there like this production won't be happy."

I step toward the counter and inspect everything in front of me. All high-end products.

"My stuff good enough for you?" Drew questions.

"Better than good." Smiling, I pick up a moisturizing cream and primer.

Looking at Cameron, I run different color combinations in my head. I inspect her face, tilting her chin with my finger. Her skin is a beautiful warm brown a shade or two darker than mine, with honey undertones. Before I get to prepping her skin, I look over at Kade and mouth a silent thank you, but he shrugs as if he didn't plan this. I'll be forever grateful that he made this happen.

"I still have to find Noah." Kade backs out of the room and Drew waves him off as she watches me with an intensity that gets my nerves going. Cameron has an earthy vibe, from her clothes to her hair. Butterfly clips are pinned throughout her burgundy locs and charms swing from the bangles on her arms. She has a natural beauty that I don't want to hide, so I play up her features. Drew has a wide variety of foundations, and I choose the one closest to her skin tone.

She's wearing a burnt orange dress, so I go with shades of gold for her highlight and browns for her eyes. She's blessed with naturally thick brows, which saves me some time. I clean them up a bit, giving her a soft arch. Her full lips have a natural pout I'd kill for. I call attention to them by using a creamy chocolate color with a pinky nude in the center and a light layer of gloss. Cameron has hooded eyes, so I'm careful to make sure she looks at me before painting her wings, going straight across the fold of skin. I've applied setting powder while I work on the swoops and swirls of her baby hair as the final touch for the look. Drew comes around humming as she evaluates my work.

"Your lines are clean and you color matched her perfectly." She mumbles.

"Thank you." I can't stop the goofy grin I'm wearing.

"I'd have gone with a softer contour. Her face shapes more squared so you don't want harsh lines." She runs her finger along Cameron's cheek and my smile drops, "Still, It's not bad. I guess Kade wasn't bullshitting me. Wasn't sure if his judgment was clouded," she eyes me warily, "But you're good. Fast too. You up to handling the next girl?"

She doesn't have to ask me twice. This is what I came here for. Serenity takes Cameron's place and I expect her to sit silently, but she's extremely particular. Apparently purples Kade's favorite color, hence the dye job on her hair. She insists we use it for her makeup too and I am grateful she isn't wearing it as well or I would have gotten *Barney* flashbacks. I go with silver accents and highlights, white eyeliner and a nude lip to tie it all together. She's a talker if Kade's the subject. The girl's a walking Kade Wikipedia page. By the time I finish with her, Drew's assistants arrive looking terrified, with Chinese takeout as a bribe.

"I should fire your asses." Drew snatches the food from their hands and they share a look of fear. "Gone ahead and say thank you to Indie, she saved your jobs today." She's already digging through the bag and the twins turn to look at me. They're both dressed in designer from head to toe, makeup done perfectly and nails freshly manicured.

"Thank you for helping my brother and I out. We owe you one. I'm Kenny." The first one offers me his hand.

"And I'm Kevin." The second one gathers me in a hug. They're identical, from their umber skin to their button noses.

The twins thank me a few more times while complimenting my work before taking over and starting on Gabby and Nicole. Watching them is like taking a master class. Kevin walks me through his thought process and Kenny asks for my input every so often. When they finish, I squeeze any bit of information out of them about the industry. They tell me how difficult it can be to break in and how crazy the hours are, but they also talk about all the cool people they get to meet and the fun projects they've worked on. Drew promises to let me help out every once in a while, and I thank them again before leaving in a daze.

That took up more time than I thought. I've got about an hour until my date, so I explore the second floor a little more. The sound of muffled talking makes me stop short. Aside from the room doubling as a makeup studio, the only person with a room up here is Kade. Closing in on the voices, I recognize Sabrina talking.

"I don't know what to do, if production finds out-" Her voice catches and a sob sounds through the cracked door. My mind races to fill in the gaps. River took me off guard at the haunted house and I forgot all about whatever he has going on with her.

The next voice is soft, "Who cares if production finds out-"

"I care Hanna. I didn't plan to fall for anyone." Sabrina's full on crying now.

"Maybe talk to River about it." Hanna responds and the sound of crying follows.

I've stumbled across something I wasn't supposed to. She's serious about River and the knowledge of that crowds my chest, making it uncomfortably tight. Quietly, I head downstairs and rub at my breastbone trying to ease the pain. What could he have said to her to make her think they were a possibility? And is it the same things he's saying to me?

# Chapter Seventeen

I've been unsure how to feel about what's happened between River and me, but I'm confident I don't want to hear about him with anyone else. Sabrina couldn't have fallen for him on her own. It takes two to tango. There is clearly something between them, and I know exactly how I feel about that.

Pissed.

The girls that don't have solo dates today are getting a group activity with Kade this afternoon, which means I have the mansion to myself, for the most part. Since my dates not until later, I cut my mic. I went from having the best day getting to work with Drew, to feeling awful. So, I make my way to my room to get my thoughts together. More than anger, I feel hurt. After Javi, I expect little from men, but this still cuts deep. When I turn down the hallway, River's leaning against my door. He smiles, but I push him out of the way, head inside and try to shut him out, but he moves his foot to block it.

"What's wrong with you?" He asks.

"I need to get ready for my date." My lie isn't a good one. My makeup is still intact from this morning, and I'm already dressed. I

push harder, and he removes his foot but braces his hand against the door instead.

"Don't tell me you actually care about this?"

"I do."

He looks down at me. "Let me in Indie."

"No." The whine in my voice makes me cringe. Avoiding his eyes, I stare at his chest, which doesn't help because then I remember how it feels to be pressed against it.

"Fine. I'll just stand here, shouting about how unfair you're being."

My face jerks up and he takes a deep breath, "Indigo Johnson—"

I slap my hand over his mouth and use my other to drag him inside, slamming the door shut. "Why would you do that?" stomping toward him, I push his chest backward.

He hardly budges, taking my wrists into his hands. "What'd I do now?"

"What aren't you telling me about Sabrina?"

River goes still. An emotion flashes across his face before I can pin it down. "It has nothing to do with you."

Even if that's true, it stings to hear.

"How can you say those things… but still start something with her?" I hate that my voice shakes toward the end, and that I can't confidently look him in the eye. The silence grows and I finally give in and face him. To my surprise, he's smiling.

"Are you jealous?"

"Seriously?" I scoff and try to pull away.

He twists us around and pushes me on top of my bed. River's body cages me in and his knee is anchored between my thighs. "It's not what you think." His hair brushes against my forehead.

"Then what is it?"

His face falls. "It's not my place to say. I need you to trust me.

When did you stop being able to do that?"

The fight leaves me. When did I start to question everything between us? One moment of weakness and it's already causing cracks. I search his face and I can see how much he wants—needs me to believe him. I'm not sure what I overheard, but I've got my own secret with Kade, so I should respect his.

"I do trust you."

His eyes soften and mine drag down to his lips, and I remember how they felt against mine. Apparently, I'm easy to read because the corners of his mouth tilt up.

"Don't even think about it." Not again. Twisting my hips, I try and fail to push him off.

"You trying to wrestle?" An adorably toothy smile spreads across his face and I can't help the laugh that finds its way out of me.

"What are we, five? Let me up."

"Sounds like an excuse, Blue. You never were able to get from under me." He pauses and wiggles his brows, inciting another laugh from me. "Maybe you never wanted to." He teases.

It's crazy how quickly he can change my mood, but I'm still frustrated. He has such a hold on me, I never feel in control. In an attempt to knock him off balance, I catch him off guard by pressing my lips against his. He doesn't move at first, but then he's matching my energy. His mouth parts slightly and I slip inside. River's lips are like silk pillows; he groans as I take his bottom one captive between my teeth, releasing his hold of my arms. I take his face in my hands, sitting forward while simultaneously guiding him into a lying position. Moving to straddle him, I take the lead for once.

And it feels good.

Finally, we come up for air. I trace a path of kisses from his mouth, down his jaw and work my way along his neck. Each one leaves a lipstick stain against his skin, and it feels like I'm marking my territory. The thought of that shouldn't send a thrill through me the way it does. His breathing becomes erratic, and his hands grip my hips. My head gets foggy, and I almost forget this was supposed to be a show of power.

However, the sounds he's making captivate me and the need to confirm how much influence I have over his body is overwhelming. Taking a page from River's book, I reach the crook of his neck and slide my tongue upward. He releases another groan, and his hands find my ass again. He takes possession of me holding me tight.

Bringing my lips to his ear, I whisper, "Did I find a weak spot?" I take his lobe between my teeth.

"Blue." His voice is ragged.

Pushing against his chest, I sit up and adjust myself only to find something hard and hot between my thighs. A small gasp escapes my lips and I squeeze my legs together because the need to feel him—to rock against him is growing and I feel like I'm losing control of the situation. Shaking my head, I scramble off of his lap.

"This was stupid of me." My dress has bunched up at my hips. I grab the bottom and pull it down while making my way to the bathroom.

"You're going to give me whiplash."

I scowl at him through the mirror as I dig through the makeup bag I left on the counter. How stupid can we be? Anyone could've walked in.

"Hey, I didn't start it this time. *You* jumped me." He clutches his chest, feigning innocence.

"Fine. I'm sorry, won't happen again." I refocus on touching up my makeup.

"You think you can have your way with me and be done?" River covers his chest as if I've scandalized him.

"That's not what I'm doing."

144

"Then shouldn't you take responsibility?"

I find a clean towel under the sink and dampen it with water. "Use this to wash up." I turn and gesture toward the lipstick smeared against his skin, but then I notice the bulge in his pants and my eyes stretch wide.

"My eyes are up here." He reaches and takes the towel from me.

"Put that thing away." I attempt to move past him, but he blocks me, holding either side of the door frame.

"I'm a man. What'd you expect?"

A knock at the door makes me jump. River frowns, rubbing the towel against his neck. Pushing past him, I move to answer it, but before I can, Jose walks in.

"Hey Indigo, it's go time. You're late." Jose freezes when he realizes I'm not alone. He points at River. "What are you doing here?"

"He came for me." I hope my words don't sound as panicked as I feel.

"And he had to come inside and shut the door to get you out?"

Shit.

"She wasn't answering when I knocked." River shrugs.

"I've been feeling overwhelmed. He caught me at a bad time."

"Are you okay babe?" Jose's concern makes me feel guilty.

"I am, and I'm ready to go." Taking his arm, I urge him out the door. He isn't giving anything away. I can't tell if he believes the crap we're spouting.

Jose looks over his shoulder, "Next time one of my girls is having a meltdown, I expect you to hit me on the radio."

River grunts in response, and we leave him behind. I'm relieved we weren't questioned further. When we arrive at the foyer, Kade and a woman wearing a smock are waiting in the middle of the room. Kade stands next to two easels wearing a black hoodie and jeans with a denim jacket layered on top.

"You look beautiful." He murmurs as we approach and guilt's making itself at home in my heart. I can't help feeling like what I just did was wrong.

"Thank you."

"I'll be working with you today." The woman smiles. She has paint smattered across her clothes. "You have your own canvases and there's also some wine." She gestures to the small table between each chair. R&B music plays from a radio on the table with our paint supplies.

"I'm not exactly good at painting." We both put on our smocks and take our seats.

"Chelsea's great. No matter how untalented you are, she'll get something decent out of you." I smack his arm. Kade laughs while pouring us each a drink. "I'm not great at it either, so don't worry."

Chelsea places some brushes and a cup of water next to me. "We'll go step by step, so take your time."

Kade's right. She's good at explaining things, patient and gives suggestions when needed. We're supposed to be painting a flower filled landscape with a cherry blossom tree and if you squint that's exactly what I've done. We've been at it for nearly an hour and Kade's content focusing on his portrait while I stress over the fact that every brush stroke seems to make mine worse.

"How's it going over there?" Kade attempts to peek, but I block his view.

"Eyes on your work." I point my brush at him like a weapon.

"It can't be that bad." He sips his wine, paint smeared across his fingers.

"I told you, I'm no good." I dip my brush in more green paint. My grass is melting into the brown of the tree trunk and looks like poop. I feel him watching me and it puts my nerves on edge. "Are you done with yours?" I ask and pick up my glass.

"Yes." He smiles. "If you're that worried about it, let me help."

I chew my lip but nod my head. He stands behind me and doesn't say anything, so I look up and he looks horrified.

"Oh, come on, it's not *that* bad." I drag my brush across the canvas, still desperately trying to fix my poop grass.

"Did you decide to paint something else instead of the cherry blossom tree?" He tilts his head sideways, as if that'll make my painting make sense.

"What are you talking about? It's right there." I point my brush at the pink blob in the center and he covers his mouth, but I can still see his lips curve up.

"I must've had more to drink than I thought. Sorry I missed it." He's fighting a smile and my face warms.

"Like yours is any better." I slide to the edge of my seat and look over at his canvas and it's a goddamn masterpiece. "You said you weren't good at this." His grass is so detailed it looks like it's billowing in the wind and the differing hues of pink on his tree make the leaves pop. Everything about it is beautiful.

"I'm not. You're just exceptionally bad. This can be salvaged, come here."

Kade grabs my hand and I watch him work. He cleans up my painting by fading some of the color with water and then hands me a clean brush. He takes my wrist and I feel his chest press against my back.

"You don't have to be so heavy handed. The less paint you have on the brush, the less likely it'll bleed." He guides my hand across the canvas. His strokes are confident and smooth. "Take your time and consider what you want on the canvas." He paints over some of the more obvious mistakes that have begun to dry and adds shadows and highlights that help form the shape of the tree.

"Look at that. I'd say we work well together." My body feels warm, and I try to pull away, but he holds on tight and wraps his other arm around my waist.

"Should we exchange paintings?" He asks.

I look over my shoulder and his mouth's inches from mine. He catches me looking and a knowing smile breaks across his face. He reaches for my painting, examining it.

"You want to keep that?" It's definitely better thanks to Kade, but compared to his, it's still not much to look at.

"You made it. I want to remember my time with you."

Why does everything he says take me off guard? "Fine."

He laughs and puts my painting down and places his fingers underneath my chin, tilting my head toward his.

"You're shyer than I thought you'd be." He smiles and those dimples will be the death of me.

"You're always saying unnecessary things." I mumble. He's still pinching my chin between his fingers, and I find I'm not as immune to Kade's ways as I thought. He leans in and my eyes dart toward the cameras. Pulling away from him when we're filming wouldn't be a good look. This is what we agreed on. Closing my eyes, I try my best not to let images of River enter my mind. He has his secrets with Sabrina. He'll understand when I explain.

Kade meets me halfway and kissing him is like standing in the middle of a storm. His hands make their way to the small of my back, sending electricity through me. I arch into him and cup his face. My heart beats loud enough to drown out everything else. With Kade, there is no apprehension. It's exhilarating. Like getting on a roller coaster—scary as hell, but you know when the ride stops, you'll be just fine. It's not until he breaks the kiss that I realize I'm in trouble. I didn't want it to stop, and that realization is jarring. It only lasted for a moment, but we're both heaving. My chest brushes against his. He takes my hand from his face and kisses the inside of my wrist.

There's so much tenderness in his touch and that's a problem, too. I take my hand from his. Kade's wearing that arrogant smile, as if he can see right through me. That kiss didn't feel like it was only for show. Deal or no deal, I need space. None of this is supposed to be real between us and I haven't begun to process what's happening between River and me.

We wrap up filming and Kade's a natural. He acts as though the kiss is no big deal, and maybe it isn't for him. We remove our mics, and he offers to walk me to my room, but instead of heading to the right, we head toward the opposite hall on the left.

"Where are we going?"

"It's a surprise."

We're not filming anymore, there's no need for the act to continue. "It's been a long day, Kade."

"It'll only take a moment. I promise it's worth it."

We arrive at the end of the hall in front of the last door, and he drags me inside. In the room is a couch with a blanket spread across it and a small tv against the wall.

Kade waves his arms around as if to say *ta da*, and I look around, confused. He rolls his eyes and bends down, reaching underneath the couch. He pulls out a beat-up box and hands it to me. When I dig inside, I find a bunch of DVDs. Upon further inspection, they're all horror films. My mouth pops open and I glance up to see him smiling down at me.

"How?" as I sit on the couch, I shuffle through them.

"The TV was already here, brought my DVD player from home and found the movies at a thrift shop."

My heart swells, "You didn't have to."

"I wanted to." He shrugs and sits next to me. His thigh presses against mine and he leans over to look through the box.

"You went to the thrift store on your own?"

"I'm allowed offsite for scheduled events. No one noticed me slip away. I wore a hat and sunglasses." He inspects a movie called *Killer Ants.*

"How'd you know what to get?"

"If it sounded terrible, I figured you'd love it." He gives me a wry smile and drops the movie back in the box.

"If you let your producer know you need alone time, they'll let you use this room. Obviously not during filming hours, but otherwise, it's yours." His smile falls, and he straightens in his seat. "Think of it as a reward for doing a good job." He looks away from me and a slight flush reaches his ears.

"Thank you, Kade." I bump his shoulder with mine.

"Did you want to watch one?" His tone is casual, but it feels like more. Everything with Kade feels like more lately. I look down at the movies in the box and all I can think about is which ones I'd want to watch with River. Watching B-horror films has always been our thing. It feels wrong to watch them with Kade.

"It's late. The other women already hate me for taking up all your time. If they find out I've stolen you through the night, they will riot."

"Who cares?" He tilts his head, genuinely baffled.

"I do. You've been picking me for everything. I think you should lay off a bit, make it less obvious." His lips purse together, and I can tell he's about to protest, so I cut him off, "Just think about it."

He gives me a curt nod, and I feel my shoulders drop. Even though this is what I wanted, it doesn't mean I enjoy pushing him away.

# Chapter Eighteen

*I*f my current self could punch my past self in the face, I'd do it. After Javi, I thought I wouldn't get attached easily. I could play the field and focus on my career after the show wrapped up. However, Ryan was right. I'm not built for this. Kade was never supposed to be an actual option, but I like him anyway. He's fun to be around, considerate, and if I'm honest with myself, things are easier with Kade. I'm scared of failing with River. I care about them both and maybe that's reason enough for me to stay away.

Kade seems to have accepted my request for space. Hanna and Serenity are the lucky ones with dates today. Gabby and I are laying on the grass out front for some fresh air.

"There's always so much tension on elimination days. Too much bad energy inside." She says.

"Are you nervous?" Kade and I never discuss his dates, but Gabby's been chosen a few times, so I figured things were going well.

"No. That's the problem."

"What do you mean?"

"Shouldn't I care? I don't know if it's still too early or if it's me."

She sighs, "I had a lot going on at home before I came here and I'm wondering if I used this to run away instead of dealing with it." Her voice wavers, "My mom passed a few months back and I'm not proud of some of the decisions I made after. I hurt a lot of people, and I thought getting away would be healing. Now I'm wondering If I should be home."

My heart hurts for her. As much as my mom and I fight, I don't know what I'd do without her. "I support whatever you decide. If you want to go home, you should. If you want to stay and dissociate from the real world a little longer then do that. I don't know about you and Kade, but your mental health comes first."

She rolls over and pulls me into a tight hug.

"Thanks for listening." She breathes and I squeeze her back.

The sound of footsteps makes us pull apart. River approaches and smiles down at us. "Can I borrow Indigo?"

"Sure thing, I'll see you tonight." Gabby stands and leaves us. River starts toward the driveway, and I follow behind him.

"Where are we going?"

"Your offsite doctors visit was approved." He points at my mic, gesturing for me to turn it off.

I reach under my shirt and flip the switch. "I feel fine."

"No. You don't, and unfortunately, this trip's going to take all afternoon." When we reach the bottom, River's truck is parked and ready to go.

"What are you planning?" I ask.

River opens the passenger door. "A date."

He offers his hand, and I take it. He helps me in the car and buckles me in.

"I could've done that." Dropping my eyes, I wring my hands because I know I should stop this, but I don't want to.

He pauses, his head hovering above mine. "I enjoy taking care of you." He shrugs and makes his way to the driver's seat.

"You gonna tell me where we're going, Riv?"

"And ruin the surprise?" He starts the engine and grins, "Enjoy the adventure, Blue." Placing his hand on the steering wheel, he hits the gas and with his free hand he wraps his fingers around my thigh. When did we reach a point where touching each other feels so natural?

"You could have given me a heads up." I chew my lip and look out the window.

"So you could try to talk me out of it?"

"We shouldn't be doing this."

"And that's exactly why I didn't tell you." His phone rings from the cupholder between us and his mother's picture pops up. River silences the phone.

"How's she doing?" I ask.

"Better. Still hasn't forgotten your promise that we'd visit. Your mom expects you now too."

Well, I set myself up for that. Talking with Gabby made me realize it's about time we had a real talk anyway. "It'll be a good trip." I say but he doesn't look like he agrees.

We're not driving for long when the car rolls to a stop in the parking lot of a small restaurant.

"I was driving after work and spotted this place." River says as he puts the truck in park.

As I peer out of the window, a sign that says *Good Eats* comes into view. He meets me on the passenger side, opening my door and we enter the restaurant. It's a small diner style spot. Booths line either side of the wall, with a few small circular tables in the center. The kitchen sits at the back where you can see the cook hard at work over a grill.

As soon as we step inside, an older woman greets us. "Just you two today?" her deep brown skin wrinkles when she smiles.

"Yes ma'am." River rests his hand on my lower back.

"Well, follow me. I'll make sure ya'll get the best seats in the house." She speaks with a cute southern twang and sashays when she walks. "Here you go." She stops at a booth and places two menus on the table. "My name is Anita and I'll be serving y'all tonight. I'll give you a few minutes to look over the menu."

The restaurant is one of the humbler establishments we've passed in this stuffy neighborhood, but that's part of its charm. The menu is stacked with my favorites, from smoked beef brisket to hotlinks and cornbread.

"All of this looks good." I'm practically drooling over the menu. One of the few things I miss about living in Texas is good BBQ. California is so hit or miss, but this seems promising.

"This place is great. What is it your moms says? They put their feet in this food."

"Foot River. They put their foot in it. Lord, please don't embarrass me in front of these people."

"It doesn't even make sense. Why would feet make it taste good?" He frowns as he scans the menu.

"Remember the first time you heard my mom say she put her foot in something and you about threw up right then and there?"

"I was ready to press charges honestly, thought she was dipping her toes in my plate." He sticks his tongue out and we both laugh at the memory.

"Did y'all figure out what you want to order?" Anita returns, placing two glasses of water on the table.

"I'm ready." My stomach feels like it's trying to eat itself. I look at River, eager to get the ball rolling.

"Go ahead." He nods.

"I'll have the brisket with toast and potato salad."

"Good choice. Our brisket is to die for." Anita yells my order over her shoulder and the burly man behind the kitchen counter grunts in acknowledgment.

"What about you baby? You need me to recommend something?" She asks River.

"Nah, I know what I want." River closes his menu. "Let me get a pulled pork sandwich with mashed potatoes and corn. I'll take an order of peach cobbler to go."

"I guess you don't need my help." Anita collects our menus and relays River's order to the cook. "You two are too cute. How long you been together?"

"Uh, well, we're not, you know…" I stumble over my words and mentally kick myself for it.

"I'm working on it." River leans forward on his elbow, his eyes firmly focused on me, daring me to contradict him.

"Ah, a man who knows what he wants in the kitchen and in a woman. Seems he's got good taste in both." She winks at me before leaving to tend to another table.

River's phone rings and after looking at the caller ID he lets me know it's work and since we're ditching he has to take it. The front entrance has large windows and through them I see River speak into his phone.

We're taking a risk by being here. Pursuing this while I'm on a reality dating show for someone else isn't great timing. I'm not sure the time will ever be right for us. River hasn't mentioned the footage of Kade and I kissing and I don't know if I'm obligated to tell him or not. We've never discussed our relationships, but we're in a weird space and I don't know the rules.

I groan and slide my hands down my face. This is River's job. This project is the gateway to the connections he needs. Getting his writing out there for everyone to see has always been his dream. The more I think about what he's risking, the antsier I feel.

He hangs up, heading toward the entrance, Two women attempt to enter at the same time. He smiles, holding the door open for them. One giggles while thanking him and the other flutters her lashes. I can't blame them. I've been on the tail end of that smile all my life and I've always felt it down to my toes when he uses it on me. River isn't the kind of guy you don't notice.

"Production wanted an update. I told them we're waiting to be seen."

"Maybe we should take the food to go." I suggest, as Anita returns with our steaming plates.

"Here ya'll go. If you need anything else, just ask." She hurries off to greet the women still stealing glances of River.

We both pick up our forks and dig in. He was right. They did put their foot in this. The meat is tender, juicy and packed with flavor. While the BBQ sauce has some heat to it without being overwhelming with a soothing sweetness that follows. The Texas toast is good but that's hard to mess up. Nice and buttery, with a crispy outside and fluffy center.

"Oh, my god." I'm practically moaning.

"Should I be jealous of your plate?"

"You know what? Yeah, you should be." Taking another bite evokes another moan and I see heat flame in River's eyes.

"I'm going to need you to stop making those sounds at this table." He shakes his head; his eyes fall to my lips and I fight the urge to lick them. Not going to let River's bedroom eyes distract me. We've been avoiding discussing the elephant in the room and that ends today.

"Why now?" I ask.

"Can I get a little more context?"

"You completely rejected me before and you never tried anything after. Why now?" I pick at the peeling leather of the booth and focus my eyes on my plate. I've spent years dancing around my feelings for him, so confronting them head on feels like I've stripped naked in front of him.

"I liked you first. I didn't understand what I felt for you initially. Ryan knew before I did."

"Ryan knew?"

"She was pissed, said I'd ruin everything. She was worried I'd mess up and you wouldn't want to be friends with us anymore. I ignored her at first because my eight year old self still thought girls were gross and Ryan was always exaggerating things." He gives me a crooked smile.

"Do you remember Dillan? From the seventh grade?"

Dillan was my bully in middle school. I nod my head. "Yeah, you fought him because he stole my backpack. You were suspended for a week." I add before taking another bite of my brisket.

"That's not why we fought. He was embarrassed when I found him with it because he was putting a note inside. We started arguing because he wouldn't let me see It, but when I got my hands on it, the next thing I knew my fist was slamming into his face. To be fair, he did push me first." There's pride in his eyes. Clearly, he didn't learn his lesson and would totally punch him again.

"What was in the note?"

"He wanted to apologize. Apparently Dillan had a crush and was never taught how to manage his emotions."

"A crush on who?" My memories of that time are fuzzy. River raises a brow.

"Me?" I jab my finger into my chest.

"Yes, you."

"Hah. Okay."

"I'm serious. When I read what Dillan had written, I was so irritated. Here he was confessing his feelings, admitting he thought you were cute—as if cute even begins to describe you—after he'd been tormenting you all year. He was apologizing, and I was still pissed off. After that fight, I knew then that I misunderstood the day you came stumbling through my door."

He straightens and fixes his eyes on me. "You asked me why now, but it's not just now, it's always been."

His words push me over the edge. They wash over me, and it feels unreal. How could I have never known?

"I held back because Ryan was going through a lot at the time. She needed you. What if I pushed you away, and she lost you too? I don't know if she would've made it without you."

His hands curl into themselves, forming tight fists. Ryan felt like her sexuality broke their home. It was like walking on eggshells whenever their father walked in a room. He wouldn't even let us shut our doors anymore, as if Ryan being queer meant she would want any girl that crossed her path. Anger flares in my chest and I understand River's need to protect her. Ryan's light was so dim back then.

"I figured I'd eventually get over it. But I still couldn't shake you, so I said yes when Elizabeth Warner asked me out the summer—"

"The summer I confessed." I whisper.

He nods. "She hated you; you know? Even though I dated her, she knew." He shakes his head.

"I thought I'd lost my chance when Javi came along. I thought I was okay with us growing apart and finding other people, but you've always been the only one. You moved in with him and I knew I made a mistake." He pauses and laughs, but there's no actual humor in it. "My timing sucks, I know that. But I've done my waiting. I want you."

A nagging feeling pinches at my chest painfully. My hands shake and my mind flashes to Kade. He's saying everything I've wanted to hear, and it hurts.

"I kissed Kade." I drop the words between us. They leave my lips light as air but fall with enough weight to crash into River like a bomb. His smile falters before sliding back into place.

"Considering the premise of the show, this was unavoidable."

My heart sinks to the pit of my stomach. I want to agree, but I don't know that it'd be the truth.

"You like him." He's not asking. My eyes lock with his and I can tell by the way he's looking at me that he's seeing what I've only recently accepted.

I have feelings for Kade too.

Hurt mars his face, his handsome features twist.

"I—" I'm not sure what to say.

"But you feel this too. I know you do." His eyes are filled with determination.

I draw in a shaky breath and nod.

"Then I haven't lost yet."

# Chapter Nineteen

he ride back is awkward, to say the least. Our conversation bounces around in my head, and I worry about how I'm supposed to deal with Kade and River in the same space. When we get back to my room, Cameron and Jasmine hop off of their beds when I open the door.

"Are you okay?" Jasmine pulls me into a hug.

"Yeah, we heard you weren't feeling well." Cameron eyes me.

"I'm fine, just bad cramps." The lie rolls off my tongue.

"Did he take you?" Cameron's eyes narrow as she looks over my head toward River. "Yeah, I told him I wasn't feeling well earlier."

"Oh. Jose's been gone all afternoon, so we thought he took you." There's an implication in Cameron's tone, one that makes me uncomfortable.

"Well, I feel fine now." I wave River off. "Thank you." He nods and leaves.

"You're telling me you spent the entire afternoon with him? Suddenly I don't feel so good." Jasmine fans her face.

"Elimination's in twenty, you might want to change." Cameron

throws over her shoulder as she leaves. She's right, Jose would kill me if I came to film in a graphic tee. Swapping my clothes for a simple black bodycon dress with rhinestone straps, I rush and add a light layer of makeup. Jasmine's kind enough to wait for me, so we head down together. Marissa's ready when we arrive with Kade at her side and jumps into action when she gets the signal.

"Hello ladies, how did the dates go for the lucky few today?" Marissa smiles with her usual faux excitement.

"We went candle making. It was fun. Mine smells just like Kade." Serenity's large round eyes expand. She stares at Kade with a level of infatuation that makes me cringe.

Marissa nods and moves on. "Hanna, how about you?"

Hanna's pale skin turns bright red. She brushes her short curls behind her ear, only for them to pop forward again. "We went for ice cream." Hanna's voice is soft.

"Come on girl, give us some details. How'd it go?" Marissa prods, barely hiding her annoyance.

"It went well. Kade and I are on the same page, so it's refreshing spending time with him." She drops her gaze to the floor, unwilling to explain any further.

"Well then, I guess it's time to discuss why we're all here." Marissa turns to Kade and slaps her hand on his shoulder. "You've been tasked with sending one of the lovely women before you home. I do not envy your position." She pauses dramatically and Kade looks bored. His eyes focus on something behind us, as if he would rather be anywhere else. "So who's it going to be?" Marissa gives his shoulder a squeeze.

Kade doesn't even look in our direction. "Serenity." He says it with no emotion, something's off about him today.

Serenity pushes her way to the front of our formation. "Me? We had a great date. Why would you send me home?"

Kade breathes heavily before turning his eyes on her. "I'm not changing my mind."

"But we have something real. You can't tell me you don't feel it."

Kade's eyes turn up to the ceiling and he mutters something under his breath before looking back down at her. "You'll have the candle to remember me by. Our time together is up."

Serenity's eyes become impossibly large. "You're saying this because you think you have to. We've stayed apart because they don't want us together." She points a shaky finger at Noah, and he gives the smallest nod, as if encouraging her to continue.

Marissa's eyes flash toward Kade. "Did you guys know each other before this?" She asks.

"I have never met this woman; I have no idea what she's rambling about." His eyes dart toward Noah.

Serenity laughs in disbelief. She runs her fingers through her hair, still staring at Kade with those wide unblinking eyes. "We met two years ago. You told me you loved me." She shakes her head and takes a step back, bumping into Nicole, who shoves her forward. This whole situation is hard to watch. Serenity is clearly confused and I'm starting to feel bad for her. I look to security and none of them are making a move to stop her.

"Are you referring to a signing event?" Kade's brows slam together.

"Why would you say you loved me if you didn't mean it?" Serenity's voice is shrill, and tears run down her face leaving streaks of mascara running down her cheeks.

"I meant in the way I say to all my fans. Why would you think I was in love with you? Is this some kind of joke?" Kade looks back at Noah, accusation clear in his eyes.

"I don't have to sit through this." Serenity rips her mic from under her dress, throwing it to the ground before stomping back toward the rooms. Jose points to one of the assistants and they run after her.

Marissa places a hand on Kade's shoulder, dragging his attention from Noah. "We'll that was unexpected."

Kade's dark eyes are cold, his fingers clench into fists. Marissa drops her hand and looks nervously at Jose who nods and signals the cameras to focus on her, dropping Kade out of the shot.

"This isn't the first meltdown this show has seen and it won't be the last—"

I don't hear the rest of what she's saying because something flies right past me, the air from the force of the object's movement pushes against my skin. Whatever it is, just nearly misses hitting Kade in the head and shatters as it hits the floor. We collectively turn towards the direction it came from to see Serenity. Her hair is disheveled and her chest heaves as she attempts to catch her breath. The assistant that followed her looks scared out of his mind, mouth hanging open and eyes fearfully locked in on Jose.

Serenity ignores everyone else in the room and points to Kade. "Don't ever embarrass me like that. I've put up with this show because you've ignored my letters and this is how you treat me?" She screams.

It takes a moment for me to register that she threw a candle with the intention of hitting Kade over the head with it. It takes me one second longer to take in the fact that if I had been standing even slightly more to the right, it would have knocked me out instead.

"Are you insane? You could have hurt him or anyone else standing here." I'm in her face before security can reach her.

"I don't want to hear from you. Whores don't get to say anything to me. We all know why Kade keeps you around." She turns her anger on me.

Every rational thought goes out the window and I pull my arm back. Just as I am about to put all my weight into wiping that look off her face, I feel a hand wrap around my fist.

"Let me go." I seethe. I'm all adrenaline at this point.

"No." Kade hisses, as he steps in front of me.

"She could have hurt you." Everything in me is begging to get to her, but Kade grabs my arm, holding me steady.

He turns to me, and the look on his face turns my blood cold. "That candle flew right past your head before it got anywhere near me. I'm pissed too." He turns back toward Serenity who shrinks into the security guard's arms when his eyes land on her. "Get her out of here now, before I lose my shit." He takes a menacing step toward Serenity, dragging me with him.

"He said you wanted me here." Serenity's eyes flit in Noah's direction.

"If you ever cross my path again, you'll regret the day you ever met me." His grip becomes painful, and I wince, drawing his attention.

"I think you should let her go." River's pushed through crowd to get to us. His eyes are locked on where Kade's hand holds onto my mine. Something's wrong. Kade's never been the friendliest, but the look in his eyes is feral, like an animal being backed into a corner.

"I don't need you telling me what to do." Kade loosens his hold on me, "You're supposed to vet these people, but you let someone like that get in. It almost hit Indigo; did you see how much force she put into that throw?"

River's jaw locks and he moves toward me despite the warning in Kade's eyes.

"Who screened her?" Kade looks past River to Noah, who's got a disgusting smile plastered on his face. He used Serenity's inability to discern reality against her.

"She's what we needed." Noah shrugs, completely unbothered.

"So, you purposefully picked an obsessed stalker? Do you know how dangerous that is? After what happened last time, how could you do something so stupid?" Kade's fuming. We both switch off our mics.

"Oh come on, don't tell me you're afraid of a woman? You were never in any real danger. What happened last time is exactly why I did it again. You can't beat that type of PR."

Kade's muscles jump under his skin as he flexes his fingers. "Again?" Kade shakes his head. "You're fired."

Noah's mouth goes slack. "You can't do that; we have a contract." Noah takes a step forward, but then gets a look at Kade's face and stops.

"I'll pay the fines; I want you gone."

Noah scoffs, "I'm finishing this project. You'll see which of us is right when it's all said and done." He stomps his way past us, careful to give Kade a wide berth.

"You still need to let her go." River repeats himself.

"Hey, I'm fine." I look to River, "I'm okay." Leveling his stare, I try to convey that he can chill out. Kade isn't hurting me, but he is who everyone should be worried about. His hand trembles and I know I need to get him out of here. "Kade, maybe we should break for the day. You can go to your room, and we can try this again when things calm down." At first, I'm unsure if he heard me, but then he looks away from River.

"We're done today." He pushes through everyone that crowded behind us, pulling me with him until I'm jerked backward, causing Kade to stumble a step back.

"She can stay here." River has captured my other arm.

Kade's fire is still burning high, his hand is moist, and the tremor I noticed earlier is becoming more severe.

"I'll go with him." I announce, and River's eyes jump to mine. There's betrayal there and the weight of it crushes me. He drops my arm like it's burned him and Kade takes me with him before I can say anything. I feel everyone's eyes on us as we make our way upstairs. We pass a few doors and enter one toward the middle of the hall. He slams it shut behind us and falls to the floor reaching for his throat, his breathing strained.

"Kade what's going on?" Rushing to kneel beside him, I brush his hair out of his eyes. He doesn't answer but his breathing's coming out as a wheeze now. "I'm going to get someone." I move to stand, but his hand juts out and anchors me next to him. His eyes are dilated and sweat beads his brow.

"Are you having a panic attack?" Ryan used to have them all the time, especially once her dad left. His breathing becomes labored, taking hold of his face I press my forehead to his. "Breathe in deep." I demonstrate, pulling air in through my nose and then letting it go through my mouth. "Just like that. You're safe, it's me and you." His large hands tighten around my wrists. "Deep and slow. We're going at your pace." I remove one hand from his cheek and message his arm. His breathing is still shallow, but it's starting to mellow out. "Do you have medicine?"

He nods against my skin.

"Okay, I'm not going to leave you, but I do need to grab it. Can you tell me where it is?"

"Top drawer beside my bed," He manages to reply.

I stand and make my way to the nightstand. A few orange medicine bottles roll around inside. I shuffle through them until I find what I'm looking for. Popping open the top, I tip the bottle until two pills roll into my hand.

"I need you to take these." I kneel beside him, and he gently plucks them from my palm.

He tosses them in his mouth and screws his eyes shut. "You can leave." He grunts as he sits back, running a hand through his hair.

I don't say anything, instead I remain rooted beside him. The moments after the panic attacks were often when Ryan felt the most vulnerable. The thoughts that would invade her mind would sometimes trigger a second attack. So, I sit quietly, observing the in and out of his breathing.

"What do you get out of this?" His hair is damp with sweat and has fallen back over his eyes.

"What are you talking about?"

"How much do I have to give you not to sell this story?"

His words dig into my heart and the pain in them slices through me. "This isn't a story, you're not a story." Leaning forward, I push his hair out of his eyes and hold until he looks at me. "This isn't something anyone should ever hold against you."

He laughs but the sound is twisted.

"Any and everything, can and will be used against you. People are greedy at their core." He knocks my hand away and stands, pulling his sweatshirt over his head.

"I don't believe that." I mumble, turning away from his bare chest.

"You must want something." I'm still kneeling when he stands in front of me. He places his hand under my chin. "Maybe what you want is already here?" His voice is low and rough, the sound of it wraps around my skin. He bends down on his haunches, leaning in. "I guess I found the form of payment you accept."

Tearing my chin from his hand, I search his face. Behind that overconfident grin and his taunting words is suffering. I can see it in the way that the light doesn't reach his eyes and in the quiet desperation of his touch. "Has someone done that to you before? Used you that way to hide your secrets?"

His smile falls and at first, I don't recognize the emotion playing across his features. Embarrassment and shame builds a wall between us. I can feel his defenses rise as he pulls away from me.

"Get out." He demands.

"No."

"Now, Indigo."

"No." I blink and he's in my face.

"I don't want you here. Sitting there judging me. You may not want money, but I'm not going to feed your savior complex either." He spits the words in my face. They feel like stab wounds against my skin, but I straighten my back and keep my eyes level with his.

"People have taken from you. Bit by bit they have pulled you apart. How much of you is left, Kade?"

He jerks away from my touch, and my hands fall to my side.

"I refuse to let them continue to take from you. Deal or no deal, you're my friend, if I let you push me away then it's the same as letting them have another part of you."

The wall he built crumbles at our feet. His eyes fall to mine. The flame in them has died and he looks so exposed. I wrap my arms around him because it feels like Kade's been holding himself together with tape and glue. Tears blur my vision. How long has he been alone? How exhausting has it been to create a new personality every time he stepped foot out of this door? He pushes away from me and his hand swipes at my tears.

"I've never had anyone cry for me before." He points a crooked smile in my direction as he leans back against the foot of the bed. "I've had a lot of crazed fans. One in particular was very... committed. She'd show up at my events and send me threatening letters. I reported her to my team so many times." His expression goes hard. "They didn't take it seriously, Noah specifically told me to ignore it. He thought I should feel lucky to have women throw themselves at me." His hands grip the carpet at his sides.

"At the time, I wasn't sure how she found the address to the hotel I was staying at. I had a sneaking suspicion Noah had something to do with it, but it seemed too extreme, even for him." He brings his eyes back to mine. "She held a knife to my throat and told me she was in love with me. She had it in her head that we were in a relationship. She didn't understand why I'd been avoiding her." He pauses, breathing deep. "Took two hours for anyone to realize I was missing before they checked my room. I could've left. I fought her off, but then she turned the knife on herself." His voice is soft. When I move to his side, I rest my head against his shoulder and wrap my hand around his. "How could I live with myself if I walked away and she didn't survive it? She was arrested, but the people around me made it seem like since I was a man, I should've been able to handle her. Instead of feeling relief that she was gone, I felt weak, like I shouldn't have even reported it." He releases a steadying breath.

"The paparazzi painted me in a sympathetic light. Noah's right, in that the incident did help my image, but the media did exactly what the woman did. Invaded my privacy, lurking behind every corner, going through my trash, exposing any private details they could get their hands on. Some of them even turned it into a joke. She was beautiful and people couldn't understand why I was complaining. Being in the public eye, sometimes the fact that I'm still human is forgotten. Seeing the look in Serenity's eyes reminded me of her."

Bringing his hand to my lips, I press a kiss against his skin. "The last thing you are is weak. This world has been cruel to you and the people around you are not your friends. What Serenity did was wrong and scary. What that woman did was demented and Noah giving your stalker the address was malicious. You've surrounded yourself with enemies at every angle, and I hope you still have it in you to let healthy relationships grow."

"Is that what this is?" He brings my hand to his chest, and I smile.

"This is the first of many. You're stuck with me Kade Ikeda."

There's relief in his eyes.

"About the panic attacks. I was thinking maybe we could have a signal."

"A signal?" His smile slides back into place.

"Yeah, to check in with each other. A way to say we're okay."

"What did you have in mind?"

I bring my fingers to my chin and wrinkle my brow. "If I scratch my nose, you tug your ear."

"What if you genuinely have an itch?"

"Do it anyway. Who cares?" I laugh and his dimples make an appearance as his smile widens.

"Yes ma'am, your orders are my command." He brings my hand to his lips, peering at me through his lashes. My skin tingles at his touch and I feel heat creep up my neck.

Thinking back to our last date, Kade asked if I was going to save him. I don't know if I can, but I'll stick beside him while I'm able.

# Chapter Twenty

Kade and I talked for what felt like hours. As much as he claims to like being alone, it felt like he needed the company. When he begins to yawn and joke about us sharing his bed, I know it's time to go.

"You're no fun." Kade clucks his tongue while opening the door for me.

"And you're trouble." I shake my head.

He grabs my hand before I can leave. "Thank you Indie." My skin tingles under his fingers. "For being a friend." He gives my hand a squeeze before letting go.

Friend. For some reason hearing that word makes my stomach twist. I need to get my life together. My mind's buzzing as I head downstairs, and I doubt I'll get any sleep.

"You finally came out."

My head snaps in the direction of River's voice. He's sitting on one of the couches in the foyer with his glasses on, typing away at his laptop.

"What are you doing here?" It's well after filming hours. I look

around and we're alone.

"Noah had me keep an eye on you two. Apparently, Kade has a habit of having women over and kicking them out after." He doesn't look at me as he continues to work. "He wanted to be sure you wouldn't cause a scene. Apparently, it happens a lot."

"You know it wasn't like that." I move to stand in front of him.

"Do I?"

"Yes. Because you know me." We stare at each other.

River eventually breaks eye contact and sighs. "I'm sorry. It's not you I don't trust." As much as I want to assure him, it's my fault things aren't clear.

"Let me make it up to you." Grabbing his arm, I drag him with me. Sleep wasn't coming for me anyway, so I drag him toward the movie room. When we get inside, I turn on the TV and grab the box of DVDs.

"How did this stuff get here?" He asks, standing in the doorway.

I hesitate, but then decide I don't want to hide anything else from him. "Kade."

"You watch movies together." He says it more to himself than to me.

"No. Kade set it up, but I haven't been here since. You're the only one I want to watch this stuff with." Holding up one of the movies I grabbed at random, I smile, hoping it's the peace offering needed to ease the tension between us.

"I can't imagine anyone else putting up with it." He smiles and I feel my heart lift. Having River angry with me weighs on me like nothing else. When he's not happy, neither am I, which is why I wish I could give in, do as he asks, and give us a chance. I don't know if I could stand to be around him if we didn't work out. My feelings for Kade are safe. It's one sided, and it isn't complex.

Easy.

"Exactly." I nod and put the movie on before plopping on the couch beside River. With a title like *Ghosts in a Coffee Shop,* I wasn't sure what to expect, but it's better than I thought it'd be. It's honestly more of a romance than a horror film. I'm about to comment on the acting when I see River's still wrapped up in his work. His fingers fly over the keys and he looks tired. I note the bags under his eyes and the sag in his shoulders.

"Are you still overworking yourself?"

He sighs, but closes the computer. "There's a lot of work to do. Not really avoidable."

"You're no good if you aren't getting enough sleep to function." I grab his laptop and move it to the arm of the couch, so it's out of reach.

"This project requires a ton of editing and some of the girls are more difficult to manage than others." He rubs his eyes with his palms and lays back against the couch.

"Who's the most difficult?" I've got my guesses, but I'm curious.

"Other than you?" He questions with genuine confusion.

"Oh please, I don't cause any problems."

"Your shots take me the longest to review." He shrugs.

"Why?" I ask, offended. I'm always camera ready.

"Working with the editing team to get you more shots that make sense is hard. I'm not always able to convince them it's not weird that your dates keep making the cut for every episode, but I do what I can." He smiles and I blink at him.

"Why would you do that?"

"You wanted to be seen. I'll do anything to get you what you want. I've got final say on what gets to Jose for approval." His eyes lock with mine. "I review everything."

"That's too much. You can't keep that up." I shake my head.

"I can."

"I don't want you to. You're stretching yourself too thin."

"Even if I wasn't looking out for you, I'd review everything. I like to know the quality of work passing through."

"I've seen Jose with assistants. Why don't you have one?"

"I do have one."

"Are you using them?"

He scratches his neck and looks away from me.

"River, come on. You can't control everything." He looks at me like he disagrees. River's always had a problem letting go. He has to try and juggle everything and now I know that's partly because he didn't have a choice growing up.

"You said you felt free when you came here and that being home was suffocating. But it feels like you traded your mother for work. Do you even know how to relax?"

He looks at me, considering my words, and then lets out a breath. "Not having control makes me feel out of control. Can we drop it for now?"

River's always been a constant in my life. He's been a big part of keeping me sane ever since the day we met. I never considered his need to take care of everything as a coping mechanism. "You were an assistant once and someone trusted you enough to give you a chance. You're holding someone back from achieving their dreams too. I'll let it go if you promise to share some of the work." I offer my pinky, and he rolls his eyes before wrapping his finger around mine. He tugs my hand towards him, pulling me closer.

"Seal it with a kiss?" One side of his mouth tilts up. Pressing our lips to our thumbs is a childish tradition we've kept.

"I trust you." I shake my head.

"It means nothing if we don't." His smile widens. His free hand cups my face.

"We're not kids anymore." My voice comes out all wispy and my heart picks up speed. My mind might be on track, but my body's veered off course. Everything in me heats, and memories of his mouth on mine invade my thoughts. He runs his thumb across my lips. My tongue flicks out involuntarily, brushing against his skin.

He leans in and I can feel the warmth radiate from his body. "Tell me to stop."

I open my mouth, but nothing comes out and that's all the answer he needs. His lips are on mine and it's as desperate as it was the first time. River's fingers trace along my jaw until they curl around my neck, and it sends a tremor through my body. His mere touch is enough to make me abandon every logical thought. He breaks the kiss and I feel like I'm gasping for air. His teeth bite into the skin at the base of my neck and a moan falls from my lips. His free hand trails down my stomach until it reaches my thigh and slips under my dress.

I gasp and move my hand over his. Our clothing is the only barrier between us. He chuckles into my neck and his breath tickles against my skin.

"Tell me to stop." He repeats himself, challenging me. He places soft kisses along the crook of my neck before opening his mouth and sucking, sending tremors of pleasure through me. My hand drops from his and he continues his pursuit until he reaches my center. When his fingers graze against me, any fight I had left starts to wane. The desire I've held back pools between my thighs. I squeeze them together trapping his hand and he smiles against my skin. He pulls my panties to the side and there he finds the evidence that he's won this battle. "How much longer are you going to run from me?" His finger circles my clit and I gasp, arching into him.

"I'm not running I—" My words tangle around themselves as he plunges a finger inside. I'm stuck between complete euphoria and disbelief as he explores parts of me in ways I've never experienced.

"What are you doing then?" He whispers into my ear before taking it into his mouth.

"Trying not to ruin what we have." My voice is weak, and he's relentless with his teasing. Building me up before slowing down, keeping me right where he wants me.

"We shouldn't—"

"I'm only doing what your body tells me to do, if only your mouth was as honest." He lets a slow smile build. At that moment, I realize I'm rocking against him. Our bodies are pressed together, and my fingers are knotted in his hair. My body reacts to his as if it has a mind of its own, eager to make contact and never let go.

Heat fills my cheeks and I try to pull away, but he slips another finger inside, curling them until he hits just the right spot knocking the air out of me. I'm seconds away from coming apart when he pulls out, and I whimper, aching for him.

"The next time he kisses you, remember how badly your body craves mine." There's a darkness in his eyes I've never seen before, and it dawns on me that he's seen the footage of my kiss with Kade. This was some kind of twisted payback. "Goodnight, Blue." He grabs his computer and leaves, shutting the door as I throw one of the couch pillows and just miss his head. Anger fills me as I adjust my dress and will my heart to slow down.

"Fuck." I wiggle my thighs together and groan in frustration. How am I supposed to remain strong when he plays dirty? Shutting off the TV, I stretch and head to my room for a restless sleep. When I step inside, I'm surprised to see Cameron awake. She has her bonnet on and a book in her hands, reading in the lamplight. Her lips press into a thin line and she glances at the clock before narrowing her eyes at me.

"Walk of shame?" Her tone's full of judgment, her nose turned up as she looks me over. I ignore her, kicking off my shoes. Technically, she's not wrong, but I'm pretty sure she has the details mixed up.

"I see through you, you know." She closes her book and sits up. Clearly she was waiting for me. "It's not fair if you're going to resort to…" Her eyes crawl over me with distaste, "Underhanded methods to get a leg up."

I'm already frustrated for *multiple* reasons, and it's been a long day. From Serenity's attempted assault to feeling like I have emotional whiplash. My patience is thin, and I have to take a slow breath before responding. "Maybe try thinking of others instead of yourself. Kade and I were talking and then I left, nothing," I lift my hands, doing air quotes, "*underhanded* happened." I slide my dress over my shoulders and reach for my bag to find some pajamas.

"You're one to talk about being self-centered." She hisses, Jasmine grunts in her sleep and Cameron switches to an aggressive whisper. "You shamelessly plug yourself any chance you get. It's obvious what you came here for."

"And why are you here, Cameron? All you brag about are the people you know and the events you're throwing."

She glares at me and then sighs, "I'm asking you to play fair." Her lips turn up in a pout. Cameron and I never really vibed since I got the feeling she looked down on what I do for a living, but seeing her all upset bothers me. Per our agreement, I do take up a lot of Kade's time.

Crossing the space between us, I sit on the edge of her bed and eye her cautiously. "Why are you here? You're asking me to back off. I need you to tell me why."

She wraps her arms around herself and hesitates before speaking. "I've never known my birth parents, not sure if they're dead or alive." She shrugs, brushing it off. But she fidgets and breaks eye contact. "Eventually I was adopted by a family who couldn't have kids. I was six years old. They were like the people you'd see on TV. House in the suburbs, golden retriever, and good jobs." She smiles sadly. "Two years after my adoption, my mother fell pregnant. It was a miracle, and I was excited, but then things changed. Attention shifted and I know what you're thinking, but I wasn't jealous." Her lips curve into a slight smile. "Okay, maybe a little. I convinced myself it was in my head, but it got to a point where no one spoke to me. It was hit or miss if they'd remember my lunches or dinner. I'd go hungry because I didn't want to complain and make them hate me more."

My heart hurts for her. Feeling alone in a house full of people is a terrible feeling. Knowing adults denied love to a child they brought to their home is incomprehensible. "I'm sorry." I'm not sure what to say, but she shakes her head.

"I'm not trying to trauma dump on you. My family housed me and financially supported me for the most part, but I always paled in comparison to my brother. They had their real child, and you can't really return a kid, so they kept me maintained. I moved away as soon as I was able and they took the opportunity to do so as well. They've never tried to find me. When I started getting attention online, it felt like it filled a hole. It opened doors and I've accomplished so much, but my mother will never know because we no longer talk."

"You don't need her to validate you." I pat her knee.

"Reality TV is her guilty pleasure. She watches this show religiously. So, I'm constantly bragging—"

"Because you're not saying it for our benefit. You're telling your mom."

She nods her head. "I want her to know that she's missing out, you know? Anyway, I mentioned my family during my audition and I think Noah liked the optics of it. He said it'd be a good story, so he's always pushing Kade to choose me. Instead of using me, Kade asked me if I was okay with it. He didn't want me to feel uncomfortable. I assured him it was fine, and you know what he did?" She pauses and the corner of her mouth tilts up, "He tells me he found my family, handed me an entire folder filled with information on them. What kind of guy does that?" She scoffs, but she's smiling at the thought.

"I came for me, but I'm staying for him. Can you say the same?" She looks at me with a challenge in her eye. When I don't respond, she pulls the blanket up to her shoulders and lays down. "I'm not trying to antagonize you, but I wanted to let you know I won't be playing fair either. Goodnight, Indigo."

# Chapter Twenty-One

It's been a week since the Serenity situation and they've brought us to an amusement park. It's a weekday, but it's still crowded.

To be honest, I think something like this is necessary after how tense things have been lately. We're waiting out front until Kade arrives so that we can all walk in together. Security surrounds us but keeps their distance for now.

"Hey Indigo, do you have a sec?" Jose hooks his arm around mine and pulls me away from the other women.

"I wanted to check in. It feels like we haven't had a conversation in a while." He tilts his head. Apparently he's doing his round of mental health checks. A little late on that one, eh?

"I'm fine." I shrug and he smiles.

"At this stage, people begin shedding their personas and the real personalities come out and sometimes they don't always mesh. I know you haven't been feeling well, and I wasn't sure if it was stress related."

"Not feeling well?"

"I recall River having to take you to see a doctor because you felt overwhelmed. Am I remembering it wrong?"

Oh, well shit.

"No, you're right. It's been a long week."

"Remember, I'm here for you. I've been busy, but I'm still keeping an eye on you." The way he says it makes me uneasy.

"Thanks Jose."

"Anytime babe." He flashes a smile and takes off.

My eyes automatically seek River, and I find him having a conversation with Sabrina. Deciding against voluntarily subjecting myself to *that*, I join the rest of the girls at the entrance of the amusement park.

"You'd think they'd at least buy out the place for the day. It's going to be packed. I know they have the money." Jasmine sucks her teeth, scanning the horde of people lining up to enter.

"You know they're cheap." Gabby adds and Nicole nods in agreement.

"Hey girl." Cameron gives me a small wave.

"Hey, Cam." I'm not sure how to handle her. Our last conversation felt like she was marking her territory, but she wasn't exactly unkind.

"Listen, I wanted to ask you for a favor." She throws her arm over my shoulder and distances us from the others. "You think you can help me get some alone time with Kade? You guys click and I thought maybe you could help me out. I wouldn't ask, but I know that out of all the girls here, you're not into him." She smiles and I'm immediately irritated.

I never said that, and I don't like having words put in my mouth. Rather than ruin this fragile unspoken truce we've put in place, I decide it's better to play nice. It shouldn't be hard getting Kade to have a conversation with the girl. "Sure." I say, forcing a smile.

"Ohmygosh thank you Indie." She jumps up and down.

"Yeah, no guarantees."

"I think you can swing it." She takes my hand, tugging me toward the rest of our crew. Kade stands at the head of our group with keeping a healthy distance.

"Alright, listen up." River folds his arms over his chest. "I know we've already said it, but everyone needs to stay together. People will try to get close once they see the cameras. To avoid any disturbances, pay attention to your surroundings." He turns his head toward Kade. "No disappearing acts."

Kade removes his sunglasses and props them atop his head, ignoring River all together.

Jose gives a signal and security ushers us inside. For the most part, things go smoothly once we're inside. Everyone gets their turn to ride an attraction with Kade and, aside from a few minor disagreements, everyone's having fun.

"Let's do that." Jasmine points to a caricature art stall while clinging to Kade's side.

He makes eye contact with me, and I scratch my nose. He rolls his eyes and tugs his ear. This is the third time I've checked in. Now that I know how overstimulating these group dates can be for him, I feel like I'm hovering.

He sits with Jasmine, and the artist starts their painting. While I know this experience hasn't been easy, he's not as distant with the others as I thought. Jasmine leans into his side and says something that makes him smile. The artist asks them to hold a pose, and she plants a kiss on his cheek. Kade doesn't pull away and they look like a couple.

Sabrina steals Kade next. She drags him to a carnival game, pointing to the largest stuffed animal available. It's basketball and the further back the hoop, the more points the shot's worth. He and Sabrina seem to have a back and forth that's comfortable for them. They aren't as physical, but they have a cute competitiveness about them.

They both take turns trying to best each other and seem to forget the rest of us are here.

They finish their game and at some point, Gabby manages to get him to wear matching hats. Hers hat has cat ears poking out the top while his has dog ears.

"I feel silly." Kade twiddles one of the floppy ears between his fingers.

"What are you talking about? This is peak fashion. I mean, after what you wore on our last date..." she trails off and Kade's eyes cut in her direction.

"Don't you dare bring that up." His words are harsh, but his tone is light. He smiles, and she breaks into a fit of laughter.

"What did he wear?" Nicole asks.

"I'm sorry. He swore me to secrecy." Gabby giggles.

Inside jokes. They have inside jokes. Kade deserves friendships, and Gabby has been nothing but kind since I met her.

"Whatever. Can we stop for food?" Nicole points to a fried food stand.

We all agree and place our orders. It's a battle royale to get the seats nearest Kade, but I ease into one at the far end of the picnic table. The sun has finally begun to set, and the breeze feels good against my skin. I ordered the fried peanut butter jelly sandwich, and it tastes like deep fried heaven.

"The fireworks should happen soon. I haven't been to a show since I was a kid," Hanna says before dipping into her ice cream.

"I'm stoked. I love seeing all the cool patterns in the sky." Gabby nods in agreement.

"We only have time for one more ride before they begin. Was there something you wanted to do?" Cameron asks Kade.

"The Ferris wheel." He puts his fork down. Cameron opens her mouth, an eager look in her eye, but Kade cuts her off.

"Indigo, would you like to ride with me?"

Six heads swivel in my direction, and I look at him with surprise. He said he'd avoid picking me to be less obvious. My eyes snap to Cameron's and she's clearly hopeful I'll decline. My refusal doesn't guarantee he'll pick her as a replacement though.

"Sure."

Cameron's mouth parts and her eyes narrow. I try to telepathically convey that I still plan to help her out, but her lips tighten anyway.

"We can head over as soon as you're finished, then." He adds. The vibe at the table's changed, and I'm ready to dip before any of the girls can push me off a cliff. I let him know we're good to go, and we make plans to meet the others later.

If it weren't for the cameras and our mics, I'd tell Kade exactly how he screwed me over. Instead, I make sure he knows I'm annoyed by giving him the cold shoulder and keeping to myself the whole time we're in line. Kade doesn't acknowledge my silent treatment. He stands there with a stupid grin on his face, pissing me off even more—which seems to humor him further. When we finally make it to the front, the amusement park staff declines production's request to set cameras inside the carriage. Kade sits on one bench, and I take the one opposite him as the door is shut behind us.

"Is there a reason you're sitting all the way over there?" He reaches under his shirt and switches off his mic, so I do the same.

"Is there a reason you picked me for this date when you said you'd lay off for a while?"

He leans forward, placing his elbows on his knees. "You told me I should, and I took that under consideration."

"Well, consider the fact that I'm staying right here."

He shrugs and moves to my side. I try to stand, but his hand encircles mine as the carriage begins to rotate, causing me to fall back into his lap. Kade wraps his arm around my middle. I try to pry him off, but my fingers slide off his muscled arm.

"Where you going? You got the best seat in the house."

"Kade." There's a warning in my voice, and he loosens his hold.

"I needed time to recharge." He rests his head against my back.

"It didn't seem like you hated today. You seem to get along with everyone."

"I don't hate them. They want different things than I do. It's exhausting pretending not to notice."

"Have you tried? You might find that you could want what they want."

"Not happening."

I tense as his free hand wraps around my thigh. "Cameron's nice."

"So's the weather." He laughs.

"Are you calling her boring?"

"Your words, not mine."

"Sit with her tonight for the fireworks show."

"You asking, or telling?"

My frown deepens, and I attempt to free myself again.

"What's the point in avoiding this?" He leans forward, his stubbled jaw scrapes against my shoulder.

"There's nothing to avoid."

"Why're you always fighting me, then?"

"You think arguing means I like you?"

"I think it means something."

Does it? Kade's pushing an issue I've been trying to ignore. "I'm holding up my end of the deal, acting as a buffer so—"

"Pretending everything between us is fake is getting old." His hand flexes before gripping my thigh, inching higher—I squeeze them together and he nuzzles my neck. I'd be lying if I said Kade doesn't make me feel anything. There is a chemistry between us regardless of if it's physical or something more.

"We're friends Kade."

"Let's test that theory." He breathes.

Wrapping my fingers around his wrist, I stop him. "I can't do this."

"You can't or you don't want to? There's a difference." He asks.

I turn and look him in the eye, and we watch each other expectantly.

"Indigo?"

One wrong move and my lips would be on his. Kade would be a fresh start. Isn't that what I need? If it doesn't work, it'd be a clean break, no messy end. My eyes drop to his lips, and they curve upward before he removes his hand from my thigh and places a finger under my chin.

"When I first saw you, I remember thinking that you were one of the most beautiful women I'd ever seen, the way that dress wrapped around you should be a crime."

"You remember what I was wearing?" A smile plays at my lips.

He cocks his head to the side. "Blue flowers. It was a dress with a slit that stopped around…" His hand travels to the top of my thigh. "Here." We're practically nose to nose breathing each other in. "Tell me you don't want to."

I can't, because I do, and I need confirmation.

His lips press against mine and for the first time since I met Kade, he hesitates. His kiss is gentle at first—unsure. When I don't pull away, his confidence builds, and the kiss deepens.

Kissing Kade makes me feel all twisted up inside. My heart isn't in it. I'm trying to be present, but my thoughts keep straying. I think about how his touch doesn't send fire through me. How even though I'm in his arms, I feel River's phantom touch all over my skin. River has succeeded in making my body call for his. Our carriage crests the top of the loop, and I move out of his lap and scoot to the opposite end of the bench. The realization of what we did hits me like a brick. This has nothing to do with our deal. There are no cameras here. For the first time, I can't lean on any of that as justification and guilt thrashes around in my chest.

"Hey, what's wrong? Did I misunderstand?" His voice is soft. I force myself to look at him. His eyes search mine and he doesn't come closer, his outstretched hand hovering between us.

"No, you didn't." I press my hands to my cheeks, and they're hot to the touch. His hand drops back to his side, and he presses his lips together. I avoid his gaze and look at all the lights shining beneath us.

"You gotta help me out here, Indie. What'd I do wrong?"

Absolutely nothing. I wanted that kiss. The problem is that the kiss changes things. This was supposed to be my one-sided fling, over as fast as it came. It was fun for me because it was simple, but if he's serious, then… "I'm not a good person." My voice cracks.

"Is that all?" He asks. I let my eyes focus on him and the corner of his mouth tilts up. "Good girls are overrated love; I wouldn't know what to do with one."

"I like you."

"I know." For once, he isn't wearing that cocky grin.

"I want you to date the other girls here, take time to get to know them."

He frowns, "I can't keep up here, Indie. Why would I do that?"

"Because I like someone else." My feelings for River haven't changed. If I'm truly honest with myself, I know they've only grown. Kade's lips thin as he absorbs what I'm saying. "I'm not asking you to wait. I'm asking you to participate like you were supposed to. The only way I won't feel like a horrible person for trying to understand what I want is if you do the same."

"Are you telling me this other person's here?" There's a rough edge to his tone. "Is it one of the other girls? Is it Cameron?"

"Are you joking?" I can't help the laugh that mangles my words.

"I mean, she's beautiful and you keep bringing her up." He pops his shoulder and looks offended.

"Unfortunately, I'm straight. So no, it's not one of the women."

"Then it's one of the crew?"

"Yes."

He's silent as he mulls it over. "Going to be honest here. This is… not what I expected."

"Never been rejected before?" I ask.

"Is that what this is?"

"This is me being honest. I'm not trying to lead you on, and we don't really know each other—"

"But you know this employee?"

"Yes."

"Fine."

"Fine?"

"You've asked me to take this seriously. I hope you're prepared for what that means. I'm not ready to let you go." Our carriage sways and he inches toward me, I freeze thinking he's going to kiss me but then he places his lips to my forehead instead and his whisky scent wraps around me as we come to a stop at the bottom. "This doesn't change our deal either." The tension I felt earlier is gone, and I relax.

"I know."

"Alright heartbreaker, you ready to face the world again?" He reaches under his shirt and switches his mic back on.

"With guns blazing."

# Chapter Twenty-Two

Cameron's not speaking to me. She had Kade all to herself during the firework display, but she's still got an attitude. Instead of sitting in awkward silence, I decide to head to the movie room. When I push open the door, I find that it's not empty. At first, I'm not sure what I'm looking at, or rather who I'm looking at. A woman with short blond curls is straddling someone on the couch. The other person's legs poke out between the blonds and the way they're tangled around each other makes it clear I've walked into something.

"Oh my gosh, I'm so sorry." At the sound of my voice, they both jump and turn. Hanna's on Sabrina's lap, her hand under Sabrina's shirt, holding her breasts. Sabrina's cheeks fill with color.

"My bad, I'm leaving." Ugh, I can't stop talking. I shield my eyes with my hands and back into the wall like an idiot. Reaching behind me, I feel blindly for the door as I hear them stumbling off each other. My hand finally lands on the cold metal of the knob. I jerk the door open and slam it shut behind me.

"What the hell?" I run my hand through my braids. Hanna and Sabrina? The sound of the door being thrown open makes my head

spin. Hanna wrenches me inside, kicking the door closed.

"Indie, please don't say anything." Her curls bounce wildly as she shakes her head.

"Where the heck is River?" Sabrina brings her knees to her chest and mumbles into her hands.

"River knew?" My voice goes up an octave.

"I can hear you guys down the hall." River hisses and I whirl around to face him as he's closing the door. His eyes bounce from me to Sabrina. He moves to her side, bending down to her level.

"I got called away. I didn't think anyone would come near here. Indigo won't say anything."

"I can't do this anymore. It's Indigo now, it'll be someone else next time." Sabrina's voice trembles.

"Hanna, take Sabrina to your room. I'll meet you guys there."

Hanna does as he says, leading Sabrina away.

"Hanna and Sabrina?" I ask River.

"Is it that surprising? They spend every second together."

Pausing, I think back on it, and he's right. They're never apart. "How long has that been going on?"

He lets out a long sigh. "Pretty much since the beginning." He angles his head toward me. "You can't say anything."

"Who do you think I am? I would never. But what are you doing, River? Do you play watch dog every time they want to hook up? This could be bad for you."

"She reminds me of Ryan. She's still figuring things out, and she has a lot going on just like…"

"Let me guess, her family isn't cool with it?"

"Ry had our moms, you and me. Sabrina has no one. Her whole family rejected the idea that she wasn't—"

"Straight?" I supply.

"Yeah."

"I don't understand. If she's not into men, why's she here?"

"You didn't come here for him either."

My stomach churns. My reasons for coming here have become murky. "You can't do this for them."

"She needs someone on her side right now. She's my assignment, but she's also a person."

River's always been the type to take care of others even when there isn't much of him left. I look into his eyes and take his face between my hands. He's still pushing himself.

"You promised to cut back, emotional labor is included in that promise."

He sighs, leaning into my touch. "I can't abandon her. Everyone else already has."

"I'll look out for Sabrina. I'm serious. Let go of the reins a little and trust me."

"You don't even like her."

"I never said that." Thought it though. He frowns because we both know I'm bullshitting. "I'm going to do it regardless of what you say, so back off."

"Yes ma'am." He smiles down at me.

"Have you gotten with your assistant yet?"

"An assistant will make mistakes I have to fix."

"It's how they learn. People are more capable than you think if you give them the room to prove it. You can't save everyone at the expense of your own sanity." While River being so willing to help Sabrina is one of the things I love about him, I'm starting to notice a pattern. First it was his mother, then it was Ryan, at times it's me and now it's Sabrina. He makes himself responsible even when he's not.

"Are we still talking about Sabrina?" He gives me that lopsided smile. "Did you know my father tried to take me with him when he left?" His smiles has lost its sincerity. River loved his dad, wanted to be just like him until he turned on their family. He never talks about how much that hurt him.

"Letting go of control is hard for me. I like to know I have a handle on all variables and this project has been a strain on me. We may curate some of the situations here, but the reactions and responses are organic. Not knowing what's going to happen next stresses me out more than it should."

"It sounds like you're feeling anxious." I touch his shoulder.

"I was always on edge when I was trying to hide my mom's depression and I feel like I forgot how to just be." He lays his hand over mine. Me being one of those uncontrollable variables isn't lost on me. My indecisiveness is likely causing him more stress, and that knowledge eats at me. "One of the last things he said to me after I refused to leave was that my mother was going to ruin me."

"You are many things, but ruined is not one of them. Having healthy relationships with your parents is overrated." I place my hands on my hips. "We can work on your anxiety. I'll keep an eye on Sabrina, and you can start giving these assistants something to do other than fetch coffee."

He smiles, and the stress seems to have lifted a bit. "I'll leave it to you then." He bends and kisses my cheek. When did that become normal for us?

"If I find out that you've broken our promise and still haven't taken advantage of your assistant, I'll think our kiss meant nothing when we made the promise." I chide.

His eyes light up, that same hungry look from before appears. "I wouldn't want you to get that idea in your head. I better go find Carl."

I pray poor Carl's ready to earn his paycheck this week.

Elimination is tonight. When I make it to the foyer the camera crew is already set up. Drew applies powder to Marissa's cheeks and Kade is slouched with his hands in his pockets.

"Everyone's here." Jose shouts as he ushers me into formation.

Marissa plasters on a camera-ready smile. "As usual, after the good we must have a bit of the bad. Today, we'll be saying goodbye to another love connection." She pouts, "Kade will—"

"Let's not drag this on, yeah? No one likes their time wasted." Kade cuts Marissa off. His eyes lock with mine. "We don't have much time left together and I need to consider who I can truly see myself with. Nicole, that isn't you."

My mouth drops open, and Nicole looks from Kade to Noah.

"What do you think you're doing?" Noah steps forward, a vein pulsing on his neck.

"It's an elimination. I'm eliminating."

"Choose someone else," Noah grinds out, his hands clenched at his side.

"No."

"You're pissed at me? Fine. But derailing everything I've planned isn't going to help you." Noah spits the words and Kade looks right through him. He may as well be talking to a brick wall.

"I just tried to send her home. Why would she stay now?" Kade shrugs.

Noah's nostrils flare, and Marissa takes a step back.

"You have more self-respect than that, don't you?" Kade looks at Nicole.

Her mouth curls in disgust. "Complete waste of my time. This is not what I was promised." She flips Kade off before stomping away with her head held high. This time, Jose looks to River and jerks his head toward Nicole's retreating form. River nods and follows after her.

"It's done. All your plants are gone." Kade's taunting smile serves to anger Noah more and his blood vessel looks like it's about to burst.

"You don't want me as your enemy."

"That's all you've ever been." Kade shrugs.

"I made you." Noah shouts.

"I never wanted to be this," Kade hisses. Silence falls over everyone. Noah and Kade are locked in a battle of wits as they stare each other down. The cameras zoom in and my hands curl into themselves. It's all good TV for them, another instance of Kade not behaving. That's all everyone sees, but to me it looks like he's pleading for Noah to hear him. To understand how trapped in this persona he has become.

Noah, however, laughs humorlessly and then points his finger at Kade. "Keep trying me." He steps forward and security mimics his action, prepared to step in. "I'm not going to touch him." Noah declares, straightening his tailored suit jacket.

Jose signals to Marissa and she jumps into host mode, her serene smile back in place. "Next time on *The Love Meltdown*, we delve into the girls past to see if they have a future here."

Now what the hell does that mean?

# Chapter Twenty-Three

After the last elimination, the halls feel empty. There are only six of us left, and the tension is growing. I decide on a knit sweater dress and boots today since the weather's been getting cooler. I've also tied my braids into pigtails and did some quick swoops on my edges.

"Indie?" Jasmine's voice floats through the bathroom door.

"Yeah?"

"Jose's asking for you."

By the time I exit the bathroom, Jasmine's back in bed, buried under the covers. When I open the door, I find Jose standing with his usual clipboard in hand.

"Hey boo, walk with me?" He jerks his head back toward the hall. "You look cute. Where were you headed?"

"Outside, I wanted to get some air."

"We can talk out there." He pushes open the front door, holding it open for me.

"What's this about?"

"Well first, how are you? I mostly wanted to check in and see how

you're doing."

"I'm good." His check ins have become more frequent lately. We stop when we find a nice patch of grass to settle into. Jose looks less than thrilled to be sitting on the ground, but he follows my lead anyway.

"That's good." He nods.

"Was there something else?"

"What about your relationships with the other women? How are things with Jasmine and Cameron?" He tilts his head.

"Jasmines great, we get along well. Cameron and I can't seem to get on the same page. Why? Is she complaining?"

"No, you guys share a space so I want to help if I can with making sure it's a comfortable environment."

"Well, I'm not asking you to say anything to her. It'll resolve itself."

"Got it, I won't meddle." He throws his hands up in surrender. "I feel like we've had a disconnect, a lot of stress and pressure comes with this and the last time you felt overwhelmed, you went to River." He lets his words hang between us.

"He just happened to be around; it wasn't intentional."

"Well, I went through your file to figure out what you liked and placed an order for your favorites to be stocked in the fridge. I'm here to look out for you, but River's probably the best person to go to if you can't find me. He's great at what he does." He smiles wider, and it seems genuine enough.

"Thanks for being in my corner."

"Of course," he nods. "And don't let the other girls get in your head. I see the way Kade looks at you. Guy is smitten if you ask me." He nudges my side. "Don't stay out here too long, we're filming soon," he says as he gets up.

Thinking about Kade has taken away any possibility of me relaxing, so I abandon the idea and head back inside. The foyer's empty except for

Sabrina who's lounging in one of the armchairs with a bottle of wine in one hand and an empty glass in the other. Her thick black hair is tied in a knot atop her head. I hesitate for a moment before moving to sit in the chair beside her.

Her eyes cut in my direction before she pours the red liquid into the glass. "What do you want?"

"Can I not sit here?"

She ignores me, swirling the wine in the glass and tucking the bottle to her side.

"I want you to know you have nothing to worry about on my end." I give her what I hope is conveyed as a genuine smile.

"I would hope so, you should be focused on your own situation before you worry about mine."

My smile drops. She's right, but she doesn't have to say it. Turning away from her, I let my head fall back and close my eyes as the pulsing at my temples grows in strength. I've been on the verge of a headache since I woke up. The love gods punishing me for being complacent probably.

I feel a light tap against my arm and open my eyes to see Sabrina offering the glass of wine to me. I accept it and take a small sip.

"You looked like you could use a drink too." She takes a swig directly from the bottle.

"What do you think is planned for us next?" I take another sip and scrunch my mouth at the bitterness. It's stronger than what I normally drink.

"Don't know, don't care."

"Can I ask you something?"

"If I knew you were a talker, I wouldn't have shared my wine." She tilts the bottle back, taking another deep drink.

"Are you—I mean, if you don't want to answer that's fine, but are you—do you like both? Like are you attracted to Kade, and…?" I let my words trail off.

Sabrina lets out a heavy breath, "I'm as gay as they come. The idea of doing anything sexual with a man makes me want to barf."

"Then?" I ask.

"Why am I here? To piss my family off. Super cliché, right?"

I mean yes, but I'm pretty sure she's asking a rhetorical question. "I'm assuming they don't approve, then."

She snorts before taking another drink.

"How bad is it?"

"The first and only woman I dated was destroyed by my family. They completely ruined her." Her grip tightens on the bottle.

"Ruined her?" I can't help the skepticism that seeps into my voice.

"I wish I was being dramatic. My family comes from old money. It would make you sick to see my family's accounts. I'm not saying that to brag, but to bring perspective. Ruining a life is nothing to them. Ending careers, black-balling someone, stopping any and every opportunity that may come their way. It's all child's play to my family. This is the last thing they expected me to do." She turns toward me, her eyes are rimmed with red.

"I told them I was going away for a while, to get my head straight." She taps just above her ear with a delicate finger. "My family doesn't care what I do unless it could possibly embarrass them or lose them money. They won't even think to check on me and by the time they do, filming will be over. My dad's going to blow his top." She breaks into a fit of laughter.

"I'm sorry you're dealing with that. But you can't deny yourself forever, can you?"

"Take it from a closeted gay. It's no fun being locked away. Hannah deserves someone that can show her off."

"I'm sorry."

"Don't be. I wouldn't want to be in your shoes either."

My headache resurfaces as my thoughts bounce between River and Kade. "How long have you known?" I ask.

"I started paying more attention to River after the first time he caught Hanna and me. It was easy to see after that. The way you guys look at each other is nauseating."

"Whatever." I whisper over my glass before taking another sip.

"I thought you were going to blow your cover at the haunted house. After River and I did all that planning."

"You were in on that?"

"River told me which routes lead to the dark room. I tried to stop Kade from looking for you, but he insisted. River has helped me with a lot."

For the first time, I think I see what Hanna sees in Sabrina. Out of the corner of my eye, I notice the other girls emerging from their rooms.

"It's about time to get into formation. You coming?"

"I have nowhere better to be." Her words tangle together, and when she puts the bottle down, it sounds empty.

"Maybe we should get you some water."

"I can handle myself."

I don't push her further, but keep an eye on her as we make our way to the back of the house. We step through the door leading to the backyard and one of the assistants directs us to stand in a line. Kade and Marissa stand among the flowers in front of us. The back yard is large and dips before turning into an incline the further back you go. A line of trees sits behind Marissa and Kade, while the cameras and lights are set up behind them. River stands with the camera crew and his mouth is set in a hard line.

I silently mouth, *"What's wrong?"* and he gives a terse shake of his head.

"I bet you're all wondering why you're here tonight." Marissa pauses dramatically.

"We're down to the final six and it's important for Kade to get to know you ladies. How can you plan a future with someone if you don't know their past?" She smiles and a man steps forward from behind the trees. He has low cropped blond hair, a polo sweater, pressed khaki pants and dress shoes. He looks like your typical country club grade A douche, with his neatly coiffed hair, luxury timepiece and condescending smile.

Sabrina sucks in a breath next to me. "Chad?"

I look between them. "You know him?"

"I'm glad I finished the bottle. That's my ex."

Dread pools in my gut and I whip my head back toward Chad. He isn't the only one making an appearance. One by one, men appear and each time the faces of the women go sour. For a moment, I think I'm safe. Javi wouldn't show up here. Not after what he did and how we ended.

However, I forgot the one thing a man will always have is the audacity and Javi is chock full of it. He walks up to stand beside the other men, a shit-eating grin on his face.

# Chapter Twenty-Four

Production is messy for this one.

The guys throw insults our way, and the women are angry. Marissa puts a finger to her lips, calling for silence. "Let's be adults here. It sounds like we have some bad blood in the water." She turns to Chad and flashes a smile in his direction. She's eating this up, enjoying all the drama she's helped create. "How does it feel to see Sabrina again?"

"Fantastic. Sabrina's a gem." His words drip with sarcasm, causing Sabrina to flip him off.

Marissa turns her sights on a man covered in tattoos and piercings with a deep tan, "Wyatt, Hanna's here to find love. Do you think she's ready for that?"

I look at Hanna, she and Wyatt look like complete opposites. Wyatt cocks his head to the side, his earrings swaying with the movement. "I underestimated how far she'd go for clout. Hanna ain't worried about love. First it was me and my band and now she's on TV." His words are venomous.

"What are you talking about? People would have to know your band

exists for me to gain anything." Hanna scoffs. Wyatt's eyes narrow, he opens his mouth to respond but Marissa cuts him off.

"Javi, you and Indie didn't have a clean break. Do you think she's ready to move on?" Marissa gives him an encouraging nod, eager to instigate.

"You don't just stop loving someone. We're not done."

Delusional. That man's not right in the head, "Is it crack Javi? Is that what you're smoking?"

I see Kade's lips twitch and River coughs into his hand.

"You all used to mean something to each other, and I think it's important to face that past. You'll go on date's with Kade and your ex at the same time, starting with Jasmine and Liam. We have a car prepared for you out front." Marissa gestures for them to follow production.

Jasmine's ex is a large man with a barrel chest and muscled arms. He's handsome—movie star handsome, with his chiseled jaw and high cheekbones. He looks at her with a burning passion. Jasmine looks annoyed as they follow Marissa's instructions.

The camera crew jumps into action, surrounding us, zooming in on our faces and dangling boom mics above our heads. My eyes move to River, and he's shooting daggers at Javi with his stare. This is the wrong time for him to have a blow up. Javi makes the first move, standing so close I can smell his cheap cologne.

I raise a finger between us. "Don't come any closer."

His smile falls, "What's your problem? It's been months."

"So, I'm supposed to forgive you?"

"I think you're behaving like a child." He shakes his head.

"Me? You're the one—"

"Back off." Cameron surprises me by stepping between us.

"Don't go getting in their business, Cam." A tall broad-shouldered man with dark skin and a low-cut fade appears at Cameron's side.

"I do what I want, Will."

Annnnnd now they're arguing.

"Can we talk?" Javi approaches me again. These cameras aren't letting anything slide today. They swarm around us and my irritation spikes.

"Sure." My tone's clipped, and I wrap my arms around myself walking away from the others.

"How have you been, Indie?"

"It's Indigo. I've been great. Turns out life is less stressful when you're not being cheated on."

His eyes flick toward the cameras before settling back on me, "Well I've missed you, I think things got out of hand. We both did things we shouldn't have—"

"What did I do wrong?" I slap my hand against my chest.

"You broke into my apartment, stole my things, and destroyed my property. Then you moved in with another guy and stopped responding to my texts."

I stop dead in my tracks. I'm not sure if he's realized River's here yet, but this conversation is dangerous enough on its own.

"I'm worried about you. You're clearly doing this to get my attention. So, I'm not sure why you're pushing this hard when I'm telling you I'm willing to take you back."

I blink once. Twice. Three times before I fully process what he's saying and then I'm laughing, like clutching my stomach, laughter, "Javi, for the last couple weeks I forgot you existed."

"You're pushing it." His eyes flick to the cameras.

"No Javi, you are. You came here knowing that you had another woman in our bed and that when I caught you cheating on me, you put my stuff outside as if I wronged you."

His head jerks back, "I didn't—"

Throwing my hands up in the air, I walk away from the conversation. I'm not sure why I let that fool get a word in. Everyone has settled at one of the stone picnic style tables in the garden, so I join them. Javi takes a seat across from me, trying to catch my eye.

"Hey girl, you good?" Gabby whispers next to me, her ex beside her. He has perfectly tousled pink hair that hangs over his eyes, soft features, pale skin, and wears a small amount of makeup.

"We're supposed to go on a date with our exes? Give me a break." I lean forward, resting my elbows on the table.

"They're so shady for this." Gabby's ex speaks with his hands and has the same musical Bronx accent as her.

"This is Benjamin, but he goes by Benny." She introduces us.

"I'm lucky to still have her in my life as my bestie, so I'm here to make sure this Kade should even breathe her air." He pulls her into his side. They seem close.

"What's your story?" Benny points between Sabrina and Chad. The tension between them is thick.

"We didn't date long." Sabrina stiffens, glancing at Hanna.

"Sabrina doesn't date anyone long." Chad adds.

"Now Chad, if you didn't meet my standards, you can't expect me to settle."

"You think you'd be settling with me? But you're on a reality dating show for some loser?"

"Aren't you guys the losers? Following us, just to get rejected again?" I speak generally, but I keep my eyes on Javi.

"What about y'all?" Gabby inclines her head toward Hanna.

"I met Wyatt on a dating app. We didn't date long before we decided we weren't—"

"We dated for nearly a year. We talked about marriage—" Wyatt interrupts.

"You asked me a hypothetical question about weddings." Hanna corrects.

"But then she left me for a woman, so I'm a little confused as to why she's here?"

"I'm bisexual Wyatt, I told you that." She massages her temples.

"You either like men or you don't. If you didn't want to be with me, you could've said so."

"Don't be an idiot just because she doesn't want you. Being bi is valid. Go home and cry about it instead of being hateful." My lips twist in disgust.

"This is between me and her." Wyatt stands and takes a step toward me.

"Back up." River calls from behind the cameras. Wyatt ignores his warning and continues forward anyway.

"I told you to back up." River's made it to my side.

"You've got to be fucking kidding me." Javi laughs, looking from River to me. "This is going to be fun."

"Alright." Jose claps to get our attention. "It's time for a break. Separate." His tone is sharp. Wyatt finally backs down, and Hanna mouths an apology.

I bury my head in my hands and sigh.

# Chapter Twenty-Five

I f you'd have told me I'd be riding in a car with my cheating ex and the new guy I've been sort of dating, while the guy I haven't been able to forget films it all, I would've told you to seek help. Yet here we are. We've been driving for about thirty minutes, and I already want to pull my hair out. Javi's been complaining since this morning.

"Where are you taking us?" Javi says from the back seat. I opted to take the passenger seat instead of sitting with him. That was the first thing he complained about.

"Aquarium." Kade's grip on the wheel tightens.

"Isn't that a little childish?"

"Not my choice."

"Aren't you supposed to be in charge?"

I pinch my lips together and grit my teeth just like my mom used to do when she scolded me as a child and turn to face Javi. "Shut. Up." I say, emphasizing each word with a jab of my finger in his direction.

"Fine." He throws his hands up and folds his arms across his chest like an upset child. Again, similar to how I'd respond when my mom

did it to me. I roll my eyes while he can still see me before twisting back around. Kade watches through the reflection of the rear-view mirror and scratches his nose. He's checking on me now? I tip my head back against the headrest to hide the smile that breaks free and tug my ear in response.

Production reaches the aquarium before we do. The crowd at the entrance stops and attempts to peer through our window.

"If you didn't feel the need to drive this gaudy car, we could've avoided all the attention. I like to keep a low profile." Javi removes his seatbelt and tugs his beanie low. Kade's car is extravagant, but everything about Kade is. The camera crew was going to draw attention regardless.

"What is it you do again?" Kade asks.

"I'm a brand. My identity is my business. I also game. Thousands watch my streams." He puffs his chest out a bit and I cringe, sinking low in my seat.

"Is this your type? I never stood a chance." Kade clucks his tongue as if reprimanding me.

"What's that supposed to mean?" Javi pokes his head between our seats.

Kade ignores Javi, opening his door and closing it behind him without another word.

"Guy's an ass, Indie." Javi says when Kade's out of earshot.

We both exit the car and the camera crew is already getting into position. Kade laces his fingers through mine, ushering me to the side entrance while Javi follows behind us, mumbling about being a third wheel.

"I've never been to an aquarium." I say as we enter. The walls are made to look like the inside of a cave, and a projector displays a video of crashing waves that surround us.

"Your last boyfriend seems to have failed in more ways than one."

"She never asked to go. I'm not a mind reader." Javi calls from behind.

Security keeps the crowd a safe distance away, but we still try to keep to one side to avoid making others uncomfortable. The first tank we come to has clownfish and blue regal tang swimming circles around each other.

"Look how cute." I wrap my arm around Kade and point at the glass.

"Very cute." He muses.

"What?" I shove his arm.

"Nothing, I just think it's adorable that you're excited over clownfish." Kade smiles.

"She's always been a little immature." Javi leans against the railing, disregarding the sign stating not to do that. I vowed not to let him get under my skin, so I bite my tongue. We come to a stop at a small pool.

"The sign says you can pet them. Would you like to?" Kade asks.

"Umm." Don't get me wrong, I love animals, but starfish aren't as cute as they look in the cartoons. Kade moves behind me, placing his hands on my waist, resting his chin on my shoulder.

"Don't tell me you're scared?"

"I'm not."

"What are you waiting for? I've got you." His lips brush against my ear. He places a kiss to the side of my neck and my cheeks warm. He's more persistent than usual.

"Are you going to touch the fish or not?" Javi grabs my wrist, pulling me from Kade.

"Hey—"

Kade rips Javi's hand away and steps between us. "Don't touch her again." Kade's muscles tense and Javi's barely tall enough to meet with the top of his chest.

"And you're just going to grope her in public? I read up on you. You think you're better than me? I cheated on Indie once. How many times have you slept around on someone?" Javi's eyes dart to Kade's fists. "You're not any better than me."

"There's an unlimited number of reasons I'm better than you."

Javi's lips flatten and his thumb curls around his fingers cracking his knuckles, a habit of his when he's frustrated. "You can't keep her from me."

He sounds like a petulant child and revulsion rolls through me as I realize the world's going to see what I used to date. Javi's eyes land on me and he reaches past Kade, shoulder checking him hard, and gripping my arm again. I blink and Kade's hand is around Javi's neck. Everything happens at once. The camera crew closes in for better angles, the crowd around us pulls out their phones and security is making their way toward us.

I wrap my arms around his chest from behind. "Kade, stop, please." It's as though he can't hear me, so I squeeze tighter, "Kade." When I say his name, my voice trembles. He looks down at me, holding on for a moment longer before letting him go.

Javi's hands go to his neck as he gasps for air. "You're going to regret that." He spits. Security grabs him by the arms and drags him out.

Focusing my attention on Kade, I move in front of him and cup his face, demanding his attention. "I promise you he's not worth it."

Our date is cut short. Javi rides back in one of the production vans while Kade and I take his car. I'm not going to lie, that scared me. Javi's like a fly that won't stop buzzing in your ear, so I get it, but he's mostly harmless. Kades silent while we drive, holding my hand.

"Can you get in trouble for that?" I break the silence. He keeps his eyes on the road.

"Doesn't matter."

"It matters. You know what they'll make that footage look like. I don't want you to look like the asshole who can't solve anything without his fists."

"I never denied the rumors, Indigo. If I'm everything they say I am, what would you do then?" He doesn't look at me, instead he watches the road and when I don't respond, he lets go of my hand. We ride in silence, and I consider his question. What would I do if the Kade I know is only a side effect of being in our own bubble and outside of here he's completely different? I try to picture that, but I can't.

"You can be those things and still have a good side. People are complex." I think more than anything Kade wants to be accepted as is.

We finally get back to the mansion and security's waiting. The cameras are hovering and anger flares in my chest. Can't they give us a break? Kade pulls to a stop, and I unbuckle my seat belt. Before I can open my door, Javi's throwing it open.

"You're going to ride with him after he put his hands on me? Regardless of what happened between us, you're choosing someone who'd do that?" His eyes are wild. I look around for security, wondering how they could let Javi get to our car. Then I see them standing nearby and I realize this is orchestrated. They want this to happen. For a moment, I let myself forget that this is a TV show and our wellbeing isn't their priority.

"Go away Javi." I warn.

"He's not safe, Indie." He shouts in my face.

Behind me I hear Kade's door open, and I panic that he'll make it around the car before I get Javi to leave.

"Javi please—"

A hand lands on Javi's shoulder, jerking his body back. River spins him around and throws him to the ground. River stands over him, blocking me from view and Javi spits at his feet.

"This is rich." Javi laughs before turning on me. "How are we any different?" Security finally graces us with their presence and hauls Javi away.

"You okay?" River says quietly. It's not until he rests his hand on mine that I realize I'm shaking.

"Why would you do that?" My voice wobbles and the tears are already falling as he swipes his thumbs across my cheeks. "This is bad, River."

"Indigo?" Kade's there, a question in his eye as he zeroes in on River. Without thinking, I pull away from him.

"Excuse me." I mumble as I move past him. Pretending I don't know River hurts every time. I exit the car on shaky legs and look between them both. River has wiped every emotion from his face while Kade's burning a hole in the back of his head.

Thank God for Jose because he breaks the tension and wraps a blanket around me. "Well girl, you do know how to bring the drama." He wraps an arm around me and angles his head toward River. "Thanks for getting to Indigo for me like I asked. I got caught up in something and couldn't get here fast enough."

River's brows knit together, but he nods anyway as if he knows what Jose's talking about. Clearly, River came here on his own. Jose keeps his hold on me and guides me inside past the onlookers.

"Jose they're gonna—"

He puts a finger to his lips and points to the mic clipped to my chest. I fumble with the cords but eventually get it off and throw it to the floor.

"They let that happen."

He doesn't deny it.

We stop walking and he places a hand on my shoulders. "This can be fixed in editing, but you need to talk to Javi. If he presses charges, then Kade may skate by, but River won't. River shouldn't have jumped in, but clearly you two have bonded." Jose pinches the bridge of his nose.

"Talk to him? What could I possibly say to him?" I hiss, my anger boiling over.

"Whatever you have to. They took him to a room and he's not mic'd right now. He also refused cameras. This is your only chance."

Both Kade and River's careers are on the line, so I suck it up and straighten my back, "Take me to him."

We stand outside the door of one of the many empty rooms. I remove the blanket Jose gave me and pass it back to him before opening the door. Javi's head whips in my direction and his expression is cold. He's sitting on the bed with his head hanging, shoulders slumped. He eventually turns away from me and we sit in stifling silence. A purple bruise has bloomed around his neck, and guilt taints my conscience. He may be a pain in my ass, but seeing him all pathetic and in pain isn't what I want either.

"I don't get it Javi, you cheated on me. I understand you trying to spin it as if I did something to deserve it, but why are you fighting Kade so hard? Why do you care what I do?"

"You weren't supposed to move on. I never wanted Abbie." He turns toward me clasping his hands together. "I didn't mean to let things go as far as they did. Abbie's the kind of girl who looks down on a guy like me. She comes from money and doesn't know what struggle feels like. She always had something stupid to say when I was trying to figure things out. When doors started opening for me, her attitude changed. She was so different when you weren't around. She'd make up reasons to stop by and it felt like confirmation I'd made it to have a girl like her want me."

He wanted to stroke his ego by cheating and keep me in his back pocket for later. He's not making this sound any better.

"When you found out, I didn't think—I just reacted. I never intended to let you leave. She was plotting from the beginning. Posting pics online knowing you'd see them and stopping at my mama's house when she knew I didn't want her there. She manipulated the whole thing."

He's pinning it on Abbie and painting himself as the victim.

"I loved you. You lied to my face and went back on everything we promised each other. You told that girl I meant nothing, that I never did. I supported you when you had nothing, and you threw my things out. In. Garbage. Bags." Saying it out loud, I realize how crazy what he did was.

"That wasn't me. That's not even how I operate. Abbie did that mess on her own. I went off on her about it, I'd never disrespect you like that. I tried texting you that."

"Oh, but fucking my friend in the first place is cool?"

He blows an air of frustration and pounds his fist against his knee. "What do you want from me Indie? I'm trying to make it right. She threatened to release messages and I'd just signed brand deals. I couldn't leave her when I wanted to, but I'm here now."

I wave my finger between us both. "We'll never be anything ever again. Not friends. Not lovers. Not anything. Make it right by letting me go. If there is any part of you that genuinely cares about me, you'd do that."

He's quiet as he takes in my words. I don't know what he sees when he looks at me, but his expression softens and he sighs. "River's here."

My heartbeat quickens and my palms begin to sweat, "Are you

going to destroy what little I have left?" I ask.

Javi looks at me with defeat in his eyes, "I broke you once, I won't do it again. If you get caught up, it won't be by my hand. But I see the way he looks at you, the way he's always looked at you and I see the way Kade looks at you too. Maybe we're not so different. Nothing's black and white. Only difference is I won't judge you for being human."

Relief floods through me, but disgust follows behind it. I'm nothing like Javi. My situation is different.

# Chapter Twenty-Six

"**D**on't worry girl, if it wasn't your ex, it'd be mine," Jasmine says before taking a bite of her eggs. This morning I'm a bundle of nerves and decided to cook everyone breakfast as a distraction. Did it work? No. Does the taste of buttery pancakes make it slightly better? Not really, but I shovel them in my mouth anyway.

Cameron stabs her eggs with her fork. "I don't know Jas, Indie can't seem to do anything without being extra. Should've called this The Indigo Show. She even has that hot producer wrapped around her finger."

Gabby nods while pouring an absurd amount of syrup over her pancakes. "Didn't know River had it in him. He was so angry, it's always the quiet ones you have to worry about."

"No seriously. It's weird right? Why'd he jump in? Security was right there." Cameron watches me like a hawk and the grip I have on my fork tightens.

"You guys couldn't see how Javi was acting. River was closest. I'm grateful he helped. Production shouldn't have let Javi get anywhere near

us." Trying my best to sound nonchalant, I cut into my cakes.

Cameron tilts her head to the side as if confused. "Doesn't that make it more odd? He works for the show, so that would mean he got in the way of what they wanted."

"Maybe if you weren't so obsessed with Indigo, you could figure out why you can't seem to get Kade to give you the time of day." Sabrina enters the kitchen and breezes past us to the fridge, pulling the door open.

"I was only asking her a question. Since when is everyone so sensitive?" Cameron throws her fork down on her plate causing a loud clatter, before leaving the table.

"I have to talk to Liam since the guys are leaving after the elimination." Jasmine picks up her plate.

Gabby does the same. "I need to speak with Kade. Benny and I talked, and it made me realize some things." Gabby takes a bite of her bacon before looking up at me. "Don't let the drama get to you Indie. I don't know why Cameron's so hellbent on getting under your skin, but I think she's also feeling the pressure." She gives a little wave before she follows Jasmine out.

"If you're hungry, there's still food on the stove." I point my fork toward the leftovers. Sabrina pulls her head out of the fridge and looks over her shoulder at me.

"I'm good." She grabs a bottle of orange juice and shuts the door. "You're telling me you made breakfast, and she still took shots at you? You're better than me, girl." She pours her drink and leans against the counter.

"How are you holding up?" I'm no longer hungry and need a distraction.

"We're not friends." Sabrina says before taking a sip.

"I know."

"I'm only going to say this to you because I have no one else."

"I know."

She bites her lip before joining me at the table. "Hanna wants to leave, but what kind of future do we have outside of here? Things will go back to before." She stretches her fingers against the table before pulling them into fists. "If I were to bring her home, they wouldn't leave her alone." She frowns at her glass of juice. "I should've gone for something with a little more kick." She mumbles before taking another gulp of her drink.

"What if you don't wait?"

"What?" She turns to me.

"What if you claimed her here? What would be the point in taking her away from you if you already came out on national television? There would be nothing left for them to hide. Keeping her a secret gives them the upper hand."

She presses her lips together and pushes her glass away. "You think I should out myself on TV?"

"I think you should take some control back."

Sabrina slouches in her chair and tilts her head back. "Everything I have is connected to my family. All my accomplishments, my job, my relationships, everything. If they cut me off, what will I do? People will treat me differently and I don't want this to be my entire identity. My father might destroy me instead out of spite."

I'll never fully understand her situation and I couldn't imagine having my family be my biggest opposition. "I'm not trying to simplify it. It's a tough decision, but it's never too late to start over. Being poor isn't the worst thing in the world. I make do." I poke her side with my finger and her lips curl.

"You do seem happy for someone with so little."

We both laugh and for the first time in a while, I feel light.

"You know, you're the last person I should take relationship advice from." She shrugs.

"Why do you say that?"

"I don't know Indie. Pot meet kettle; look in the mirror. I've gotten to know River; I even consider him a friend. So, I'm saying I'm not the only one with things to figure out."

"I hear you." Definitely don't need Sabrina reminding me. I pick up my plate and move to the sink to clean up.

***

I adjust the strap of my dress for what feels like the millionth time as it doesn't quite fit me, and we've been standing around for longer than usual. When the exes arrive, Javi's not accounted for. My eyes search for River and I find him standing with some of the camera crew behind Kade and Marissa. Some of the pressure on my chest lifts. Even though Javi said he wouldn't push the issue, there's no way I could take his word for it.

Drew stands next to Marissa, touching up her lip gloss. An assistant calls out that everything is ready and Marissa smacks Drew's hand, dismissing her. Drew gives her a death glare, but steps out of the shot.

Marissa is the picture of devastation. Her lips turned down and her hand over her chest. "As some of you may have noticed, one of our guests is no longer here. After yesterday's incident, we thought it'd be best if Javi went home and he agreed. We don't condone anyone putting their hands on another and we think this outcome is what's best for everyone's safety." Marissa looks to Kade. "Our team reviewed the tapes, and the footage confirmed that Javi shoved Kade to get to Indigo and that Kade reacted in self-defense. While we didn't get a good angle of the altercation that involved our crew," she waves a hand in River's general direction. "Javi himself confirmed that when he was being pulled away from the vehicle, he tripped over his own feet."

Blinking, I look at River, who already has his eyes on me. Javi lied to protect us, or rather, he lied to protect me. I guess I did mean something to him at some point, and that knowledge is like salve on a wound I didn't know I was still nursing.

"Even with everything that has occurred, the show must go on. Kade, today you must send two women home."

He nods, and for the first time, he seems to hesitate.

"Gabby."

At first, I think I've misheard, but the only one who doesn't look shocked is Gabby herself. She smiles even as her eyes shine with tears.

"Gabby and I have had multiple conversations about this. While I find her to be beautiful, we never—"

"We don't want to bone each other," Gabby cuts him off with a soft laugh. "I'm thrilled I came here because I met people I hope to remain friends with, and Kade is one of those people."

"You want to be my friend?" Kade looks genuinely bewildered.

"If you'll have me."

His smile widens, and it takes me a moment to realize I'm smiling like a fool too because this is what Kade needs, friends. He makes his way to Gabby, and she gathers him into a hug. They rock back and forth and she giggles. Gabby pulls away with tears fully falling now. She turns to me and practically jumps into my arms. Gabby has been a constant since I got here and I'm not happy to see her go. Jasmine joins, wrapping us into a tight group hug.

"I'll call y'all when you bust out of here." Gabby pulls away and hugs Cameron before taking Benny with her through the front door.

"Five girls remain. One more must go." Marissa looks to Kade and gestures for him to continue.

Hanna steps forward before Kade can proceed, and my heart sinks.

My eyes flick toward Sabrina and her mouth parts.

"It's my time to leave. I don't think we'll be able to go any further, and it's not right for me to stay."

"If that's what you want, who am I to stop you? Is there anyone else?" Kade looks over Hanna at the rest of us. His gaze lingers on Sabrina, and I realize I must be dense because what the hell—does Kade know too? No one else seems to pick up on what he's implying as the silence stretches. Hanna's practically holding her breath, but Sabrina says nothing. The room remains silent. Hanna's face falls and my heart aches for her.

"Looks like it's just me." Her voice cracks and she folds her hands together. "Thank you for having me." She gives Kade a quick hug and turns on her heel, Wyatt trailing after her. I steal a glance at Sabrina, and her face is devoid of emotion.

"Five girls remain. Only one can be chosen. Good luck ladies, the pressure gets worse from here."

# Chapter Twenty-Seven

We're filming this afternoon, but we have nothing but free time this morning. I head toward the movie room for some alone time to get my head straight, however the universe will not let me be. Kade's spread out across the couch, legs kicked up on the armrest. I debate backing out of the room, but his eyes fall to mine before I can decide. His head tilts in my direction, curls falling over his eyes.

"Hey heartbreaker." He closes the book he's holding, resting it on his chest.

"I guess you beat me here." I make to leave, but Kade sits up on his elbows.

"Where you running off to?"

"I'm not running." Changing direction, I slide back inside, shutting the door behind me.

"Glad to hear it."

I move toward the couch, and he pulls his legs in, only to spread them back out and rest them in my lap after I sit.

"You read?" I ask.

"I'm a man of many talents." He places the book on the floor.

"What are you doing here?"

"Waiting for you."

"Don't start."

He laughs and straightens in his seat as I push his legs off my lap. "How're you holding up? Your boy left with a bang."

"I'm fine. We talked, and it went better than I thought it would. I was worried…" Biting my lip, I turn to him. "It could've been a big deal."

"I'm glad that producer stepped in."

I avert my gaze. "Yeah, he seems to take his job seriously."

"But he takes extra care with you." He inches closer so that our thighs press together.

"I looked into this River Beck. He's worked to help produce a lot of big projects. It's weird though, because reality TV doesn't seem to be his thing. Why now?"

"I mean, I wouldn't know?" I shrug.

"Now, when did we start lying to each other?" He places his fingers around my chin and turns my face toward him, "It's him, isn't it?"

My stomach drops. This is a rhetorical question, Kade knows.

"When I saw him last night I knew, and then I remembered all the other times I saw him with you, and I don't know how I didn't catch on sooner."

"It's not like—"

"I've been such an idiot." He laughs humorlessly.

"What?"

He pulls me closer, our lips a breath away from each other. "You set me up. What did Noah promise him? Were you in on it? They get you to keep me in check?" He drops his hand.

"I don't know what you're talking about. River didn't even want me to be here."

"How do I know you're not lying? That you didn't get close to me with some hidden agenda?"

My mouth falls open and before I can give it a second thought, I pop him on the back of the head. "You're the whole reason I'm here. You approached me." Jabbing my finger into my chest, I stare at him incredulously. He rubs the spot I hit and glowers at me. "Even with you paying me double, this show doesn't pay me enough to put up with your crap." I give him the same evil eye he's throwing my way.

"Noah never approached you?" He repeats himself and it pisses me off.

I reach for his ear, tugging it lightly. "Kade relax. River didn't know I applied, and when he found out he wasn't happy. I wasn't sure If I was going to go through with it after the audition and I definitely wouldn't have done it if I knew it was going to be you." Thinking about how vastly my opinion of him has changed makes me smile.

"I don't think I can take you not being real, Indie."

I press my lips together and send a puff of air through my nose. "I meant what I said about taking control of my life. No one could make me do this, and I would never manipulate you. You're my friend."

Kade's frown deepens. "You negotiated in bad faith heartbreaker. That man's in love with you."

"He's not in love with me."

"You believe that?" He chuckles under his breath.

"It's the truth." The words don't come with the confidence I intended.

"Then I almost feel sorry for the guy. So he's the reason you won't let me choose you at the end of this thing?"

"None of this has anything to do with that. I put a man before my dreams once and it wasn't worth it."

"Ah, I get it now." A slow smile spread across his face as he leans in close. "Your heart was broken and now you've sworn off love. Is that it?" His fingers draw circles around my knee before traveling up my thigh, making it hard to think.

"It's just not a priority right now." I place my hand over his. There's no denying my physical attraction to Kade. If I'm not careful, I'll end up following his lead.

"I have no intention of getting in your way. I want you to have everything you desire."

"But I—"

"Have sworn off men. I get it." He laughs, brushing my braids behind my hair. "I told you from the beginning you wouldn't have to worry about me falling in love with you."

"Then what do you want from me?"

"You. In whatever form that is. Friend, lover, whichever way you want to define it. I'm not ready to let you go." His words rattle inside me uncomfortably. Muffled talking emits from his earbud and his hand goes to his ear. I feel a strange sense of relief at the interruption.

"What is it?"

Kade stands. "They're saying they need me now. I'll see you tonight for filming. You still have your end of the deal to uphold."

"I know. I'm not backing out, but we need to talk." We need to set boundaries. He needs a friend, and I'm not sure if what we're doing is right anymore. I'm doing my best to be honest with him, but he's not the only one I need to be upfront with. Kade smiles, but it has none of the bravado I'm used to.

After parting with Kade I thought I'd have a moment alone with my thoughts, but Cameron steps into our shared room and pauses at the door at the site of me. We have to film in twenty minutes, and I don't have the mental capacity to go another round with her. I get up to leave, but she raises her hands.

"I come in peace." She closes the door and sits on the foot of my bed. "I wanted to apologize for snapping at you the other day. Things aren't going as smoothly as I'd like, and I took it out on you." She folds her hands in her lap and gives me a small smile. "That's no excuse, so I wanted to say sorry. I might have been slightly jealous."

I watch her, and she looks genuinely embarrassed. Her eyes drop to the floor, and we sit in an awkward silence. Despite everything, she cares for Kade and that's what's important.

"This environment is stressful. I think we all deserve some grace." I smile.

She perks up and nods her head. "I think the pressure that comes with being here reveals things about ourselves we didn't know were there. At the end of the day, I hope the woman that will make Kade the happiest wins. He deserves that." Her eyes meet mine.

Why couldn't he have set his sights on her? She's jealous of me, but I'm envious of how confident she is. She knows what she wants, and she's going for it. How can I not admire that? I've spent most of my friendship with River downplaying my feelings and now I'm struggling to let myself accept it.

"Indigo?" Sabrina's voice sounds from the other side of the door.

"Yeah?"

"They want us out front for filming. We're all supposed to walk out as a group."

"We're coming." I call back. Cameron and I stand. I readjust my dress so that it sits neatly and slip my heels back on. The camera crew is ready to go when we make it to the foyer, and Kade and Marissa are nowhere in sight.

"Alright ladies. We are on go, please head outside." Jose points toward the front doors. I take the first step and the rest follow. When we push open the doors, another group of women are all standing in the middle of the courtyard. Among them, I see a familiar head of golden-brown hair and bright green eyes.

"Ryan." My legs are moving before my brain can catch up. We slam into each other and the moment we connect I'm crying.

"Indie, who do I need to fight girl?"

"No one, I just missed you." It feels like everything inside of me unravels and all the emotions I've held tightly in place fall forward. I'm crying in her arms for a multitude of reasons, the main one being that I'm happy she's here.

"I missed you too."

# Chapter Twenty-Eight

The air fills with squeals and shrieks as women hug each other.

"We figured after recent events, you could each use someone in your corner." Marissa smiles as she watches us, and I'm still holding on to Ryan for dear life. Beside her is Kade and another man with black skin rich in color. He's incredibly handsome, with plump lips, high cheekbones, and a neatly trimmed beard. His twists fall to his shoulders, thick like a lion's mane.

"Damn." Ryan whispers in my ear, "Who the hell is that?"

"No idea." The man ruffles Kade's hair, and his laughter is deep and full. Kade pushes him away, but there's a lightness to his eyes.

"I'm sorry to say that we weren't able to bring anyone here for you, Sabrina." Marissa presses her hand over her heart, feigning empathy.

Kade locks eyes with her. "You won't be alone; we're going to have a good time tonight."

Sabrina gives a curt nod and wraps her arms around herself.

Marissa places a hand on Kade's shoulder. "Tonight, we're sending you out for a little fun. Kade, do you want to let them in on the details?"

"What's up ladies, my names, Shemar." He cuts Kade off and rubs

his hands together, causing some girls to giggle.

Kade pushes Shemar out of the way. "This is my cousin. Please ignore him." He frowns and shakes his head; Shemar throws his hands up in mock defeat. "Tonight, we're hoping to show you a good time. We've brought your best friends here so that I can get to know them." Kade's eyes flash toward Ryan, and I wonder if he can tell who she is. Ryan and River could be twins.

Shemar jumps in front of Kade. "Most importantly, I don't want to see anyone holding back. Bottles popping and everyone's dancing tonight." He shakes his hair and does a little dance. Kade runs his hand down his face and closes his eyes.

"Well, what are you ladies waiting for? Go get dressed." Marissa waves us away.

When we make it upstairs, Ryan and Jasmine click right away. Ryan practically drools over the dress Jasmine has on, and Jasmine is gagging over the limited-edition heels Ryan has paired with her outfit.

I readjust the straps of the dress Ryan forced me into. It's simple in design; a camel color embellished with sparkles. It glitters with every movement, like diamonds in the sand. The cups are cut low and put the girls on full display. Tugging at the hem of the dress, I step into the matching heels.

"Stop pulling it down." Ryan swats my hand away.

"It's too short Ry."

"It's not. You just have a lot going on back here." She slaps my backside.

"If I had an ass like that, no one could tell me nothing." Jasmine throws over her shoulder as she helps her friend, Kailanni, apply boob tape to her chest to complement the plunging neckline of the dress she's wearing.

"They're right. It looks good, Indie." Cameron offers.

"Thanks Cam."

"I have a bracelet that would match." She turns from me and digs in her bag until she pulls a black box out of it. "This would look great on you." Inside is a bracelet with beautiful clear stones in gold plating, it shines like my dress does in the light.

"Wow, it's gorgeous. I can't wear this. It's too nice."

Cameron moves to snap it around my wrist. "It's totally fine," she leans in close and whispers, "The diamonds aren't real." She shrugs. "Supporting each other makes our time here a little easier. It's almost over and I want to have fun tonight."

"Me too."

She smiles up at me. "I'll see you downstairs." She reaches for her friend, and they leave together.

"Thank god, it's about time you guys squashed the weird energy. I'm ready to turn up. No drama." Jasmine helps adjust Kailanni's dress after finishing with the tape.

"I'd hope she knows better than to talk crazy when I'm here. Indies soft, I'm not." Ryan finishes tying my braids into a top knot bun while I finish swooping my baby hairs with gel.

"You ready Sabrina?" I do my best to sound casual, but it's painfully apparent that she's the only one without a visitor. Ever since Hanna left, she's been on mute.

"I'm always ready." Sabrina looks stunning. Not a hair out of place, a light smokey eye and liner to accentuate her eye shape.

Jasmine leads the way downstairs. Once we reach the foyer, all the other girls are already waiting. Some of them hang onto Shemar's every word—and he has a lot of them—while the others surround Kade.

"As soon as everyone's here, we can leave." Kade lifts his wrist and peers at his watch.

"I think we're the last ones." Tucking my clutch under my arm, I come to a stop at his side. His head jerks up at the sound of my voice. His eyes follow the lines of my curves. This dress feels like a second skin, and I feel exposed. "We can leave now." I pat him on the shoulder, and he seems to regain his composure.

Shemar throws his arm over Kade's shoulder. "Let's get this party started."

The music's loud, and the club's packed. We're in our own roped off VIP section and because of the building's capacity, we have a smaller camera crew and security detail with us. Cameron found her way onto Kade's lap. She flicks her hair over her shoulder and rests a hand on his chest. The bottle girls arrive waving flashing lights and wearing matching lingerie. One girl offers a tray of shots, and Ryan and I happily take one each, clinking our glasses together before throwing them back. I'm not sure how many I've had so far, but they haven't caught up with me yet.

"You want to hit the floor?" Ryan doesn't wait for an answer. We hold hands and dance with the beat, finding the rhythm and letting it move through us. Ryan's hands go to my waist, and I wrap my arms around her neck as she bounces. A hand skims my ass and then grabs a handful. The hand in question is way too large to be Ryan's. My head whips around and a man I don't know is leaning over the ropes into our section with a goofy smile on his face.

"What the hell do you think you're doing?" I yell over the music.

"Oh, come on, don't be stuck up. You think you're too good?" His eyes are glassy, and he sways on his feet.

"You're drunk."

"I've hardly drank." His words meld together.

"Hey." Kade cuts in. He places a hand on my stomach and moves me behind him. "I'm going to need you to back up." Everything about

Kade right now screams threat, from his stance to his tone.

"Hey man, you're in the way." The guy reaches over the rope and attempts to push Kade to the side. To avoid a repeat of what happened with Javi, I grab Kade's arm.

"He's drunk. I don't think he even knows what he's doing."

Kade points a finger at him. "Find something safe to do. I don't want to see you near our section again."

Shemar puts himself between the drunk and Kade, shooting Kade a confused look before addressing the intruder. "Hey man, you got any friends?"

The man looks like he doesn't understand Shemar, but then begins rambling about something.

"Let Shemar handle it." I yell over the music.

"Distract me." His voice is rough, and his eyes look at me hungrily.

"Well, come on. Let's see if I can hold your attention." Walking backwards, I pull him with me to the main floor. The music switches to an intoxicating beat. It's slow and sensual. I let Kade's hands go and sway my hips. Kade's always wound so tight. I want to see him have fun. The corners of his lips tilt up and my brain says dancing with Kade's a bad idea, especially since we still need to talk, but the alcohol has me in a teasing mood. I wrap my fingers around his belt and tug him closer. The drinks are definitely hitting. I feel light and airy.

"How much have you had to drink, beautiful?" He calls over the music. Reaching for my waist, he holds me steady.

"I'm fine. Why don't you loosen up?" I run my hands through his neatly combed hair. "Dance with me Kade, who knows when we'll get to do this again." I wrap my arms around his neck and his eyes narrow.

"You planning on running from me?" He asks, tilting my face toward his as we sway to the music.

"Indie." Ryan shouts over the music as she makes her way over.

"Sorry buddy, I need to steal my girl." She reaches for my hand and pulls me away when Kade grabs my arm. Without thinking, I shake him off and I immediately regret it when I see the hurt that flashes across his features.

"Sorry, I just—I need to see what she wants." I shout over the music.

His lips press into a thin line, and he nods before we disappear into the crowd. Ryan's a woman on a mission. She pushes through people with no remorse. The drinks are kicking in now. The floor feels unsteady. We end up in a small hallway with a restroom and Ryan practically kicks the door open. She lets go of my hand and starts checking under each stall.

"What are you doing?"

When she's satisfied no one's inside with us, she locks the door. "What was that?" She hisses while stomping toward me.

"What was what?" Blinking, I take a step back. "Are you drunk too?"

"Don't even try to blame what I just saw on the alcohol. You fucking like him?"

I shake my head and mentally kick myself for having so much to drink.

"Indie no, you can't. What about—" She stops mid-sentence and looks at the mic firmly attached to her dress. She dips her hand underneath and rips hers off, using her thumb to flip the switch. She lets the mic fall to her feet before surprising me by digging her hands inside the cups of my dress and tearing mine off too.

"What are you doing?" My words trip over each other. She's moving too fast for my alcohol drenched brain.

"You've been holding out on me, Indie. What's going on here? That man's looking at you like he's starving, and he bit that guy's head off for touching you."

This is not a conversation we should be having. Not when I can barely keep my thoughts together. I lean against the sink and sigh.

"Kade and I have a connection, but we're just friends."

"This is my fault." She whispers and brings her hands to her mouth. "What about River, Indie? He loves you."

That's the second time someone's told me that. If River's in love with me, why hasn't he said it?

"Indie, did I force my brother to watch you fall in love with someone else?" Her voice breaks and her eyes glisten. River and I haven't even figured things out yet, and it's already causing our relationships to shift.

"I'm not in love with Kade."

"But you're attracted to him? Don't answer that. I don't know why I'm asking. Of course you are, shit I am too."

"None of this is your fault Ry. I'm not even sure what to call what Kade and I have." Closing the distance between us, I hug her tight.

"River got confused because my life's been such a train wreck lately. He's mixing up wanting to help me with wanting me."

"River has never been confused. My brother has been wrapped around your finger since you met. This is my fault." She pulls away, sliding against the wall until she hits the floor, bringing her knees to her chest. I sit beside her, and she rests her head on my shoulder.

"I was jealous of how close you guys were when we were little." She sniffles and swipes her wrist against her nose. "I hated myself for a long time after my father left. My parents loved each other, and our dad was River's hero. I was the one thing standing between them." She scoots closer, snuggling into my side. "My mom and River don't love me any less for it, but it still didn't change the fact that I felt like I took something important from them. I lost friends too. I didn't tell you guys, but people acted so different when they found out. It wasn't as common to be out like it is now."

"Your father was a grown man; you were a child. You didn't take him from them. He left on his own. They aren't the only ones he abandoned. You loved him too."

She sits up and faces me. Her cheeks are wet and a trail of eyeliner and mascara marks the path her tears have fallen.

"I know, but I didn't know that then. I thought that if you and River got together, there wouldn't be any room for me." Her chin trembles and I reach my hand to swipe at the tears that keep building.

"I was young and immature. I'm not trying to make excuses."

"Ryan..."

"I made River promise he wouldn't." She covers her face with her hands. "We grew up and I kind of forgot about it. I thought River moved on. You both dated separately, and he never mentioned it again. But it was different after you met Javi. You never made things official like that, and your relationships never affected your friendship before." She wipes at her tears again.

"I thought River was okay with it but when you moved out—when you pulled away from him... He wasn't okay, Indie."

Everything feels off center and my chest feels heavy. He was always so busy with work I didn't think it bothered him when I pulled away. Ryan places both hands on my shoulders.

"You're my friend. You'll always be my friend. Stop worrying about how this will affect us because it won't. You'll never get rid of me. So, tell me what's been going on. Talk to me as your best friend, not River's sister. What's so great about this Kade?"

We both lean against the wall, and I take her hand in mine.

Telling Ryan everything feels good. As awkward as it is, she keeps her word and remains neutral. She listens quietly, only speaking to ask for more clarity. Kade feels like someone I've known for a long time, but I can't see him around my feelings for River, and that's something I wish I could have admitted to myself sooner.

"You really do care about Kade." She comments.

"I do."

"Now tell me how you feel about River."

"He's… River feels like home. Every time I'm near him I feel like I can breathe. Like it doesn't matter what's happening in the world because I know he's always got me, you know? River never makes me feel like I'm not enough. If anything, he makes me feel like the most valuable thing he's ever held on to. When I'm with him, I'm constantly waiting on the other shoe to drop because it feels too right. How can someone be that perfect?"

"How long have you loved my brother?"

"Ryan we can't." I shake my head.

"Why not? Stop using me and our family as an excuse." Her tears are gone, replaced by determination.

"It's time for you to woman up and do what you want. I'm sorry Indie, but our worlds don't revolve around you guys. If you break up, I promise our moms and I will survive and the world will keep spinning." She laughs. "I'd be disappointed, but not enough to destroy what we've built. You're my sister. Not by blood, but because I love you. Give us some credit, will ya? We can handle it."

"I'm scared I'll lose him. If he changes his mind or we find out we're not compatible, it would break me."

"What if it's exactly what you needed? What if you two are the best love story ever written? Are you not going to try? My brother won't let you go easily. Anything worth having takes a leap of faith."

Coming home to River every day and knowing that we belong to each other sounds like a beautiful dream. The thought of it fills me with a joy I can't describe.

"The timing is…" I'm still on a reality dating show vying for another man's attention and I'm still a risk to River's job.

"Do you want to be with Kade, or do you want to be there for him? You mentioned thinking River was confused. Aren't you the one misunderstanding your feelings?"

"When I think of River and compare it to my feelings for Kade, I know I'm not in love with him. I think it's more like how I love you. I want him to be happy. He grew on me, Ry."

"Indie…"

"I think I could have fallen for Kade. I wanted to try because being with him is comfortable, but being with River scares me to death because I want it so bad. There is no room left in my heart when River exists."

Ryan gives me a sad smile. "It sounds like you aren't confused at all, then."

She's right, I've been a coward. Standing, I brush the back of my dress off.

"Where are you going?" She asks.

"I'm done running Ry." I unlock the door and set off with my mind made. It's time to end this and face River.

# Chapter Twenty-Nine

I forgot how loud the club was after being held captive by Ryan in the restroom. Standing on my toes, I try to look over the crowd.

After a bit of searching, I spot Kade back in our section talking with Jasmine. My stomach is in knots, but it's better to rip the Band-Aid off. Unfortunately, I don't notice Cameron in my path. We bump into each other and what's left of her drink splashes the front of her dress.

"Oh my gosh, I'm so sorry." I pat at the wet spot with my hand, but she waves me off.

"Don't worry about it. You want to dance with us?" Cameron bounces back and forth with her friend at her side.

"I can't, I need to—"

"Indigo puh-lease. Let someone else have time with Kade. If you're not hogging him, then he's in a bad mood waiting for you to come back around. For once, he's giving everyone else a chance. Don't ruin it." Cameron rolls her eyes.

She's kind of right. Waiting a few more hours won't hurt. I scan the room again, finding Sabrina at the bar. I'd forgotten she was alone, and

I had intended to keep her company tonight.

"I'll catch you guys later." I tell Cameron before making my way to Sabrina.

The bar's dark, and further away from the dance floor so it's less packed. I take the stool next to Sabrina and lean forward on my elbows. "How's your night going sexy?" I whisper in her ear.

She looks alarmed at first, but then recognition settles. She laughs before taking the last swig of her drink. "Like shit."

She looks it too. Perfectly put together, but cracking underneath. Her eyes are puffy and a frown has been permanently stamped on her face.

"It's not too late. You can still leave." I bump her shoulder with mine.

"I don't want to hear that from you." She pushes her glass forward and crosses her arms over her chest.

"I know I'm the last person who should give anyone relationship advice—"

"Have you figured that out yet, by the way?" She asks, changing the subject.

"I think so." My eyes drift to Kade, and she follows my line of sight.

"They're both good guys."

"I know."

"I wouldn't want to be you." She cracks a smile.

"You think you're doing any better than me?"

"You're right. Hey," she taps the counter with the palm of her hand. "Two more of these." She shouts over the music, pointing at her glass and waving to get the barkeeps attention. He grunts in response before filling two glasses with whatever cocktail she was having before I came. He drops them in front of us before tending to another customer. Really shouldn't have another, but what the hell, why not?

Sabrina picks up one glass and hands me the other. "To us figuring out our shit."

"To us."

Apparently, Ryan can get along with anyone. Sabrina warmed up to her way quicker than she did me. We spent the night dancing, and it was just what I needed. Kade seemed to be having unfiltered fun. I don't know if it was the drinks, his cousin being there or him finally letting go, but how could I ruin that?

It's close to two in the morning when we pull up to the mansion after stopping for burgers on the way back. Sabrina's holding on to Ryan for support as we hobble out of the limo. Kade finds my hand while the other girls laugh, stumbling up the steps.

"Where are we going?" I ask as he hauls me behind him.

"I don't want the night to end. Stay up a little longer for me?" He reaches under his shirt and flips his mic off.

I watch his back and grip his hand tighter. I'm not sure if we'll have another night like this, so I turn my mic off and let him pull me along. We make it around the back and step into the garden where the floor's less even and Kade sways on his feet, so I drape his arm around my shoulders for support.

"Thank you, beautiful."

"Who invites someone on a walk when they can hardly stand?" I ask.

"I can stand just fine. Maybe getting close to you was the plan."

Neither of us is paying attention, so when the ground begins to incline slightly, we both stumble. As we fall, Kade twists his body, so that I land on top of him.

"Crap, sorry." I attempt to move, but he grabs my hips.

"The floor's moving more than I expected is all." He mumbles.

"Oh sure, yes, that's it." The words bounce around with my laughter.

He smiles softly and caresses my cheek.

"Why are you looking at me like that?" I ask.

"This is how I always look at you." He shrugs.

"Well, stop it."

"I've tried."

Rolling my eyes, I sigh and lift my chin. "I'm happy I met you." I'm not sure how to start, but I want him to know that. More than anything, I hope we could still be friends after this.

"It's been a long time since I've had someone on my side." He smiles up at me. "Shemar and I are close, but he was always traveling for military business until recently. My mom and dad retired to Japan and aren't in the states often and as you know, I'm a terrible judge of character." Even though his tone is light, his eyes are sad.

"I'll always root for you to win. You deserve a win."

His hand drops from my face. "I gave up on trying to do that a long time ago. So I took a step back from acting because my panic attacks made it nearly impossible. I got caught up in what I thought I had to be." He focuses on the night sky above us. "I signed contracts I didn't understand and tied myself to Noah and his team. At first, I tried to ruin my image, figured they couldn't sell a damaged product."

Hearing him describe himself as if he's not a person with feelings breaks my heart.

"Then they used the money angle, threatening to empty my bank accounts with penalties and fines. They soon learned I didn't care about the money. I just want to be free to act without any of their agendas tying me down. I stopped going to auditions, started bailing on jobs, went to therapy and my panic attacks got better." A ghost of a smile breaks across his features.

"It didn't last long. Turns out I needed the money more than I thought. I bought my parents' home and couldn't afford it, the route I was taking."

"How can a contract be so one-sided?"

"People only look out for themselves."

"That's not true."

The stars shine bright and reflect in his eyes.

"I'll give the world what they want. Not me, but the manufactured version my management team has created. This show's supposed to show a softer side of me. Not exactly working in their favor, is it?" He smirks, but it's all smoke and mirrors.

"The world's missing out."

"I don't need the world." He twines his fingers through mine, and I feel like I'm falling and the landing is going to be excruciating.

"I'm happy to orbit your universe, but it can't just be me. You need a solar system." I can feel that I'm hurtling toward the floor and the painful crash is coming, so I brace myself. "Kade we–"

"How long are you going to stay on top of me?" He smiles and his eyes drift down to my chest still pressed against his.

"Oh god, my bad." I scramble to my feet and offer him my hand. He still seems a little off balance, so I lean his weight against me. Asking him to break our deal now feels like I'd be twisting the knife already stuck in his back. I'll leave it alone for tonight and try again tomorrow. It's a slow trek back to the mansion, dragging Kade up the stairs was an obstacle all its own. When we finally make it inside his room, I drop him to the floor with a huff.

"That wasn't gentle at all." He chuckles.

"Were you even trying" I pant as I throw his blankets back. He laughs harder, which leads me to believe he wasn't.

"Come on, time to sleep." I tow him toward the bed. Pushing at his chest so he falls backward onto the sheets.

"Are you going to tuck me in?" He teases.

Pulling his shoes off, I roll my eyes and then reach for the blanket as he twists his body so his legs aren't hanging over the side. I push the covers underneath his arms as tight as I can and fluff his pillow roughly, so his head bounces violently.

"Is that good?"

He laughs and wiggles his arms free.

"You better remember this in the morning." I mumble. I kick off my heels and grab them in my hands as I start towards the door.

"I'm happy I met you too."

I stop and look over my shoulder. Kade's smiling at me, and he looks so exposed. Like he's expecting me to make him regret it instead. I should tell him now. End things before they go any further, but I don't. Not when he's looking at me like that.

I mirror his expression the best I can. "We'll talk tomorrow." He nods and I leave. Every opportunity was missed tonight.

When I turn away from the door, I stop dead in my tracks because River stands in front of me.

# Chapter Thirty

River stands across from me, eyes cold. "Why are you coming out of his room?"

"River, it's not—"

"Did he touch you?" His voice takes on a deadly tone.

"Stop it. Nothing happened." Deciding it'd be better not to have this conversation outside of Kade's room, I march to where River is standing and yank him away. He doesn't protest and falls in step behind me. A puff of air flows through my nose, and I stomp my feet with each step. The accusation in his eyes has me running hot. "Why are you following me around, anyway?" I throw over my shoulder. He doesn't answer. I want to face River after clearing things up with Kade, so we could have a clean slate. However, River's patience with me seems to have run out and I don't know if I can avoid it much longer. We make it down the stairs and I start toward my room, when River jerks me backward, causing me to fall into his chest. Before I can right myself, he's bending his knees and throwing me over his shoulder.

"What the hell are you doing?" My head whips around, scanning the area for any witnesses, and the tension dancing along my muscles

relax when I see the coast is clear. "I told you nothing happened." His hold on me is iron tight, so I give up. We enter one of the empty rooms and he stops at the bed tossing me on top of it. "What is your problem?" Anger causes me to trip over myself before I'm able to get to my feet.

He closes the distance between us. We're so close my nose is practically at his chest. I raise my chin and look up at him—I'm met with unfiltered anguish. Whatever strength he had left has been used up, he's not holding back anymore.

"My problem is that I had to watch you walk out this door on his arm dressed like this." His hand goes to my thigh, slipping underneath the skirt of my dress. He trails upward, bringing the flimsy material with him until he reaches the curve of my hips, the air's cold against my skin. "I had to sit back, knowing he was going to have his hands on you." His voice is thick and the pads of his fingers trail along the hem of my panties. "My problem is you not pushing him away and letting it happen." His eyes bore into mine.

Whatever barricade I had restraining my feelings for River vanishes and all my pent-up feelings come rushing forward like water breaking through a dam. "And I had to go years thinking you didn't want me. How many women did I watch you date? How many women did you bring home, and I had to smile in their faces?"

"I was trying to move on." He grits out.

"So was I."

"Is that what you're doing now?" He looks at me like he's bracing himself.

I channel all my anger into pushing him away. All my frustration is spilling out and I can't stop it. "Fuck you, River. I had a plan. No attachments, no stress and nothing that could bite me in the ass later. I promised I'd never give someone that kind of power over me again." He grabs at my wrists. I don't know when I started crying, but the tears are flowing now, and I can't find the off switch. "Fuck you. Because I'm so in love with you, I don't care about the consequences."

He wrenches me forward and his mouth is on mine. Any words I had left die on his lips. My tongue meets his greedily. His hands wrap around my braids before he tightens his hold, pulling them back so that my head tilts up.

"I had it in my head since we were kids that you were mine. I've been in love with you since before I was old enough to know what love was."

His words send my heart into overdrive. He dips his head—his lips covering my rapid pulse at the base of my neck. River is a torrent of overwhelming need. His kisses send rivulets of pleasure through me and my knees grow weak. His hands go to my waist and the moment my feet leave the floor, I wrap my legs around his hips. I take his face in my hands, meeting him blow for blow. Our kisses are desperate. I feel like I can't get enough of him.

His fingers flex as he takes a handful of my ass into each hand and I feel his desire for me grow, hot and hard. I rock against him, and he moans against my mouth, causing my own desire to pool between my thighs. He takes rushed steps toward the bed before laying me down. He stands over me, tugging his shirt over his shoulders and all the wind is knocked out of me. Everything about him is beautiful.

My legs are still wrapped around him, I use them to bring him closer before I push myself up to undo his belt. When I finally manage to get the buckle and buttons undone, my fingers tremble as I pinch the zipper between my fingers.

The metal glides over the bulge that's grown underneath and I swipe my tongue against my lips, peering up through my lashes. River's smile is teasing, and I flush under his gaze. He tries to guide me back on the bed, but instead I take his hand and pull him down, maneuvering us so he's on his back.

His mouth parts as he watches me, and my lips turn up as I run my hands slowly from my chin, down my neck, along my collarbone and underneath the straps of my dress. Pulling one down, I turn my back to him and slide the other off as well.

Looking over my shoulder, I see longing in his eyes, and it only encourages me. I let the dress fall at my feet. I hear his intake of breath behind me, and goose bumps crawl up my skin from the thrill of baring myself to him.

Placing my hands on my hips, I dip my fingers underneath the waistband of my panties, pulling them down to my knees and bending all the way forward so he has a full view as I step out of them.

"Get over here." River's strong arm loops around me, and he presses kisses down my spine. Each one leaves a tingling sensation in its wake as I arch into them. "You're so perfect." He mumbles as his lips reach my lower back. I gasp in response and twist in his arms.

River Beck's on his knees in front of me. Suddenly I feel shy, and my hand moves to cover myself.

"You can't put a meal in front of a starving man and then take it away." His touch is gentle as he uncovers me. "From the looks of things, you want this too." He glides a finger down my slit, when he pulls away, it's covered in my arousal.

"River." His name comes out breathless, and I twitch with anticipation.

"Say my name, just like that."

He drags his tongue along my center, tasting how much I want him. Pleasure rocks through me and my hands go to his hair to keep me grounded. He swirls his tongue around my clit, and I feel like I'm losing the ability to stand. He pushes inside of me, pumping in and out, while one of his fingers applies a rhythmic pressure.

"Oh my god" The words are a strangled mess as they fall from my mouth. He replaces his tongue with a finger from his free hand and my legs shake as he places a kiss on my inner thigh.

"I love the sounds you make." He kisses me again as he inserts another digit and I feel myself tighten around his fingers as he pumps faster and harder. My breathing has become ragged, and I lean on his shoulders for support.

"The way your body reacts to me drives me mad."

His fingers curl and hit just the right spot, lighting every nerve ending on fire as he hits it over and over again.

"River." I moan as my entire body falls apart; all my nerves are on fire as he continues to work me into oblivion. My body feels completely boneless as I fall to my knees and take his face into my hands. He kisses me and I can taste my pleasure on his lips. We break apart, and I look down to see his erection standing between us. Immediately, my body aches for more.

"I want this too." Running my hand up his length with one hand, I lean forward and place a kiss on his cheek before standing.

I guide him back toward the bed. Once he's laying down, the full size of him has me a little intimidated. The corners of his mouth tilt up as he takes the base of his shaft into one hand.

"Scared, Blue?" He asks.

"For you maybe."

I knock his hand away and wrap my fingers around him as the heat from his erection seeps into my skin. Leaning forward, I slide my tongue along the tip, and I hear his breathing deepen. My want overshadows any nerves still lingering and I take him into my mouth, swirling my tongue and making sure to wet every inch before I begin slow steady strokes. I'm careful to cover my teeth as I work him from top to bottom. His hands go to my braids, keeping them out of my face.

His head rolls back as his breathing becomes haggard.

I pick up the pace and stroke him faster, wringing my hands around his length as I take him even deeper.

"Fuck."

I smile around him as begins to pump in and out of me. My own need builds. I dip my fingers inside myself, but it's not enough. I moan and he stills. Pushing away, I look into his eyes, and they're hooded with lust.

"Let me take care of you." His eyes are on my fingers, still inside of me. Removing them, I crawl over, straddling his waist.

"Put it in." He commands, and it sends shivers down my spine. After all the time I wasted fighting him, all I want to do is obey. I lift my knees and position him at my entrance. Just the tip grazing my slit is enough to make every part of my body sing.

"Look at me while you do it."

My eyes snap to his, our desperate breathing and the sound of the sheets beneath us fill the room. Slowly I sink, spreading my legs wide as he stretches every part of me. He grinds his teeth, and my mouth opens into a small "o" shape as I realize how much of him there is. I whimper as I take every inch.

"Good girl." He moans.

His hands palm my breasts, and I lean forward capturing his mouth. All while feeling him inside me. My body's a ball of pleasure. Any place he touches comes to life. My mind is filled with too many thoughts for me to catch a steady stream of consciousness.

Lifting slightly, I feel him slide out of me just before I slam back down only for him to release a strangled gasp. I do it again and pick up the pace as I ride him, I want to see him come undone the same way I have. River isn't one to let me do all the work though. He lifts his hips to meet me stroke for stroke.

"Shit." He grabs my waist, stopping me from moving only to pound into me hard. I fall forward on his chest as he continues to grind into me. My nails drag along his chest. I feel my orgasm building as I clench around him and his fingers bite into my ass as he slams me down on top of him before he lifts me completely off and we both cum together. He uses the last of his strength to help keep me steady above him.

"I love you so much." I feel like I can't say it enough. Like I have a back order of love to give and not enough supply. I want him to understand he means so much to me.

"I'll never let you go now, Blue."

And I believe him.

"Hey, Indie. Wake up." River's standing over me, shaking my shoulder. The memories from last night come crashing into me and I jolt forward. The blanket falls, revealing my breasts and his eyes drop to watch them causing my nipples to harden. I marvel at how natural it feels to be naked in front of him. How could I ever think being with him this way would feel anything but?

"I could get used to waking up to that." He smiles like a kid on Christmas.

"What time is it?" If anyone finds us like this, it's over.

"Relax, it's still early, but you need to get ready for elimination." He tosses a small duffle bag on the bed.

"I had Ryan pack that for you last night. Initially I brought you here because all the girls passed out in your room." River's already dressed in jeans and a sweatshirt, his hair is combed back neatly and he's brushing his teeth.

"How long have you been up?" I unzip the bag and pull out the clothes hoping for something comfortable, only to be disappointed. I don't know why I expected anything else, style over comfort is Ryan's motto.

"A while, I didn't want to wake you." He smiles with toothpaste still on his lips. He returns to the bathroom, and I follow behind him with the clothes Ryan packed draped across my arm.

River rinses his mouth then turns to me. "I have to leave before people start waking up." He brushes a finger across my lips. "I want you to come home with me."

My stomach knots as I remember the rest of the world outside this room. "I have to talk to Kade."

His mouth thins, but he doesn't say anything about it. He tells me he loves me and brushes a kiss against my lips before leaving. After taking a quick shower and freshen up before sliding on the cream racerback bodysuit and high waisted burnt orange flare pants. I sigh as I add the uncomfortable heels to the ensemble before heading out. I'm the first one there, but I don't wait long before the rest of the girls exit our bedroom. Ryan clings to my side, yawning, resting her head on my shoulder.

Kade enters with Marissa and I feel nausea roll through me. I've made my choice, and I don't regret it, but Kade's friendship means a lot to me. I shouldn't have tried to ignore how I felt for River. All my attempts to catch his eye fail. If I didn't know any better, I'd say Kade was avoiding looking at me.

The camera crew finishes getting into place and Marissa fluffs her curls with her fingers. Jose adjusts our formation to accommodate for our guests and checks all our mics.

"We're ready when you are." Jose gives a thumbs up.

Marissa plasters a smile on her face and pops her hands on her hips. "Welcome back to *The Love Melt Down*. We're down to the wire here. Everyone has developed their own unique connection, but it's time for

Kade to sever one. Who'll it be?"

For once, Kade doesn't look completely emotionless. He sighs and looks hesitant.

"I'm truly sorry, Jasmine. Your time here ends today."

A gasp escapes me, and my hands cover my mouth. Jasmine blinks up at Kade as if she's unsure she heard him correctly. Cameron reaches for her hand, but Jasmine knocks it away.

"Why?" Her voice is steady as she faces him.

"There are only so many of you left. I don't believe we have enough in common to move forward." Kade slides his hands in his pockets and levels her stare with one of his own. Jasmine bites her lip and allows Kailanni to hug her.

"Jasmine—" I start.

"Indie, do your best." Jasmine looks over her friend's shoulder and smiles.

"Yeah, of course." I'm not able to look her in the eye because I plan to drop out and I should've done it last night.

"You too Cameron, and for heaven's sake, be kind to each other." Cameron replaces Kailanni, embracing Jasmine. Guilt holds me back and I don't hug her, even though I want to. Sabrina silently observes, I don't think her head's been in this since Hanna left.

One of the staff members takes Jasmine away and Marissa claps her hands before continuing, "Congratulations. Cameron, Sabrina and Indigo, you're officially in the final three. We'll be filming the finale episode in a week. Kade will go on two dates. One of you will be eliminated after the first date and the last date will end in the choosing ceremony. The cars will arrive to take your friends to the airport shortly, so make sure to say your goodbyes."

When everyone separates, I turn to Ryan. "I have to talk to Kade. I'll try to be back before you leave, I'm sorry."

"Don't worry about it. Do what you have to." She drops my hand and immediately I miss the strength her nearness gives me as I step toward Kade. Finally, his eyes meet mine, but I feel a hand land on my shoulder and I spin around to see Jose behind me.

"I need to speak with you."

"Can it wait?" I move forward, but Jose steps around me, blocking my path.

"I think you'll want to take care of this now." His eyes go to the bracelet Cameron lent me. "You shouldn't have slept with him, babe."

# Chapter Thirty-One

Jose's words knock the wind right out of me. I feel completely off balance and I'm sure I look it too.

"I'd rather handle this privately." His eyes dart around us and I swallow hard, managing a nod. We head to the front doors when Sabrina blocks our path.

"Where are you going?" She narrows her gaze.

"We have to discuss a personal matter." Jose attempts to walk around her, but she side-steps.

"Are you okay Indie?" She completely ignores Jose and focuses on me. I'm not sure what she sees when she looks at me, but her lips tighten.

"I'm fine. I'll see you when I get back." I maneuver around her with Jose trailing behind.

"There's a guest house over that way. It's a short walk. We do a lot of our editing there." He sounds chipper. I'm unsure if he's trying to ease my nerves, but it's only rattling me more.

"How did you know?" I remember the way he eyed the bracelet and my stomach drops. "Is there some kind of weird camera on this thing?"

"There's no camera, but there's audio." He doesn't look at me.

They heard everything. The moment between River and I means so much to me and it wasn't private at all. Something inside me cracks. Thinking back to when Cameron gave me this thing, I relive any other conversations I've had.

"How'd she get her hands on a recording device? We're not allowed electronics, and I doubt this was premeditated." The more I think about it, the less it makes sense. "Did you give this to her?" I wait for him to deny it. To laugh and tell me how ridiculous it is that I even asked, but he doesn't.

"It's better if we hash out the details when we get inside, babe."

Everything in me recoils at the sound of the playful nickname. "Don't call me that."

We continue in silence until the house comes into view. When we enter, the crew is walking around with phones pressed to their ears and stacks of papers. Everyone looks busy and no one seems to notice us.

"This way." He gestures for me to follow. We stop at a room at the very back and Jose steps to the side. "After you." He doesn't smile this time. I guess he's done pretending. My spine stiffens and I step inside, head held high. Noah sits in the middle of the room looking at me with his mouth twisted into a sneer.

"Let's get straight to the point. You're trying to leave, but that's not happening. You'll stay and convince Kade to choose you."

I glance around at the few others in the room to see if any additional information will be offered up, but they remain silent. "I don't understand. Why would you want that?"

He sighs as if I've asked the most asinine question he's heard. Leaning back in his seat with his legs cocked open, he swirls the amber liquid in his glass. "I was hired by Kade's team to help him succeed, regardless of whether or not he wants that. There's a lot of potential money to be made off of his back and he's too stupid to get with the program. He's all but ruined his reputation and he hasn't done a good job fixing that with his attitude on this show either." He pauses to take a drink.

"You think choosing me will help Kade?" My confusion is evident.

Noah laughs, "Sweetheart, don't think so highly of yourself."

"I'm asking Kade to cut me. I don't want to be here a second longer." I glare in Jose's direction, but he only smiles, which pisses me off.

"Allow me to show you exactly why you'll do what I'm asking you." Behind Noah are a bunch of screens mounted to the wall in neat columns. He reaches for the remote in his lap and presses a button. The first image that pops up is grainy and unsteady, clearly some kind of body camera. It takes a while for the footage to settle, but then River and I come into view. The video shows us getting into his truck and pulling off. The video cuts out and comes back outside the restaurant we had lunch at.

"We thought you were sick that day, but apparently that was a lie?" Noah asks and I don't dignify it with a response.

"You followed us." My eyes stay on Jose, searching for any sign of remorse, but there is none.

"I told you I keep an eye on all my girls." Jose shrugs and I want to punch him in the face.

Noah presses another button, and an audio clip plays. It doesn't take long for me to figure out that it's the conversation River and I had in the movie room.

"Set up some equipment in there just in case." Noah almost sounds bored as he takes another sip before cutting the audio. A new video appears and this one's clear and obviously recorded on a hidden camera based on the angle. At first, I don't recognize the room, but then Javi bursts in with Jose. Noah fast forwards until Jose leaves and I walk in next. The weight of Jose's betrayal starts to sink in. He didn't just catch me with River, he set me up.

"You told me that was the only time I could have a private conversation with him. That there'd be no cameras."

"I said a lot of things." Jose waves me off.

Noah turns up the volume, and we listen to Javi and I admit to my connection with River. "Let's not forget this little gem you gifted us."

The screen goes black but an audio plays. My moans reverberate from the speakers.

"Turn it off now." I scream at the top of my lungs. Flames fill my chest and I see nothing but red.

"Of course." Noah presses a button, shutting the audio off just as I am calling River's name. Embarrassment and shame threaten to suffocate me, but I force my tears back. A moment I never wanted to forget is tainted forever. I feel completely naked in front of them.

"Can I ask, does Kade know about last night?" Noah takes the last swig of his drink, placing the glass on the table beside him.

"Why are you doing this?" I'm so emotionally beat down.

"Money. When Kade chooses you, and they see how much he loves you it'll be a new side to him no one's seen before. We plan to release edits of all your lies either way, but at least if you do this, you'll be helping him. You were going to break his heart anyway, weren't you? People will feel bad for him. Sympathy works wonders."

"If you're going to do what you want regardless, why would I help you?"

"Do as I say, and I'll make sure the edit falls completely on you. The whore that couldn't keep her legs closed, manipulating the successful men around her to get what she wants. Won't be too far from the truth." Noah is smug. Jose and the others in the room laugh, egging him on, and I feel so small.

"Kade's got deals I won't allow to fall through. As long as the money's coming in he's not getting rid of me. River's good at what he does. This will be a blip on his record, and I'll still introduce him to my connections like I promised if you do what you're told. If not, I'll make it very hard for him to find work after this." Noah folds his hands in his lap and his eyes crawl all over me. "Society is cruel to women, I can admit that. If I get River in front of the right people, and he bides his time people will forget his part in it. I mean, how can anyone blame him for falling for your tactics? Even I can see you're beautiful."

There's no other option, I don't need to hear any more. It's either I ruin River's career or go along with what he wants. "I'll do it."

Noah claps his hands together and sits forward, "Good Girl." Noah's smile is cruel and the way he says it makes my skin crawl. "Why do you look upset? Based on what I heard, I thought you liked to be called that."

Rage and pain courses through me. "Don't you ever bring that up again." I don't even recognize the voice that comes out of me. I've never been this angry. Balling my hands into fists, I turn around and go back the way I came.

When I make it to the double doors of the mansion, my heart hammers in my ear like a drum and I furiously wipe the tears that have escaped despite my efforts. I can't go in looking how I feel. The cracks along my heart continue to fracture and the pain feels so real, I clutch my chest. I have to pull myself together and find Kade.

I want to tell him the truth because if there's anything we've been consistent about it's being upfront with each other, but I suspect that if I told him what's going on he wouldn't go along with it either. When I feel like I have a handle on my emotions, at least outwardly, I push open the door. Ryan's lounging on one of the couches with her bags at her side.

"Indie," her smile falters when she sees me. "You okay?"

Apparently, I'm not as in control as I thought. "Totally fine."

She nods, but she looks me over as if searching for any evidence of harm.

"I have to find Kade."

She stops short. Something in my eyes makes her frown. "He was looking for you. He went upstairs when I told him you still hadn't come back."

"Thanks Ry."

"No worries. I'll be here when you're done."

I pull her into my arms and squeeze tight, trying my best to soak up all the love she gives me. The walk up the stairs fills me with dread. All my messed-up emotions tumble low in my belly as I knock on Kade's door. When he opens it, he's in nothing but a towel and his curls hold droplets of water. He hardly looks at me before walking away.

Taking that as an invitation, I step inside and shut the door. Kade grabs a shirt and some sweats from the drawer, "Do you mind?" He looks pointedly at his towel.

"Oh. Sorry." I spin around. Behind me I can hear him slip into his sweats.

"You can look now."

When I turn, he's sliding his shirt over his head. "We need to talk." He's still not looking at me, "I know we have a final two deal—"

"You backing out, heartbreaker?" He asks with that familiar sly smile. Something about his demeanor reminds me of the day we met at the casting call. Before I got to know him underneath the arrogance. He finishes pushing his arms through his shirt.

"That's not what I came to say. I want to stay."

Kade's entire body stills. "Why would you want to do that?" He speaks in a measured tone.

"Because I want you to choose me."

Kade faces me and the look he gives me deals the final blow. The fractures on my heart splinter and shatter what's left. Closing my eyes, I try to force the image of anger I saw in his eyes out of my head.

"And why would you want that? You understand they'd expect us to be together."

"I want to be with you." The words burn on their way out.

"Didn't take you for a liar. Let's call this what it is." He steps toward me, reaching for a few of my braids and twisting them around his fingers.

"What do you mean?"

"You decided the money was more important. I'm not mad at it. River can give you what I can't."

I look into his eyes, and they seem so unfamiliar. "But I thought you…"

"From the beginning I said that I wasn't capable of loving you." He drops my hair. "I told you I'd have you in any form, but I gotta say the games you're playing are a bit much, even for me. I've been wracking my brain trying to figure out how to keep you and I didn't realize I just hadn't offered you enough." He laughs under his breath.

"I don't want the money." The tears are falling, and I know I look as broken as I feel. I'm having a hard time pinning down Kade's emotions.

"Aw c'mon, Indie. Crying's dirty."

"If you're closed off, why do you even want me?" I ask, shaking my head.

His jaw tenses and the muscles under his skin flex. "I didn't plan to like being around you. To look forward to our time together or laugh at the ridiculous shit you say, and I really didn't expect to trust you. How could I let that go?" He looks genuinely confused.

"But you don't love me?" I ask, trying to piece this puzzle together. He stares at me and I realize why I've felt so unsettled. Not once has

Kade ever stated that he wanted to be with me or that anything he felt was romantic. He just doesn't want to let go.

"Do you think that if we're not together that, that's it? All or nothing?" My mind jumps back to the day of the panic attack. Kade's been used for not only his money but for his body as well. He offered it to me like it was nothing, and he's doing it again. "Oh Kade…" I didn't think my heart could hurt anymore, but it continues to bleed.

"But I was wrong about you. You almost had me." His eyes darken and his voice takes on a frosty edge. "When you left I went after you. I saw you go in that room with him, and you never came back out."

Another blow to my psyche. I don't know how much more I can take. Knowing that something so special has been twisted and is causing pain to someone I care about is fucking with me right now. "I don't understand, why'd you come after me?"

He looks away and I've felt enough embarrassment today to recognize it play across his features. "I knew what you were trying to tell me that night, so I let you walk out that door, but I couldn't leave it like that. I didn't want to shut you out."

"You knew?" My voice is barely above a whisper.

"When he stood up for you against your asshole ex, I knew he was in love with you, but it's also when I noticed you looked at him the same way. I thought for sure I'd lost you, but you're not who I thought you were. You said you'd never manipulate me." He's looking at me like he doesn't know me.

"That's not what this is." My words come out choked. I'm full-on sobbing now.

"No, don't backtrack." He steps toward me, tipping my face up with his finger. "You could've told me you wanted to ride this out. Obviously me picking you will lead to opportunities. I would have done it for you, Indie. I wouldn't have said no, but you pretended you wanted me."

"I'm sorry."

"Don't be. I'll do it. I'll choose you." He drops his hand and steps back. "Oh, and you won't be seeing your boyfriend for a while, so get it out of your system. We have images to maintain. Welcome to my world, heartbreaker. I hope it's worth it." He brushes past me and opens the door. "Leave." There's no warmth in his eyes. The only giveaway to how this is affecting him is the slight tremor in his hands. In trying to protect him, I did exactly what Noah's done by trying to puppeteer the situation. Wiping my tears, I walk to his nightstand and open the drawer. Grabbing his medicine bottle, I move to stand before him as confidently as I can.

"I don't want your money. I'll reject every opportunity and do whatever else I have to, to prove that to you." I shove the bottle against his chest. "They've damaged your perception of relationships. You already had me, and you weren't going to lose me. Were friends."

"We're nothing." He takes the pills and I walk out the door feeling empty inside.

# Chapter Thirty-Two

How did I get here? I guess that's a stupid question. I've made plenty of horrible decisions that have led to this moment. Feeling so much hatred from Kade guts me, but what I have to do next will empty whatever's left.

"You okay?" Ryan's still where I left her. I don't even remember making it downstairs.

"I'm good." My smile feels fake. I should practice, my day isn't over yet.

"I'll be counting down the minutes until you come home. I don't care what happens here. Nothing changes when you get back."

The muscles in my cheeks ache with the effort of keeping up the charade. I won't be going back. River won't want me there after this. "Yeah, I can't wait."

Ryan's phone pings. "Looks like my ride's here. I love you, Indie." She gathers me in a hug before rolling her bags out the door.

The sound of footsteps makes me look up and River's with Cameron, a camera crew shadowing them. Taking a seat, I sit back and watch as he flits through his questions. Cameron seems excited to talk about how

she feels to still be here and my blood boils at the sight of her. River's eyes meet mine and I'm too much of a coward to hold his gaze. They're dangling everything he's worked for in front of me. I've been selfish and karma's come to collect.

It's been the longest day and the sun's starting to set by the time he finishes. I give a pathetic wave to grab his attention. When I have it, I nod my head toward the back garden and do my best not to garner any attention as I make my way over. He doesn't make me wait for long. As he enters, he closes the door quietly behind him. He takes my face into his hands and his kisses are like a sweet caress. I miss his warmth when he pulls away.

"I'll never tire of doing that." He gives me a boyish grin. "Since we're down to the final three, most of the crew's gone for the day. I have something I want to show you." He drags me behind him toward the back of the property.

"We need to talk." I dig my feet in, attempting to slow his pace, but he forges forward.

"We'll do plenty of that. Talking to you is one of my favorite things."

Giving up, I let him pull me along. One last moment before the end is all I can ask for, so I do my best to push what I have to do to the back of my mind. "Where are we going?"

He looks over his shoulder and gives me a brief smile. "Do you know how far back this land goes?"

"Should I?"

"I guess not, but I had to stay late one night, and I did some exploring. Found something I want to show you." Of course he did. River would live outside if he could.

"You're not going to get us lost again, right? It would be kind of embarrassing to call for help."

His shoulders shake as a laugh rolls through him. When we were little, River took me exploring and at some point, lost track of where we were. Instead of telling me we were lost, he confidently kept going saying, *"We're almost there."* Until we finally made it back home well after curfew.

"We got in a lot of trouble that night." He murmurs.

"You cried as soon as our moms answered the door."

"I thought we'd never find our way back." He laughs and a real smile spreads across my face.

"Why didn't you say you were lost?"

He's quiet for a moment before answering. "You were always a little afraid to be so far out, but I made you come anyway. Add in the fact that you're afraid of the dark and I didn't want to frighten you." He pauses and looks over his shoulder. "If I'm being totally honest. There was a part of me that was embarrassed and didn't want to look like I couldn't take care of you." He turns away, breaking eye contact as the terrain becomes uneven.

"We were kids Riv. I never expected you to take care of me."

He shrugs, "You cried when we first met, and I remember thinking I only wanted to see you smile. It stuck with me."

My heart stutters and I feel the familiar flutter in my belly, but guilt twists in my chest. We're losing light and the shade from the trees makes it difficult to see. I lose my footing, slamming into his back and he twists, steadying me. "Watch your step."

"Isn't your warning a little late?" I breathe.

The corners of his mouth turn up and his large hand captures mine. "Try to follow my footsteps. We're almost there."

I can't help the laugh that escapes me. "Are we? Or is that code for 'we're lost and I should alert the search party'?"

"Ha, ha. We're really almost there."

The trees have thickened, and we're headed up an incline. The mansion's built up a hill and the walk has me winded. When the ground finally begins to level out we come to a stop.

"Okay, close your eyes."

"What?"

"Come on, indulge me."

I do as he says and cover my eyes. His soft steps come from behind and his hands find my waist as he guides me forward.

"I won't let you fall." His breath is warm against my neck and sends goosebumps crawling up my skin. We walk for a short while longer before coming to a stop.

"Open your eyes." He whispers into my ear, and I drop my hands smiling at his theatrics.

Laid out before me is a plush blanket, containers of fruit, muffins, cookies and juice. My eyes jump from the display to River, and he scratches the back of his neck while keeping his eyes on the floor.

"You can't leave yet, so I thought we could spend the night together." His brown curls slide through his fingers as he runs his hands through them. A nervous tick he's never fixed. My smile falters as I look from him to the picnic.

"River… you didn't have to."

"I wanted to."

"They'll notice that I'm gone."

"No one noticed we were missing last night."

Ah. I shouldn't have let him bring me here. "Two nights in a row is pushing it."

"You worried about production or Kade?" His tone has a bite to it.

"Both."

The muscles in his jaw tighten as he considers my words. "You're right. I'm sorry for pushing. I'm so damn ready to have you home." He closes the distance between us and brings my hand to his lips and I do my best to memorize what it's like to have him touch me.

"I'm not going back with you." I manage to keep my voice even. His brows knit together, and he cocks his head to the side. "I talked with Kade, and after discussing how we felt—I'll be staying." I swallow and do him the decency of looking him in the eye. He looks as though I've grown a second head. I can see his mind trying to process my words.

"What're you talking about?"

"What I have with Kade. It means more than I thought it did." More lies, Javi would be proud. Kade's right, I'm a manipulative piece of crap.

"Why are you doing this?" I have never seen River look at me the way he is right now. His eyes search mine for any answer other than the one I'm able to give. If I tell him the truth, he'd want me to leave and let Noah blackball him after all his hard work.

"We've had too long to get this right." The words feel like poison on my tongue.

"You're choosing him over me?" The weight of the emotion in his voice makes me flinch and I turn away. "No. You're woman enough to do this, then you're woman enough to say it out loud." He cups my face in his hands and I'm forced to face him. There's nothing but skepticism staring back at me. He doesn't believe a word I'm saying. "Now, Indigo."

I dig my nails into my arm to gain control, I can't do this halfway. "I want Kade. He makes me happy. Let's go back to how things were."

His hands fall away, and he shakes his head. "What's going on? You told me you loved me last night."

"I shouldn't have said that, and we shouldn't have done what we did. You told me if I wanted you to stop, that if I decided I didn't want you, you'd walk away." I lift my chin and ignore the urge to scream that I'm lying and that I take everything back. "I'm asking you to do that for the sake of our friendship." I might as well have carved his heart out myself. I can see how I feel inside, reflected on his face. He stumbles back a step, and it feels like a punch in the gut.

"You said you loved me this morning."

"I do love you. I've always loved you. Just not in the way that you want." My voice feels disembodied. Like someone else has taken control, and I'm a spectator.

"We belong together, and you know that. What makes you think I could hold you and ever walk away? Whatever's gotten into you, I'm going to figure it out."

"Figure it out without me, River. Give me space."

He looks like he wants to argue, or drag me out of here and if he acted on that urge I don't know if I'd be able to keep pretending. But he doesn't. He gives me a small nod and heads back down the incline without another glance in my direction.

When I'm certain he's long gone, I fall to my knees and allow myself to feel all of it. The pain washes over me and I allow it to wrap around my throat as I gasp for air. Tears blur my vision, but it still doesn't block the image of River's face as I threw those lies between us.

Eventually my tears dry up. It's completely dark by the time I make my way down. When I finally come close enough to the mansion, I can see Sabrina sitting on one of the benches with a blanket folded across her lap. She jumps to her feet when she sees me, throwing the blanket over my shoulders.

"Why are you out here?" My throat feels raw from crying.

"River sent me."

The sound of his name breaks something inside of me, and the tears start falling again.

Sabrina wraps her arms around me, patting my back gently.

"What's going on? First River has me sitting out here for an hour on the pretense that you'll need me, and then you come crawling out of the woods looking like hell." She pushes me away gently to get a good look at my face. "Indie, tell me what's happened."

"I can't."

"I'm not mic'd. Tell me what's going on."

I run my hands through my braids and pace back and forth trying to get my thoughts in order. I did it. I pushed him away.

My breathing becomes erratic and I'm not sure when Sabrina got in front of me, but she shakes my shoulders roughly. "Get a grip. You're freaking me out."

"I. Can't. Tell. You." I spit the words out. I know I'm directing my anger in the wrong place, but I have nowhere else to put it.

"Fine. You can't tell me. Does it have something to do with Jose pulling you earlier?"

I glare at her and she shoots one back and we stay like that, locked in a stalemate. Finally, she gives in, pinching the bridge of her nose.

"We can revisit this later. I may not be the easiest person to talk to but when you're ready, come to me. For some reason you can't talk to River, so I'll stand in. Just do me a favor and take it easy on him. He didn't look good either. Let's get you back to your room."

The mention of my room reminds me that Cameron is there and my mind goes to a dark place. "I can't sleep there."

"You can stay with me. That way if you get the urge to clue me in on what's going on you won't have to go far." She doesn't give me a chance to respond, she pushes me inside and when we make it to my room, it's empty. Maybe Cameron had the same idea. Sabrina leans against the doorway as I pack my things. I throw my bag over my shoulder and pause as I look down at my wrist. I'm still wearing the bracelet. I'd completely forgotten about it, but I guess it doesn't matter at this point.

The metal's cool against my skin. I hesitate for just a moment before unclasping it from my wrist.

"Hey, you alright?" Sabrina eyes the bracelet with disdain.

"Can you give this back to Cameron?" I hand it to her, and she pinches it between her fingers as if it bites. If only she knew.

# Chapter Thirty-Three

T ime is my biggest enemy right now. It crawls at a snail's pace and eats away at my sanity. I want out of this house, but the truth is I'm not sure if things will be much better when I leave. I've spent the last couple of days holed up in my room. Aside from a few extremely awkward forced conversations I've filmed with Kade, I've lived beneath my blankets.

"Alright, it's time to get up. I'm over it." Sabrina rips them off of me. "I mean this in the rudest way possible, so please take offense, but you need to shower. When I said you could stay with me, I didn't think I was inviting the swamp monster.

"Leave me alone, Sabrina." I reach for the blankets, but she snatches them.

"My room, my rules. I want you clean."

"I'm tired."

"Fine, River can deal with you."

My eyes pop open, and I sit up. "You're pushy, you know that?"

She shrugs. "It gets me what I want. I'm getting us food while you shower."

Final interviews are today, and Kade's true to his word. He's not letting me off easy. Everything he says to me bites and leaves its mark, but it's nothing compared to the expression River wears anytime he sees me. I catch my reflection in the mirror before hopping in the shower, and I can see why Sabrina was so stubborn. I've been wearing the same sweatshirt to bed since everything happened and it's gotten a few stains. My eyes have bags, a few small stress zits have appeared, and my braids have run their course. I look as defeated as I've felt. The water from the shower feels good against my skin, I can feel my worries roll down my back and my mind clears. I made my decision and it's time to face the consequences.

"Wow, clean looks good on you." Sabrina's picking at a muffin when I step out of the shower.

"You want to help me unbraid my hair?" Ignoring her jab, I pick a grape off her plate.

"I guess I can spare the time."

Shuffling through my hair supplies, I set all the necessities out. After eating, Sabrina sits on my bed, and I take a seat on the floor between her legs. I've learned a lot about her in the last couple of days and she's surprisingly very nurturing. Even though I haven't left the room unless required, she's made sure I haven't missed a meal. When I do have to leave, she finds a reason to need River and pulls him in the opposite direction. Even though I haven't told her about Jose, she takes a dig at him any chance she gets on my behalf.

We finally unravel the last braid, and she falls back onto the bed. "That was a job. I should've charged you."

"Thank you for your service." I pat her thigh as I get up.

"We have a little over an hour before we have to be downstairs. Get dressed." She demands. Tonight, the dress code is formal, so I go with a wine colored off the shoulder dress with a tulle skirt that starts short at the front, showcasing my legs and gets longer toward the back. I've twisted my hair into bantu knots and tamed my baby hairs into soft waves that frame my face. The girl looking back at me is strong, bold and wouldn't take any of the things I've let slide. I know I have that in me, but it's been so damn hard lately. I'm pretty sure Cameron's avoiding me. If I were her, I'd avoid me too.

"We need you downstairs." The sound of River's voice startles me, and my mic slips through my fingers. I pick it up and get it clipped on and when I open the door River's still standing there. His eyes widen when he gets a look at me. My heart still hasn't learned not to react at the sight of him. I don't think it ever will.

He doesn't say anything, and I can't bring myself to either, so I walk past him, and the sound of his footsteps lets me know he's following. We make it to the foyer and the room has been completely redone. They changed the seating and decor to look homier, like a living room set up. Lights and cameras all point toward a couch and angled beside it is a loveseat where Marissa sits shuffling through her cue cards.

"You ready?" Kade's beside me, offering his hand. I can feel River watching so I straighten my spine because we must be believable.

"As long as you're with me." I place my hand in his and we take a seat in front of the cameras.

"You two good to go?" Marissa smiles. "The questions are straightforward, so this should be painless."

River speaks into his mic before grabbing our attention. "Try your best to ignore the cameras and keep your eyes on Marissa when talking." Apparently he's going to stand front and center for the entire thing.

Great.

"Welcome back to *The Love Melt Down*. Things are certainly heating up. We're down to the final three and I have Indigo here, who seems to have fallen head over heels for our bachelor. Did you think you'd make it this far?"

Kade gives my thigh a squeeze and I welcome the comfort. I know this is all an act for him and he's still pissed, but the small gesture gives me courage. "No, there were so many beautiful women here, I wasn't sure I'd be able to get his attention."

Marissa laughs, "Oh stop, as if you don't know how gorgeous you are. Being on the show is intense. People don't understand how quickly feelings grow because it's not a normal environment. Right now, at this moment, how do you feel about Kade?"

My eyes involuntarily flick toward River. His expression is unreadable.

"Indigo?" Marissa brings my attention back to her.

I lean against Kade's chest and place my hand over his. "Is it too early to say the L word?" I smile and I know it looks real because I've practiced it. It wouldn't look good for River to be around me once this is over, so I need him to want anything but that.

Marissa giggles into her hands and shakes her head. "If you know, you know. I don't think you can put a time stamp on it. Then it's safe to say you can see a future with Kade?"

I turn to him, and he eyes me warily. I want him to know that despite everything, he does mean a lot to me. "I'd be lucky to have Kade in my life no matter the circumstances. Meeting him is one of the best things to come out of this experience." I turn back to Marissa and she has her hand over her heart. "It doesn't matter how this ends. I won't regret it." And I mean that. I'm okay taking the brunt of the backlash because Kade's been through enough.

Marissa looks to Kade. "How does it feel to hear that?"

"Like I've got a tough decision to make."

"Are you saying that you have no idea who you're choosing?" She asks with wide eyes.

"I'm saying there's a lot to consider." He folds his arms over his chest and the look he gives Marissa clearly screams "back off."

Her eyes bounce from Kade to me. "Your ex, Javi, said some concerning things about your motivation to be with Kade since he has a promising career. Do you think he has a right to be weary?"

It's not like I didn't expect some questions to be messy, I just didn't expect to have to discuss Javi. I may not forgive him, but he did me a favor and I want to move past it. "We all guard our hearts for a variety of reasons. Kade's not the only one with something on the line here. If you're asking if I want anything from Kade other than the connection we've fostered, then the answers is no."

The sound of someone scoffing makes me turn and I see Jose behind the cameras. He's looking down his nose at me. The sight of him causes my hands to shake, but Kade places a hand on my knee and my body relaxes.

"Bear it for a bit longer," he breathes low enough, so that only I can hear. I blink up at him, but he keeps his eyes on Marissa. That's the first slightly non-pissed thing he has said to me in a while.

"While we're discussing trust, Kade's work makes it so he may not be home often. Eyes tend to wander in situations like that. Is this something you guys have discussed?"

Ah. I'm going to look like such a liar once the edits drop. These questions are clearly targeted. Marissa's handing me the shovel so I can dig my own grave. I straighten in my seat and lift my chin. "If he chooses me then there is no one else. My understanding is that you're well versed in infidelity, if your recent divorce is any indication. Maybe you can speak to the matter more eloquently than I could?" I'm grateful Gabby gifted me with that nugget of information. Marissa drops the act and looks like I've slapped her with the way her mouth hangs open. I'm ready for this to end and Kade mercifully takes over.

"I'm not concerned. Indigo hasn't given me a reason not to trust her." He looks at me and smiles and it looks just as practiced as mine.

Marissa recovers and places her cue cards in her lap. "That's all I have for you two. In-depth interviews will happen one on one with each of you after the finale. Kade hang tight. We're bringing Sabrina in next." Marissa says while flippantly calling Drew over to touch up her makeup.

Grateful that it's over, I unclip my mic and hop off the couch, eager to get out of the spotlight. River blocks my path before I can escape.

"You didn't mean any of that." His voice is strained, and his eyes travel across my face. No one seems to be paying attention to us, but I point toward his mic.

"You think I care if they hear me? I don't give a damn about this job." River's voice echoes in the space between us. No one was looking before, but they are now. Jose speaks into his headset and signals for the nearby cameras to swing in our direction. This conversation needs to end. Now.

"If he chooses me, I'll be moving in with him. I love him."

I'm too much of a coward to look River in the eye, so I push past him and he doesn't stop me this time. When I look up, Sabrina's there, clearly close enough to have caught our conversation. Her expression is sad and she shakes her head at me before heading toward Marissa. I move to the opposite side of the room and wrap my arms around myself. We're supposed to have a group interview, so I can't hide away yet.

Sabrina sits stoically and doesn't play into Marissa's cheery demeanor. Her answers are short, and she doesn't give Marissa much to work with. Kade attempts to make up for her lack of enthusiasm by laying on the charm, but it just highlights Sabrina's disinterest.

"How do you feel about Kade?" Marissa tries again to pull her into the conversation.

Sabrina laughs. It's the first real emotion she's shown. "You know what? I don't love you, and you know that." She gives Kade an incredulous look before turning back to Marissa. "I don't know why I'm still here. The person I wanted already left." She leans forward and looks directly into the camera.

"Hanna, by the time this airs I hope we're together. I hope we get to see the moment I realized how stupid I've been. I'm coming for you because if I've learned anything being here, it's that you shouldn't let go of someone you can't imagine yourself without." Sabrina shoots me a pointed look. "It'd be a mistake to lose someone like that over this." She waves her hands around her head and stands.

"What do you think you're doing?" Noah stomps forward, but she ignores him and removes her mic. "I didn't say you could leave." He points his finger in her face and she breezes past him.

"You're breaking contract, you'll be fined."

"I can afford it." She tosses over her shoulder.

I run to catch up with her and Noah's still on a rampage behind us. The crew tries to calm him down and a few make sure the cameras swing to catch Sabrina stomping away. We make it to our room and she drops to her knees, dragging her suitcase from under her bed.

"What are you doing? What about your family?" I move into the room and start helping her round up all her scattered items.

She throws a pair of heels into her bag and looks at me wide-eyed, with her mouth hanging open.

"What am I doing? What are *you* doing?" She gets up and snatches what I've gathered out of my hands. "Watching you piss all over a good thing made me realize I don't want to make the same mistake."

My hands drop to my sides, and I shake my head. "You don't know what you're talking about."

"River would do anything for you. You're making all the decisions on your own when you don't have to. I don't know what they have on you, but you're making the wrong choice." Sabrina slams her suitcase shut and zips it closed. "Hit me up when you come to your senses. I don't like how you're handling this, but I guess I consider you a friend, so I still care." She surprises me by pulling me into a hug. It's brief and to the point, which is just like her. "See you later Indie." She rolls her bag out of the room and shuts the door behind her.

Her parting words burn. I'm not sure if I'm making the right decision, but it's the one that does the least amount of damage.

# Chapter Thirty-Four

The days following Sabrina's departure are especially lonely. River has finally given up on me. I haven't seen him since our last conversation. It's what I wanted, but it hurts more than I could've imagined. He may say he doesn't care about this job, but that's a lie. He took it hoping it would lead him to something bigger.

We have a photo shoot this morning and lunch this afternoon before the choosing ceremony and I've decided to let the makeup team take care of me today. Before coming, I washed and moisturized my face and undid my bantu knots so my hair sits in perfect spirals around my face.

"Thought I'd never get you in my chair." Drew spins my seat to face the mirror.

"I couldn't leave without getting to experience your work." I close my eyes as she preps my skin with her perfumy creams. Really, I'm just so done with everything. I didn't have it in me to do my own.

"I've had the same thoughts about you. Kade was right. You're talented. I screamed when I saw the look you did for your interview the other day, but you had me gagging when you gathered Marissa

together. I hope they air that." She laughs as she dips her brush into an eye shadow pallet. "She's the worst, never satisfied." She dabs the color on my lids, and the corners of my lips quirk up. It's the closest I've come to smiling. Drew reads my mood and turns on some R&B music to fill the silence while she continues to work. This is the last day and instead of feeling relief I feel... I don't know how I feel, but my stomach's constantly nauseous and I've got this feeling of dread I can't shake.

"Close your eyes for me." Drew interrupts my thoughts. I do as she says, and she applies a mist of setting spray. "What do you think?" She stands back and I look myself over.

Production chose a sleeveless velvet royal blue mermaid dress with matching opera gloves. I don't wear blue often because part of me always felt it was corny because of my name. However, the dress is stunning. It shows off my hourglass shape and enough cleavage to remain tasteful. Drew matched the color perfectly with my eyeshadow, adding it to my lids and beneath my lower lash line. Silver sits on the inner corners of my eyes and dances along my cheeks in the light. My cheek bones are made prominent by her masterful contour and my lips are a glossy pink nude color.

"It's beautiful. Thank you so much."

"Girl, let me snag a pic to post on my page and we're even."

I give her my permission and she takes a few videos and photos. When she's content I move to leave, but she stops me. "Listen, I don't normally do this. I don't like to mix my business, but you're good and I like you." She shrugs while smiling. "If you're looking for work when this is over, I could use another assistant for the next couple of projects I'm working on."

It takes me a moment to absorb what she's offering me. I blink at her and she laughs. "I mean, if you're not interested..." She waves me off playfully.

"It's not that I—"

"Take it."

We both turn at the sound of Kade's voice. He stands in the doorway, adjusting the buttons on the cuff of his shirt. He's breathtakingly handsome. Curls pulled back, suit tailored to show off every muscle and eyes dark and cold when they connect with mine. He walks over to me and twists one of my curls around his finger. "You've worked hard. You more than deserve it." The corners of his lips tilt up, but I wouldn't classify it as a smile.

Drew gently takes my wrist and places the card in my hand. "Call me if you're interested."

"They're ready for us." He takes my hand before I can respond to Drew. As soon as we leave the room, he lets me go.

I move to his side and look at the card in my hand. "I wasn't going to take it."

"Why not?"

"I'm not doing this to gain anything from being around you."

He stops and for a moment and looks at me like I'm a puzzle he's trying to put together, but then Cameron approaches and he shuts back down.

"Kade," she beams up at him with open arms and they wrap around each other, "You look good." She says with a lustful look in her eyes as she looks him up and down. Since when are they so close? He's never been rude to Cameron, but he's never seemed that interested either. She finally notices me and a look of fear flashes across her face before she can hide it. She's kept her distance, and this is the closest we have come together.

"Cameron." Giving her one of my practiced smiles, I nod. She's thrown off by the greeting and looks to Kade for reassurance. Oh please, if I wanted to hurt her, he wouldn't be able to stop me. "You look… nice." I let out a small laugh just to fuck with her. But in all honesty, someone in wardrobe must hate her. The dress is a hideous shade of green that clashes with the red in her locs.

She smiles back at me. "Jose's been real busy lately. He's been short staffed since that one guy… what was his name? The producer you were always hanging around?" She tilts her head to feign confusion.

I'm not usually a violent person, but every time I see her, that's all I want to be. Memories of Noah playing the audio and knowing she played a part in their plan sets me on fire. I step toward her and she glances at Kade. "I've let you slide—"

"Indigo." Kade steps in front of her. "Why don't you stay here and cool off?" We stare at each other and when he's sure I won't try anything, he takes Cameron's hand and walks away. Even though I know he's angry with me, it hurts that he's on her side. Taking a deep breath, I give my head a shake and head downstairs to get this photoshoot over with.

The photoshoot was awkward, but Kade was professional. If you look at the pictures, you'd think he was in love with me while I look… constipated at best. Now, they've dragged us to this restaurant for brunch, but no one bothered to tell me Kade's parents would be here. Immediately, my stomach begins churning. Even with the lies I have to continue to spin, I'm happy Kade gets to see them. They seem to mean a lot to him.

We sit at the table as he smiles wider than I've ever seen while listening to his mom, Catherine, speak. She's an older woman with golden brown skin and beautiful grey hair styled into big movie star waves. Her lips are painted ruby red, and she carries herself with a level of elegance I can only hope to achieve one day.

Kade's father, Hiro, sits beside her. He's more reserved. I see Kade in him, or rather, I see him in Kade. They both have the same strong jaw and broad shoulders. His skin is a few shades lighter than Kade's and he's classically handsome with a salt and pepper beard.

His parents are kind, they clearly dote on their son and are content mostly focusing their attention on him. I'm seated next to Kade and do my best to keep my head down, pushing my steak and eggs around my plate.

"Indie, please eat," he whispers, but I ignore him. Kade's unbothered by my indifference. He takes my plate and begins cutting into my meat while maintaining conversation. Without missing a beat, he stabs into one sliver of steak and offers it to me.

"Are you trying to feed me?" I ask, unable to keep the dismay out of my voice. Finally, he turns away from his mother and leans in close.

"You're the one that wanted to do this," he whispers. I let out a frustrated breath before I give in and take his offering. My cheeks burn when I notice his mother smiling from ear to ear as she watches our exchange.

"So, Indigo, out of curiosity, what is your timeline for marriage and when do you plan on having kids?" Catherine asks, and I choke on my food. Kade slaps my back and the corner of his lips twitch.

"Um, I'm not sure. I guess it depends. Kade has plans for his career and I fully support that. I have my own plans as well." I dab my lips with my napkin.

"But you do want that? Marriage and kids, I mean. Neither of you are getting any younger." She clucks her tongue.

"Mom, please." Kade complains, but there's no real fight behind his words.

"Oh hush. I'm just asking her where her head is at." She turns to face Cameron. "What about you?"

"I can't wait to get married. I want a big family, so kids would definitely be in our future."

"Hey everyone, how was the meal?" Marissa saunters over. The production company rented out the entire restaurant, so we're the only ones here.

"I thought it was delicious, and we had great company." Kade's mother smiles brightly.

"I'm so glad. I wish we could give you more time to get to know the ladies, but I think Kade needs some alone time to help him make the next decision. If you'll come with me, I'll make sure you guys have some privacy."

"It was nice meeting you both." Catherine's smile is genuine. Hiro's a man of few words, but he nods as if he agrees before Kade and his parents follow behind Marissa.

I'm left alone with Cameron and I'm not letting this moment pass. "So, does it feel good? Doing what you did to me?" I move seats to sit directly across from her.

"I don't know what you're talking about."

"You set me up."

"If you weren't breaking any rules, then you wouldn't have any issues. Don't blame me for your problems."

"Do you think doing this makes him want you? It's pathetic that you'd be so desperate."

That gets a reaction out of her. Her eyes snap to mine and her face twists into an ugly sneer.

"You think everyone's worried about every little thing you do? News flash. You're not that important." She slams her hands on the table, causing the dishes to rattle. The camera crew is zooming in, catching every word. Doesn't matter now, they already have everything they need on me.

"I'm important to you. You're my biggest fan. Taking me down doesn't make you better than me. It just makes you a loser."

"Better a loser than a whore."

I release a slow breath, and my fingers curl into fists. "You pretended to want to get close to me, and for what? I felt bad for you, and I still do. Find peace."

"Paint me to be the bad guy all you want, and maybe I am, but don't you for a second think your hands are clean. You're not stupid, but you like to pretend you are. Kade wasn't enough, so you had to sleep around with the crew. Figure out your own drama before you come to me." Her skin is flush with anger. The truth of her words sear my heart.

"You're right. I'm selfish. I was taken advantage of and I decided to put myself first. I won't let anyone make me feel bad about that. So, while you may be obsessed enough with me to make me the villain in your story, you didn't even exist in mine. Get a fucking life. I hope you know I won't stay quiet about your part in this. We'll let the public decide who's the bad guy."

Her mouth falls open, and her eyes dart to the cameras.

"Did you think Jose and Noah would protect you? You let yourself be used. You came here to show off your accomplishments and it'll be overshadowed by this petty rivalry. The most pathetic part of it all is we both did exactly what they wanted."

Cameron's eyes glisten and she chews on her bottom lip as we both fall into silence. Marissa returns and informs us we're going to meet Kade at the choosing ceremony. Cameron jumps out of her seat as if she can't get away from me fast enough. The silence during the ride back is stifling.

I think about every moment since I stepped out of that limo on premiere night. Are there things I'd do differently? If I knew what I know now, then without a doubt I would. I was too wrapped up in my own wants and needs to see what was in front of me.

When we arrive back at the mansion, an assistant directs us to stand side-by-side at the bottom of the steps. This is where it all began. I was nervous about what might be, and now I fear what is to come. Kade stands beside Marissa, looking down at us. He rolls his shoulders and looks like he's counting down the seconds until this is over. Marissa whispers something beside him, but she might as well be talking to a wall. Kade doesn't acknowledge her at all.

Jose signals a thumbs up from behind the camera and Marissa brightens. She places a hand on Kade's shoulder. "It's time for you to decide. Who will it be?" Marissa's gaze glides over us. The crew is completely silent, and I feel the pressure building in my chest.

"I thought this decision might be difficult. That I might feel torn, or undecided, but I don't." He pauses and his eyes are on me.

"I choose neither of them."

Marissa gasps.

"What the hell are you doing?" Noah stomps over.

"If you'd chosen quality women, this wouldn't have happened. You're pissed, but you've wasted my time with this subpar group." He looks back at Cameron and me. "It was never going to be either of you." Kade steps past a still yelling Noah and stops in front of me. "I told you from the beginning not to trust me. You let money blind you. It doesn't matter how much you're struggling; you should have some dignity."

I'm completely lost. I knew Kade was angry with me, but he looks like he hates me. "Why are you doing this?"

"Let me ask you a question. How much would I have had to offer you to get you to sleep with me?"

My hand connects with his face before I can even register what I'm doing. The slap is loud and hard enough to hurt. He unclips his mic and lets it fall to his feet. "Did you think I would want to chain myself to a liar? That I'd let you use me?"

"This isn't you." My voice trembles and the corners of his lips tick up.

"I told you who I was. You're the one that created a side of me that never existed." He slides his hands in his pockets and brushes past me.

"You get back here, or you're done. I'll make sure of it," Noah screams at the top of his lungs.

"Kade!" His name rips through my throat, and he pauses before looking over his shoulder.

"There's no way everything you told me was a lie. I hope one day you allow yourself to be more than what they've turned you into." I rip off my mic and turn my back on him. I've had enough betrayals to last me a lifetime.

# Chapter Thirty-Five

hen Noah finally came to terms with the fact that Kade wasn't returning, we were dismissed to start release paperwork. Waiting for all of it to be drawn up and filling it out took hours. "Here," one of the staff members hands me my phone. "Sign this last page and you're good to go." He slides the document toward me.

I do as he says and pass it back. Pulling my suitcase behind me, I walk out the mansion doors for the last time. Sitting on the steps, I watch the sun as it sets. With everything that happened, I forgot that I'm practically homeless. Taking a deep breath, I unlock my phone and pull up my contacts. I call my mom and put it on speaker so I can bring up my browser while the ringer trills.

"Hey baby, is it finally over?" My mom's voice relaxes me. Even though I know she will have her own opinions about everything, she's one of the few people that don't hate me right now.

"Yeah, it's over. I'm going to be flying in. Can you pick me up from the airport?" I bring up the next available flight and it's nearly four hundred dollars for a ticket.

"Will River be with you?"

Hearing his name makes me feel incredibly empty inside. I swallow hard and clear my throat. "No mom, just me." My bank app finally loads, and my eyes stretch wide. "Dammit, Kade." I breathe.

"What honey?"

"Nothing." I refresh the page to make sure it's not a glitch, but the same number pops up when it reloads. He was paying me way more than we agreed. I'm not sure I'll ever understand him.

"Why isn't River coming? Tiffany will be disappointed."

"I need to get away, no questions asked. Can we do that, mom?"

She goes silent and my stomach twists. I'm barely keeping it together. I need her to drop it.

"We don't have to talk about it. Come stay as long as you need."

"When I tell you, just know I already understand I made mistakes, so—"

"Indie, I don't care that you make mistakes. Our last talk didn't go how I wanted, and you didn't even call me before you left. It made me realize I might be projecting a little." She laughs softly. "Sometimes I see you making mistakes I made, and I try to stop it before it happens when I need to let you learn. No matter what's going on, I'll be there to listen."

I don't realize I'm crying until I feel the tears falling.

"Thank you. I'm excited to go home." I'm unable to say more than that or I'll break down on these steps.

"I look forward to it baby. I'll see you tonight."

The line goes dead and I book my flight, order my car and put my phone on DND. Teasers of the show have already dropped, and my notifications have been going off nonstop.

I pull my knees to my chest and drop my head between my knees. It's hard to stop my thoughts from drifting to dark places when I have nothing to focus on. I'll have to figure out how to get my things from River's place. I'll have to call Ryan and explain how badly I messed up too. My chest feels like it's caving in, and my eyes burn. Acting normal on the phone took a lot out of me, and thinking of tying up all my loose ends is overwhelming.

"Here."

Cameron stands with her arm stretched toward me, a tissue in her hand. I turn away from her and check my phone for an update on my ride.

She sighs and sits next to me. "Take it." She nudges my shoulder.

What evil can she do with a tissue? I accept it and wipe at my nose.

"You were right. He never cared about me. Hell, I'm not even sure he liked me. He made me think..." She pauses and turns to face me. "I thought I was helping him. I truly liked Kade Indigo, so when Jose told me about you, I just didn't want him to get hurt. However, I didn't relish doing it. Kade knew, you know? He came to me wanting to rehash the details. He said he wanted to be sure there were no loose ends."

"Are you saying he knew about what you did? About what Noah and Jose planned?"

"He didn't seem surprised by anything I told him." She frowns at the memory. "Anyway, I don't expect you to forgive me, but I wanted to tell you anyway."

"Do you think we have some type of camaraderie now? You say Kade knew, so what were you guys doing? Laughing at me behind my back? He didn't choose you, so you think we have something in common?" The laugh that comes out of me is a little crazed and she looks taken aback.

"I know it's hard for you to believe, but we didn't spend our time talking about you. He asked me how I did it and after I told him, that was it. We didn't discuss you again."

Nothing she's saying makes any sense. It's like I never knew Kade. But even as I think it, I know that's not true. There is no way everything we shared was fake, which is why what he did at the finale took me by surprise.

"Here I am, trying to make you feel better and you bite my head off." She huffs.

My phone chimes, alerting me that the car's pulling up soon. "Fuck you, Cameron. Hope to never see you again. Everything you said about me, you meant, so stand on that. No need to be fake about it now." Pulling the handle on my suitcase, I start down the steps.

"I overheard your call. Running away will only make it worse."

"You've invaded my privacy enough, Cameron."

A sleek black car pulls into the driveway. I throw my bag in the trunk and then hop in the back seat. The man driving looks at me through his mirror. "Headed to the airport, huh? Going on vacation?"

"Not exactly." Closing my eyes, I lean back in my seat, hoping he'll take the hint. The driver gives me the small mercy of silence for the remainder of the trip. It's a quick ride to the airport. I feel nausea as I stand in front of the doors. I tug at my sweatshirt and give my head a shake as I step inside.

Checking my bag is easy enough. Going through security is the stressful part. They shout, and people stumble about in confusion as we're directed into differing lines. When I make it to my gate, I'm left with nothing but my thoughts to occupy me. After almost two hours of trying to read a book and failing, I pull my phone out of my pocket and swipe up on the screen. I've got multiple notifications from Ryan. Biting my lip, I dismiss them and open my camera roll.

I scroll through my photos and come across the pictures we took at the beach. In one, I'm wrapped in River's arms and he's smiling against my hair. In the next photo, River, Ryan and I have on her pastel colored wigs and we're all making silly faces. A small laugh escapes me as I run a finger along the screen. This day seems so long ago. Swiping again reveals a video Ryan must've taken after I passed out. River has me hoisted on his back and Ryan must be walking backward because the video's pointed at us and the footage bounces with each of her steps.

*"Why are you recording?" River asks and squints at the flash beaming from my phone. My arms are wrapped limply around his neck, and my head lolls to the side.*

*"Because tonight was a great night little bro. Why wouldn't we want to remember it?" Ryan's voice floats from behind the camera.*

*"The night's over." River grunts and adjusts my weight as he walks.*

*"That it is, and you didn't make a move." Ryan throws back. "I'll be traveling for work soon and I'm worried you're not going to make progress."*

*"It's not the right time."*

*"When will it be? Are you going to be okay if she starts dating again? I won't be here to hold your hand through it." They both stop walking and River's jaw clenches.*

*"You need to tell her." She lets her hands fall to her side and the camera angles toward the ground so that we're out of frame.*

*"She just got out of a relationship; I'm not going to prey on her emotions." The camera's still pointed at the ground, but I hear their footsteps start back up.*

*"Aren't you afraid you'll lose her?" She points the camera at his back.*

*"No. I'll never lose her. I never let her go to begin with."*

*"She should know that you like her."*

*River laughs and looks over his shoulder. "Like her? I'm in love with her, Ry."*

*"Then how can you stand this?"*

*"Because she's in love with me, too. It's only a matter of time."*

*Ryan stops walking and flips the camera on herself. "I guess I'll have to give you guys a little push. I hope you put that application in."*

My vision blurs as the video cuts out. Tears slide down my phone screen. I love him so much. Without him, a part of me is missing. River's been so ingrained in my life, the thought of him being gone forever feels like a gaping hole has been cut into my chest.

One of the airline employees announces over the intercom that my flight will begin boarding soon and it hits me that I'm really leaving. The people around me stand in preparation. Some of them laugh, others carry on conversations or scroll on their phones. It's so weird how the world continues as normal when everything inside you is collapsing. I'm so in love with River Beck and he knew it before I could even comprehend it.

My boarding group is called, and I wipe at my tears before getting in line. I've said too many hurtful things to go back. I'm a coward.

*"I'll never lose her. I never let her go to begin with."*

Ah.

How horrible am I? River put everything he had into showing me he was serious and I'm giving up because I'm scared to be rejected.

Pathetic.

"Ma'am, can you step forward and pull your ticket up for me?" The employee taps his foot impatiently.

"No."

"Excuse me?" He asks while looking at the long line behind me.

"I'm not getting on the flight."

"Indigo!"

My head whips toward whoever is calling my name. The stress must be getting to me because it looks like River is running toward me.

"Indigo Johnson." He yells and pushes through a crowd of people attempting to get to their gate.

"River?" I step out of line.

He finally reaches me and his body slams into mine. His powerful arms pull me in so tight it's almost painful, but it feels so good.

"Why are you here?" I'm crying into his chest, and it feels so safe, like he's not just holding me, but putting me back together.

"I'm here for you."

I push against him, but he refuses to let go. "Why would you come?" My voice cracks.

"Why would you leave?" He's still holding me, and I look up through my wet lashes and his eyes stare down at me without a trace of anger. There's so much damn warmth there.

"How'd you know I was here?"

"Kade called."

Kade? I open my mouth to ask about it, but River continues.

"When I got to the mansion, you were gone, but Cameron was still there. She told me where to find you, so I booked a flight."

"You bought a plane ticket?"

"They don't let just anybody in here."

I look down and he is indeed in just his socks, sneakers in hand. He must have run from security. My eyes water again.

"I don't deserve you." I whisper and mean it. He's too good for me.

"You don't."

My head jerks up, and he's smiling. He brushes away my tears with his free hand.

"You deserve so much more than what I can give you. Someone who wouldn't be slow to act, and who would tell you he loves you from the moment he felt it. Someone who would never turn you away when you were brave enough to say it first, regardless of the reason." He presses a kiss to my forehead, and it's so soft, but I feel it with every fiber of my being. "Unfortunately, you'll have to settle for me. I told you I'd never let you go, and I meant that."

"I'm so sorry for everything. I didn't mean any of it and—"

His lips meet mine, and every last thought disappears. His mouth on mine feels like I've found sanctuary. The thoughts that plagued me moments before, release their hold on me. River pulls away and places his forehead against mine.

"You think I don't know when you're lying? I've known you my whole life and you've never been good at it."

"But you left."

"When Noah asked me to help with this project, I didn't really know him. After seeing how he operated, I didn't want to work with him. I was able to get my script reviewed by someone else who seems to be interested. I quit and planned to find you once filming wrapped up."

"Why didn't you say anything?" My mind is reeling.

"I wanted it to be a sure thing."

"And is it?"

He smiles and I jump back into his arms. My knees feel weak with relief. The amount of happiness I feel for River is immeasurable. Someone crashes against us, wrapping their arms around me. I look over my shoulder and Ryan's crying as bad as I am. I twist in her arms and pull her into a hug.

"How could you try to leave me? If you're on the run, so am I." She's got a backpack slung over her shoulder and she's in pajama pants with a ribbed tank. She looks like she rolled out of bed and came straight here.

"I'm sorry. I was trying to get my head straight. Next time it's you and me."

River grabs her shirt, dragging her out of my arms. "Why would she take you over me?"

"Best friends come first." She shrugs. The speakers sound with a last call for our flight and River checks his watch.

"We're going to be left behind if we don't hurry." He drops his shoes and kicks them on.

"We're not getting on that plane."

"You want to go home?" He looks confused and rightfully so, but if Kade called him, that means I was wrong about more than a few things. The puzzle pieces are finally fitting together.

"Tell me about your call with Kade."

# Chapter Thirty-Six

"I need to know everything Kade said." At the mention of Kade, River stiffens.

"He said you were waiting for me and hung up." He looks at me warily.

"He knows everything." I mumble to myself and the knowledge of that rocks me. None of what Cameron told me made sense, because if he was willing to destroy me to fix his image, why would he sabotage himself in the end? The vile things he said at the elimination will only hurt him… "I'll look justified for turning away from him." I look at River and it all clicks. No one would blame me after hearing the things he said.

River rubs his thumb across my furrowed brow. "Indie, what's wrong?" He asks, and Ryan looks just as worried.

"I know this is the last thing you want to do, and I want nothing more than to just be with you." Ryan makes a gagging gesture and I roll my eyes. "But I have some things to make right."

Without missing a beat, River nods, "What do you need from me?"

"I'll explain on the way. Send me Kade's number." Turning on my

heel, I head for the exit. My phone pings, and it's a text from River.
Immediately, I call Kade as we dip and dodge our way through the
crowd, only to get his voicemail repeatedly. When we make it to River's
truck, he opens the passenger door for me and I curse under my breath
as I get the same automated message. When Ryan gets settled in the
back seat and River gets the engine going, I give up on calling and
google Kade's address.

"Found it." The screen loads with an article detailing the luxury
homes within a community that Kade supposedly resides in. It's not his
exact address, but close enough.

"Want to tell me where we're headed?"

"Sent the address." I sigh and drop my head against the headrest.
River taps at his screen, plugging it into the GPS.

"You ready to tell me what this is about?"

Not at all. Telling him means reliving everything again, but I do
it anyway. From my deal with Kade, to Noah's plotting, and Jose and
Cameron's betrayal. River becomes more tense as I relay the details,
and by the time I finish, he's got a white knuckled grip on the steering
wheel. Ryan reaches from the back seat to hold my hand. I hadn't
realized I was shaking. I skipped over what exactly they caught on the
recordings because I'm embarrassed and, logically; I know it's not my
fault, but I still feel responsible.

"Kade somehow found out and sabotaged what Noah had planned.
I need to know how to fix this." My voice catches and I'm just so damn
mentally exhausted.

"None of this is your fault." River's fingers flex and I can tell he's
seething.

"He's right. If Kade thought you were a horrible person, I doubt he
would've done it. He knew and made an informed decision." Ryan rubs
my arm.

I'm able to calm down some by the time we roll to a stop at the large gate of Kade's community. We pull up to the security box and a guard greets us. "Who are you here for?" The plump man's hand hovers over the phone.

"Kade Ikeda." River supplies.

The guard nods as he dials a number. After a brief conversation, he hangs up. "Mr. Ikeda isn't receiving guests. Please turn around."

"Excuse me," unbuckling my seatbelt, I lean across River. "Tell Mr. Ikeda to call the cops because I'm not leaving." I drop back into my seat and send a text to Kade's phone, relaying the same message.

River puts the car in park and looks at the guard. "We're not trying to be rude, it's important. Can you please try again?" He asks.

The guard throws his hands up. "I don't get paid enough for this." He picks up the phone and this time after a few words he presses a button, and the gate opens. "Take the first left, go straight until you hit the stop sign, and he's on your right. 622 Windridge Lane."

"Thank you," I call as we pull off. I'm genuinely stunned when we park in front of Kade's home. It puts the mansion we filmed in to shame. Ryan whistles as she attempts to peer through one of the windows.

"He's loaded. You sure you want my brother?"

Ignoring her, I make my way to the front door and knock. It swings open, revealing a severely unhappy looking Kade.

"You knew." I fold my arms across my chest.

"I did." We could be strangers with the way he looks at me.

"Since when?" I'm not backing down.

"Does it matter?"

"Can you just tell her? She's not going to let it go." River's patience is growing thin.

Irritation flickers across Kade's features before he looks back at me. "After you came to me, I kept an eye on you, and you acted as though you signed up for your own funeral. Not like someone who manipulated their way to something they wanted. Once I started digging, it wasn't hard to get information out of Cameron. She didn't know exactly what they had on you, but she knew enough for me to piece it together and Sabrina filled in the gaps."

"What does Sabrina have to do with it?" River asks defensively. He's protective of her and I'm not sure where Kade's going with this.

"She gave me the bracelet. Before she left, she told me about her suspicions of Jose and Cameron. She wasn't sure if the bracelet was special or not, but after talking to Cameron..." He pauses and looks to River, then back at me, "There was a micro SD card inside with all the recordings." He pulls out an envelope and holds it between us.

My lips part, and I stare at it. Everything in me wants to run the opposite direction. Guilt seeps into my bones, because as special as that night with River was, thinking of it hurts. "I was wearing it when they told me to lie to you. Is that on there?" I ask Kade and he nods. "Why didn't you use this? You have everything you need to show how corrupt this whole thing has been." The envelope hovers awkwardly between us. He could have used the recordings to save himself. There's no way Noah want's to be outed for blackmail and intimidation.

"It wasn't mine to use. I figured you wouldn't want anyone else to hear it." Kade gives me a hard look.

"What's on there, Blue?" River zeroes in on me, sensing I've left something out.

I take a shaky breath, and Ryan gives my hand a squeeze. "They caught us when..." My voice trembles and I look at my feet, trying to catch my breath.

"You were wearing the bracelet that night." My eyes lock with River's and I can see him connect the dots.

"They recorded everything. They made what we did into a

nightmare. I feel like they were in the room with us. It was only audio, but it feels like…" I cross my arms over my chest, completely breaking down. I'm tired of holding the pain in alone, so I reach for him and he takes me in his arms, tucking my head underneath his chin.

"I want you to know that when I think of that night, I will forever remember it as the day I gave myself to you. They weren't a part of that. I won't allow them to be," River whispers.

Ryan drops my hand, stepping to Kade. "They can't get away with it." I can already see her mind working a mile a minute on the different ways to make them suffer.

"We need to use the audio." I force my voice to be strong.

"No." Kade and River say in unison.

Kade shakes his head. "The media isn't kind. Some will support you, but others will try to spin it."

"I'm not letting Noah make you the villain. After what you did, it won't be hard for him to do that." I push against River's chest and look him in the eye. "The recordings are between you and me. If you're okay with it, I want to use it."

# Chapter Thirty-Seven

e decided confronting Noah as soon as possible was the best option, so after reviewing as much of the audio as we could yesterday, we got some rest and set out early this morning. I'm confident in my decision to be here, but standing outside the door of Noah's office building makes my stomach twist uncomfortably. I feel like I haven't had a moment to absorb everything. River stands to my left and gives my hand a squeeze while Kade is to my right. It took everything I had to convince Ryan not to come. I couldn't trust her not to get riled up. I glance at River and he's just as tightly wound as Kade is.

Telling River about the recordings is vastly different than listening to them. Hearing Noah mock and distort our relationship into something vile had him angrier than anything I'd ever seen. I still can't think about *that* night without tying it to all the events that occurred afterwards. The embarrassment I feel over the situation makes me feel more guilty because it's centered on my first time with River. It should make me feel special and fill me with warmth. Instead, it fills me with dread and instead of being in his arms, I'm standing outside the office

of the man who forcibly inserted himself into my memory of that night.

When we step inside, there's a woman behind the front desk. An elevator sits to her right, but the first floor is otherwise empty. She looks up and smiles at the site of Kade, but he ignores her and uses his keycard to buzz us into the elevator. We ride up in silence and the sick feeling in my stomach intensifies. I didn't think I'd have to see Noah again.

The elevator doors slide open. This floor has a few cubicles where employees sit, typing away at their computers. River and Kade lead the way toward an office at the back.

A man sits at a desk nearby and smiles as we approach. "Hey River, Noah told me you have a 10 a.m. scheduled. He's ready for you inside." The man jerks his head toward the door. As far as Noah knows, River and I aren't speaking, and he is here to discuss his script. River nods and pushes the door open.

Noah smiles from behind his desk when he sees River, but when Kade and I follow behind him, his face falls. Jose sits in a chair across from Noah with a stack of papers in his lap. Noah looks at Kade. "Are you here to beg for my forgiveness?"

"We're here to talk business." Kade hands Noah his phone.

"What am I supposed to do with this?" He looks amused.

Kade reaches over the desk and taps the screen. Noah's voice sounds from the speaker. River tenses and I grab his arm and feel him relax at my touch. Hearing him extort me and be so god damn giddy about it makes my blood run hot. The fucker got off on trying to hurt me that day.

"How do they have this?" Noah turns to Jose.

"I don't know." Jose shrinks in his chair.

"You don't know?" Noah's voice is ice cold.

"The bracelet was a backup. I didn't think she'd look inside it. Plus we've been busy."

Noah stands and slams his fist against the table. "You didn't think to take it back?" Noah throws his hands in the air. Jose's eyes widen and he jerks back in his seat.

"Get the hell out of my office." Noah yells.

Jose scrambles out of the chair, but before he leaves, he pauses at the door, "Will you still be sending the contract tonight?" Jose ask's despite the fear in his eyes.

"You think I'd still work with you? You're done." Noah throws his stapler and Jose slams the door just before it hits him. "Now, what do you two want?" He grits out.

His eyes fall on me and I fight to maintain his eye contact. "Cancel the show."

"That's not within my control." He rubs his temples.

"Then maybe you're not who we need to speak to. I have a feeling you've been making decisions on your own, but you have a boss you report to, just like the rest of us." Kade takes Jose's vacated seat.

River takes a step forward and Noah meets his gaze. "I know how this industry works, so I know stunts like this and worse happen every day. However, getting caught is an entirely different story. The same people you brag about knowing for years will turn their backs on you if they think being around you will taint their image. How many times have you seen someone at the top of their game fall because of one slip up?"

Noah's vein pulses, "They will not cancel the show. Too much money and time was put into this for me to talk them into that, and Kade, no amount of editing will have you looking good by the end of it."

"Cancel my contract. I want to be done. Figure out a way for me to be completely out from underneath you and my management team.

Fix it so these two are left out of it." Kade sits calmly, it's clear we have the advantage.

I place my hand on Kade's shoulder and open my mouth to protest, but he cuts his eyes at me and I snap it shut.

Noah sighs and then looks to Kade. "Fine, I'll draft the paperwork by the end of the week, and I want this to be the last time we see each other." His eyes flash in my direction. "I'll make sure your girlfriend gets a favorable edit."

"If the audio ever leaks, we go public with everything you did. No one will want to touch you after that." Kade pauses. After a beat of silence, Noah nods his understanding.

Kade stands so I take that as our cue to leave, but before we can Noah gets one last dig in.

"All this for some whore. If all you wanted was a good lay, I could have introduced you to some quality women."

His words don't fully register before River's no longer at my side and his fist is connecting with Noah's face. River's arm draws back and then slams back into Noah's jaw. Kade is there in an instant and pull's at River's shirt, but River rips out of Kade's grip and lands one more, knocking Noah completely out of his chair.

"Let that be the last time you say anything about her." River stares at him with burning anger. I step around Kade and gently take River's hand in mine, tugging him toward me.

"We need to go. We got what we came here for." I pull harder and he relents, letting me guide him out the door. After the shouting they've heard, the employees watch us with wide eyes as we make our way to the elevator. As much as I've wanted to hit Noah myself, I'm ready to go home and put this behind us.

When we exit the building Kade starts toward his car without a word. I look to River and he nods, so I drop his hand and catch up to

Kade.

"Hey," I call after him. He pauses with his hand on the handle of his door. "Thank you. For looking out for me. I haven't had the chance to say that."

"Noah was trying to sabotage on my behalf. It makes sense that I'd step in." Kade lifts his shoulders like it's not a big deal. Like him turning himself into what the media has always thought him to be isn't going to come with a lot of blow back.

"Or maybe it makes sense that we look out for each other because we're friends." I mimic his stance, arms crossed and head held high.

"People won't understand why you'd stick around once they see how I treated you."

"They'll never get to see how you treated me, because none of the stuff that matters will make air." I shrug.

River walks up to my side, dropping his arm around my shoulders. "Indigo isn't going to leave you alone to do the whole brooding thing. Just give in."

"Are you asking to be my friend too?" Kade taunts River as he opens his car door. When he gets inside, he turns the engine on and rolls down the window. "You've got my number." Kade throws up the peace sign and speeds off.

River looks down at me as he leads us to his truck. "You think he's going to be okay?"

I watch as Kade's car disappears and I smile. It won't be easy, but he's free now. We could all use a do over.

"Yeah. He'll be alright."

Ryan sent a text letting us know she would be gone the next couple days, so when we make it home, the apartment is empty. It's the first time I've been alone with River since everything happened and I feel so unsure of myself. I place a bag of ice against his knuckles, and he winces. "Ryan wasn't allowed to come because I knew she'd react this way. I never expected you to." I reach for the bottle of water on the table and hand it to him along with some pain relief pills.

"I thought I'd be able to hold myself back, but he tested my limits." River swallows the pills and chases them with a drink of water. Thinking about Noah brings back that sick feeling in my stomach. River has always been able to read my emotions, so when he gets a look at my face, he sits up and takes my hand in his. "How are you doing with all this?" He pulls me into his side and it's the safest I have felt in a while. "We haven't talked about any of it."

The words feel stuck in my throat and my mouth feels dry, but I force them out anyway. "They turned our first time into something horrible." My words come out as a whisper.

"They could never do that. Come here." He guides me onto his lap, and I loop my arms around his neck. "They don't have the power to corrupt that night for me. I'll never forget anything about it. The things we said to each other, and the way you felt in my arms, are things I can't forget." He cups my face so that I'm looking him in the eyes. "I can't undo the trauma they caused by weaponizing our feelings for each other, but I can give you a new memory." His hands fall from my face and trail up my thigh. Despite my insecurities, his touch makes me feel grounded.

He grips the hem of my shirt, pulling it over my head and my hands move to cover my breasts, but he catches my wrists. He looks at me with unfiltered adoration and I'm reminded again how much I love this man.

"I'll give you so many good memories there won't be any room for the bad ones to exist." He speaks between kisses he leaves along my shoulder. His feather light touches leave me breathless. I could become addicted to this in the worst way.

"Having you in my arms will always feel like the first time." He twines our fingers together and kisses the back of my hands. "I'll give you as many first times as you need."

"How did I get so lucky?" I'm genuinely in awe of him.

"I'm the lucky one. I can die a happy man knowing I've held even a small piece of your affection."

He kisses me, and it's intoxicating. Our bodies meld together, and I still want more. He breaks our kiss and takes my breasts into his hands. Rolling my nipples between his fingers, he watches me as he leans forward and glides his tongue across them and I moan at the pleasure that washes through me. He grazes his teeth along my sensitive skin, turning my breathing uneven.

My thighs squeeze around him, and I can feel the warmth of him between us. My hips rock against him, needing to feel the friction of our bodies being pressed together. He groans in my ear, and I can feel my arousal building between my legs.

He lifts me up and I frown at the loss of the feel of him. He unzips his pants and I smile at how ready he is for me. After everything, our bodies are still so in tune with each other. I kneel over him, twitching in anticipation. He pulls my panties to the side and glides himself back and forth at a torturously slow pace along my slit and I release a slow breath. "River, please."

He rubs my clit with his free hand as he continues to slide his erection against me. "Please, what?" He tilts his head back, his green eyes hooded with lust.

"Put it in."

His mouth curls upward, and his eyes never leave mine as he lowers me around him. He fills me to capacity, and I rest my head on his shoulder. I tighten around him and he grunts, dropping his head back.

"I'll never get over how good it feels to be inside you."

I kiss his neck and rock slowly, adjusting to the size of him. I push him as far as I can, teasing and biting all while hardly being able to contain the sounds that come from my mouth. Without warning, he flips us over so that I am on my back. He pulls out. Gripping my hips, he turns me over and lifts me, so I am on my hands and knees. I look over my shoulder and the corners of his lips tilt up. He runs a hand down my spine before pushing into me and I gasp at how much fuller I feel in this position.

His fingers tangle in my hair and he pulls back as he rams into me. Shockwaves of pleasure jolt through my body.

"I love you." He breathes and I feel my eyes roll back when he reaches around to massage circles across my clit. I feel like I'm overdosing on euphoria. It's all too much and I try to crawl away, but he pulls me all the way back so that I'm pressed against his chest. "No more running. It's me and you from now on." He kisses my neck as he slams into me, emphasizing his point. We hit our highs together, and he was right.

That felt like a new beginning for us, the first time I've given myself to him with no uncertainties. I think of all the other firsts to come, and I can't help but smile.

# Epilogue

## ONE YEAR LATER

*N*o matter how much I love California, coming home to Texas always feels nice. However, what I didn't miss was the humidity. Currently, River and I are standing outside the Dallas airport melting while we wait on the car we ordered. When I look at River, he's tapping away at his phone. He's been anxious about this trip all month. He and his mother have been working on their relationship, but he still reverts into a ball of anxiety when we visit.

I place my hand on his shoulder, and he looks up at me. "My mom says she has everything handled. Your mom's home and has no idea we're coming." Today's Tiffany's birthday and we're surprising her by showing up on her doorstep. "She's been doing so well with her therapy. You can relax a little."

River sighs and drops his shoulders. "I am relaxed." He gives me a lopsided smile.

"I'd hate to see you tense." I laugh and adjust my backpack. We packed light by sticking to one bag each, since it's a weekend trip, but the weights biting into my skin.

River loops his finger underneath one of my straps and slides it off my shoulders. "I'm good, I just want her to be surprised."

"She will be." I grab his hand and give it a squeeze. "I still can't believe that Ryan accepted a job the same week as your mom's birthday."

"She promised she'd make it up to her later." River's eyes leave mine and focus on something behind me. When I turn to look, two teen girls are approaching, giggling into their hands.

"We're so sorry to interrupt but…" the blond one looks at her friend.

"We had to come ask for a picture," her friend finishes for her.

I'm still not used to being recognized in public. "Of course." I smile. Both girls turn to each other and squeal. It's a high-pitched sound that garners a few annoyed looks in our direction.

They both jump to either side of me. The blond holds her phone out to River. "Do you mind?" The girl asks, not unkindly. River takes the phone and they both hug me tight as he snaps a few photos. I learned quickly that physical boundaries are crossed easily and often by people that don't know you when you get a little bit of the limelight.

The brunette takes her phone back and smiles up at me. "You were our favorite. We thought Kade was going to choose you. I guess he did you a favor." They both look at River and laugh.

I never know what to say to comments like that. Kade got the brunt of the bad press. I got the favorable edit we were promised and he came out looking like the villain. Fans of the show are divided between Cameron and me. The ones that love her tend to hate me, but they can all agree on their disdain toward Kade. The show raked in high ratings and even though it cemented the negative outlook everyone has on him; his popularity is at an all-time high. Everyone wants to know what he'll do next.

The girls thank me again before running off as our car pulls to a stop in front of us. We slide into the back seat and the driver pulls off.

"We're running late." River comments, his shoulders tense again. Relaxed my ass. We have reservations at his mother's favorite restaurant later this afternoon. Both our phones ping, alerting us of a text.

**RYAN**

Did you two land okay?

**ME**

We have. We're in the car now on our way to your mom's house.

**SABRINA**

Bring me back a souvenir.

**GABBY**

Get her a cowboy hat. I'd pay money to see her in one of those.

**KADE**

Who keeps adding me back to this group chat?

**RIVER**

If I have to be in it, so do you.

**CARTER**

So Kade... you DO respond to texts. I have been calling you. We have a meeting in an hour. If you're not there, I swear to god...

*Kade has left the chat*

Carter is the publicist Ryan introduced Kade to. She's nice and seems to know what she's doing, but their personalities are like oil and water. "You think those two will be okay? I've never seen two people argue the way they do."

"They'll be fine." River's still typing something into his phone.

As we make our way to his mother's house, we pass sign after sign for the Texas State Fair. "I wish we could stay for the fair next weekend."

"If you didn't have the fashion show, we could have extended our stay." He locks his phone, sliding it into his back pocket.

I'm filled with unease at the mention of the upcoming event. I was trying not to think about it. It'll be my first time without Drew, Kenny or Kevin. I've learned a lot over the last year. The show's popularity brought an influx of attention to my socials and I've been booked and busy, learning under Drew and taking on more clients than ever before. But I've never led a team.

Sensing my nerves, River pulls me to his side and kisses the top of my head. "It's going to be great." The car rolls to a stop and we've arrived. River takes both of our bags as we get out of the car.

"She's going to be so happy when she sees you." My excitement peaks and I jump on my toes.

We make it to the porch and River unlocks the door, gesturing for me to go first. I can't help the huge smile on my face as I step inside. "Surprise!" I yell at the top of my lungs, but then I blink, and the room fills with laughter. In front of me stand my mother and Tiffany, who are holding on to each other, but surrounding them is Sabrina, Gabby, Jasmine, and Ryan.

"What are you all doing here?" Confusion has my head on a swivel as I look around the room, trying to make sense of what's going on. My eyes fall back to our mothers, and they look like they're both trying to keep the other from falling apart. Their eyes glisten and their chins tremble. "Mom?" Their eyes all fall from mine and stare behind me. I turn around and River is bent on one knee, holding a small black box between us. All the air leaves my body and my heart dances in my chest.

"I've wanted to do this for so long, to make you mine—give you my last name and see our families come together. Since we've been together, you've helped me learn how to be human again. I forgot how to live freely and it's ironic because the one person I never want to lose taught me how to let go. Indigo Johnson, I don't remember a time before you and I don't want to know one after you. I want to grow old with my best friend and the woman I love. Will you join me in a forever together?" River opens the box and inside is a princess cut engagement ring with a halo of diamonds along the band. It's absolutely stunning. His eyes are clear and sure as he looks at me, but I can tell by the slight tremor in his hands and the deep swallow he takes that he's nervous.

I'm not sure when the tears started, but there's no stopping them now. A small laugh leaves my lips as I reach for his face. How could he ever think I'd say no? My voice fails me and all I can manage is to nod my head.

"Is that a yes?" He laughs.

"It is."

Everyone behind us cheers. Ryan, of course, is the loudest one. He slides the ring onto my finger, and I hear both our mothers sob harder behind me. Warmth feels my chest as the weight of the ring settles against my finger.

I feel arms wrap around me from behind me and when I look over my shoulder, it's Ryan pulling me into a hug. "You knew." I twist in her arms and punch her shoulder.

"Of course, I did." Ryan rolls her eyes.

My mother steps up next, tears still falling. "I'm so proud of the woman you have become. I see the hard work you put in and you deserve someone that will stand by you. I'm happy for you." Her words soak into my soul, and I let them fill me with so much joy.

Tiffany stands beside my mom and takes one of both River and I's hands in her own. "Seeing you two finally come to your senses is a dream I've had for years. My babies…" Her voice tapers off and turns into a soft cry as she looks between us, overwhelmed with emotion. My mom pats Tiffany's back and guides her back to the couch.

I turn to River and loop my arms around his neck. "When did you have time to put this all together?"

"Started planning months ago. Had to make sure everyone's schedules would line up."

I tilt my head to the side, narrowing my eyes, "We've only been together a year."

Sabrina cuts in, "Ask him when he bought the ring."

River's skin becomes flush. "A week after filming ended."

"That long ago?" Of course he did. River's been sure of us before there was an *us* to consider.

"I always knew you'd be my wife." There's nothing but love in his eyes, and I feel it in every fiber of my being. A year ago, I never thought I'd end up here, but I am grateful for every misfortune that led us to this moment.

Stepping on my tiptoes, I place a kiss against his lips, and he presses me against him. The sound of a camera click makes us pull apart. My mom laughs as she looks at the image on her digital camera. "You guys are so cute." She points toward the dining area, "Come eat, we made all your favorites."

I look back at River, and my lipstick stains his lips. I swipe at them with my thumb, and he smiles. "You ready?" He asks, taking my hand. I look at him and all our friends and family gathering at the table and nod my head.

"I'm more than ready."

I let my fear keep us apart and I'll always regret the time lost, but the journey it took to get here makes it all worth it. I won't waste another second.

### Thank You!

If you enjoyed Lipstick & Camera Clicks, please consider leaving a review! Any review, however short, helps spread the word about my books to other readers.

For all the romance and bookish updates, join me over on Instagram.

### Scan to join the fun.

## D.J.MURPHYWRITES

### What's Next?

Kade's story is far from over. He's got something to prove and no one to tell him how to do it. If only his publicist wasn't on his ass about everything...

# Acknowledgments

Cynthia, thank you for suffering through the earlier drafts and being one of my biggest cheerleaders. Knowing you were waiting on new updates helped push me to finish writing Indigo and River's story when I lost the confidence to do so. I hope you continue to enjoy the imaginary worlds that fall from my brain to the page.

Sandrine, thank you for being my oldest friend and telling me what I need to hear. Your honesty helped make L&CC what it is today, and I'll be forever grateful for that. From the late-night talks going over my doubts to agonizing over the title together. Thank you for sticking through it with me, and I hope you're ready to do it all over again with the next book.

To all the beta readers who helped shape this story with your honest reactions, THANK YOU. This book has passed through many hands before publishing and every time it changed for the better. I couldn't have done this on my own.

Made in the USA
Las Vegas, NV
17 January 2025

16533335R00187